SINNER'S GIN

RHYS FORD

Dreamspinner Press

Published by
Dreamspinner Press
5032 Capital Circle SW
Ste 2, PMB# 279
Tallahassee, FL 32305-7886
USA
http://www.dreamspinnerpress.com/

Sinner's Gin

Cover Art by Reece Notley
reece@vitaenoir.com

ISBN: 978-1-62380-248-6

Printed in the United States of America
First Edition
December 2012

eBook edition available
eBook ISBN: 978-1-62380-249-3

Sinner's Gin is dedicated to Reetoditee Mazumdar, Bianca Janian, Tiffany Tran, and Lisa Horan (listed in order of appearance into my life). You four have kept my head on straight and looked at me funny when I went off the rails. This one's for you.

ACKNOWLEDGMENTS

OKAY, the Five—or rather four of the Five—Penn, Lea, Tamm, and Jenn. Because damn it, you are going to be in every single book I write because I carry you with me always. Also in my heart, Ree and Ren, my two beloved baby sisters.

On the business side, Elizabeth North. Dude, you keep me in Korean music and my cat in insulin. Also kudos to the Dreamspinner Press staff who have to put up with me: Lynn, Julianne, Ginnifer, Anne, Mara, Julili, and everyone else who pitches in to make me look good, thank you. Couldn't get here from there without you.

I also need to give a shout-out to everyone who has bought my books. Thank you. Hell, thank you doesn't even cover it. You all rock.

Lastly, I have to extend so much gratitude to the men and women who kept me sane when I was growing up and a little bit beyond. In no particular order and probably forgetting a shitload of names they are: Steve Tyler, Mr. Joe Perry, and the rest of the boys in Aerosmith, Janis Joplin, Stevie Ray Vaughan, AC/DC, The Police, Tool, Metallica, Flotsam and Jetsam, Jake and Elwood Blues, Etta James, and whoever else helped stopper up my brain leaks. Thanks for the sanity, even when it was only in my imagination.

PROLOGUE

MIKI ST. JOHN was riding high.

Half drunk from whiskey and the other half pure adrenaline, he stuck himself out of the limo's moonroof and screamed into the pouring rain. Shouts came from below, mostly curses, and strong hands yanked him down, grabbing the heavy gold trophy from his cold, wet fingers. Nearly deafened from the rush of wind he'd stood in, Miki grinned up at his best friend, Damien, reaching for the bottle of Jack they'd opened to celebrate.

After ten years of dragging their equipment and tired bodies from venue to venue, tonight's celebration made it all worthwhile. They'd stood on stage, humbled and numb following their band's name being read off by a legendary loose-lipped singer, and were handed four old-style record players cast in gold to hold until they got off stage. Miki couldn't remember what he said—if he said anything at all—mostly nodding when reporters asked him if he was excited or proud of the band he'd formed with a guy he met behind a bar one day. How could he tell the blank-faced journalists that his heart probably wouldn't start beating again until he got home to San Francisco, or that the three men standing around and behind him were the family he needed to be proud of him?

So he nodded and stumbled out past the hordes of people and flashing lights, letting himself be guided to the limo by Damien to be whisked off to an after-party being thrown by someone he didn't know.

Two blocks away from the theater, Johnny pulled out a trophy he'd nicked from one of the backstage tables and tossed it into Dave's lap. The drummer yelped, then harangued and scolded the bassist as he hefted the stolen statue, turning it over in his hands before passing it to Damien.

"This." Damien held up the award, saluting it with the bottle of Jack Daniels he'd taken from the limo's wet bar. "This is our payoff for every shitty night—"

"And our stuff getting ripped off," Johnny howled, wiggling over the long bench seat to reach one of the beers from the limo's mini-cooler. The New York Italian popped off the cap and flipped it over his knuckles. "And every goddamned gig with only three people!"

"God, those were shitty times," Dave murmured, quiet as always, but the gleam in his eyes was a proud one. He took the bottle from Damien, tilted it back for a swig, and swallowed as he handed it to their singer. With his soft Southern accent, he drawled, "To our Miki… for kicking ass and taking names."

"To our Miki," Damien whispered in agreement. He pressed the trophy into Miki's hands and took the bottle of JD back from Dave.

They were as different as cheese and chalk. Damien—with his cocksure, blue-eyed all-American swagger—was a sharp contrast to Miki's street-bred Asian mongrel, and if not for a chance meeting one foggy day when Miki stepped out to grab a hit off a clove cigarette between shifts, they'd never have crossed paths. But when the guitarist overheard the growling, sultry voice belting out blues rock as he cut through a back alley of Chinatown, he knew he'd found his singer, even if he had to coax a very reluctant Miki off of a fire escape to come down to talk to him. Damien became the closest thing to a brother Miki ever knew, and as the guitarist leaned over to hug him tightly, Miki clenched Damien close to him, refusing to let go.

"You wrote the songs with me," he whispered into his best friend's ear. "Those are my words, but it's your music too."

"Yeah, but I didn't slither across the stage in black leather pants and ink to sell it," Damien teased, pushing Miki away with a semi-gentle shove. "You're the reason our name's on that thing. You're why Sinner's Gin's name was read off tonight. Take a bow, kid. It's all on you, dude."

The moonroof seemed to be the only place wide enough to take a bow, and, his head spinning from the sheer joy of the night, Miki took it. The Los Angeles rain was cold. Not as frigid as the storms up north, but cold enough to make him shiver. The buildings around them were tall and lit up, and to his right, a wall of colorful LEDs hawked a soft drink for a few seconds before undulating over to a clothing store advertisement. He screamed a thank-you to the universe, barely able to get the words out before he was pulled back down, heady and soaking wet from the downpour.

Johnny and Dave fought over the roof's switch, flipping it back and forth with stuttering jerks, and Damien pulled Miki close, cradling his friend against him as he took a mouthful of whiskey.

"You did good, kid," Damien whispered, barely audible over the rough banter from their other two band members. "From here on out, we're going to have a wild ride."

Miki turned to tell Damien their name wasn't on the trophy because Johnny had taken one of the props, and if they were lucky, they'd be sent theirs without anyone finding out they stole the other one to begin with, but the words never left his mouth. He blinked, and suddenly Damien was gone.

Then everything went black.

NP News—Tragedy struck the music world late last night when three members of the rock band Sinner's Gin were killed nearly immediately following their win at the Grammys. Initial accident reports detail a collision between their limousine and a semi truck carrying supplies for a nearby construction site. Lost in the crash were founding member and lead guitarist Damien Mitchell, drummer Dave Nichols, and bassist Johnny *González,* along with the driver of the limousine, Jordan Wheeler. All were pronounced dead on the scene.

The sole survivor of the early morning crash is reported to be the band's singer, Mieko "Miki" St. John, who was life-flighted to a local hospital, with life-threatening injuries. A spokesman for the group's record label reports Mr. St. John is in a coma and listed as being in critical condition.

Witnesses state the truck failed to yield to a red light, thus colliding with the band's vehicle and an additional car. Other than the occupants of the limousine, no other injuries were reported.

While rain may have been a factor in the crash, a police spokesman issued a report stating the driver of the semi has been arrested for driving under the influence and will be charged with multiple counts of vehicular manslaughter.

CHAPTER ONE

Took a blind man to tell me I was something to see.
Took a man crossing his heart to tell me where to begin.
And the kiss in the rain you last gave to me,
Was the holy water I needed to erase all my sin.

—Blind Man Crossing

THE fucking dog was back again.

Kane Morgan eyed the scruffy blond terrier suspiciously. It sat at the edge of the cement pad, right under where the rolling door to the converted docking bay would land if it were closed. He'd already lost a chamois to the mutt, and God knew what else when his back was turned. The thing was a thief and a menace.

And irritatingly enough, the dog always seemed to be laughing at him.

"Leave my stuff alone, mutt," Kane growled and pointed warningly at the smiling terrier. "Just cause I rent this place doesn't mean I'm one of those tree-hugging hippie artists who'll let your shit slide. I'm a cop. I've got a gun. Keep stealing my shit and I'll shoot you."

He'd chosen to rent the work space from an art gallery and co-op mostly because it was close to his apartment. The space's quiet was soothing despite the added bonus of a thieving neighborhood terrier. The majority of the brick building's space had been turned into a long showroom on the main floor and art studios on the second level, while its three docking bays, sunk halfway down from the first floor, had been framed out and drywalled to use as studios. Kane had taken the end dock space, liking how the industrial, square windows overlooked the San Francisco Bay below.

He didn't know at the time it came with a furry blond pirate.

With the windows open, a faint hint of the shore reached him as he worked. The perfume of the exotic woods he worked with mingled pleasantly with the permeated metal scent of the ex-ironwork's girders, and the converted docking bay was big enough to hold his larger lathe, something he'd been itching to use since he got it out of storage. After fitting a seasoned, slab of a red-brown burl, Kane locked the wood into place, easing the scissor clamps in until the teeth lightly bit into the slab to keep it from flying free of the lathe as it spun.

Despite the cold lingering in the late morning air, Kane left the docking bay door open as he worked the wood. Kane could almost see the graceful lines of a bowl under the burl's mass, with the shape of the lip framed in the burl's rough bark. Setting his foot onto the lathe's pedal, he could lean into the grain's curve, his shoulders and arms straining to keep his carving tool firm against the hard wood. The whine of the motor lulled him as he worked, the tip of his blade finding the form he wanted to bring out of the amboyna burl.

That's when he noticed the dog with its nose buried deep in the shelves where he kept his exotics.

"Fucking son of a bitch," Kane spat out as the terrier dashed out of the workshop with a large chunk of koa clamped in its jaws. Stopping only long enough to roll down the bay door, Kane dashed after it.

The warehouse next door was built by the same architect as the gallery, a mirrored version of the co-op's. A small alley, barely large enough for two men to walk shoulder-to-shoulder, separated the buildings' back walls and, unlike the co-op, the other warehouse had been transformed into a home. The warehouse's long alley wall retained its solid brick lower level, and the frosted glass square panels on the second level had been left in place, effectively preventing anyone from looking into the home from the gallery's broad glass windows. Only two of the four docking bays seemed to remain, with thick blackened steel doors instead of the bright white the gallery chose. The warehouse's old front glass panels were gone, replaced with long art-nouveau-style windows, but Kane couldn't see past the thick curtains that swaddled the glass from the inside.

"Damn it," Kane swore as he spotted the dog slipping under a bay door left open only a foot, enough for a blond terrier to squeeze through. He'd almost caught up with the mutt, but it was gone, and a tug on the metal rolling door only rattled it loudly. He squatted and tried to look through the opening but saw nothing, only darkness.

"Padlocked! Okay, let's find out who owns this mutt."

He paced down the front sidewalk and stared at the thick wooden door with its elaborate curlicue ironwork. There didn't seem to be a doorbell, or at least not one Kane could see. Frowning, Kane was about to turn around and head back to the studio, but the koa'd been a bitch to get.

"And it's not my damned problem that dog's not on a leash," he muttered angrily. "Fuck it. Time for whoever owns it to reap what they sow."

FIRST, the pounding woke Miki up. It echoed through the converted warehouse until it seemed like the bricks picked up the beat and bounced it back on top of him. Mumbling in disgust, he turned over on the bed, pulling the soft sheets over his naked body. His bones ached in the cold San Francisco morning, and from the throb pulsating through his right leg, Miki knew in his gut that fog rolled in thick over the water, and there would be hell to pay in pain if he crawled out of his warm cocoon.

A wet tongue wormed into Miki's ear, and he recoiled, spitting softly in disgust. The ripeness of the waterfront's salty stink tickled his nose, and he reached out to shove the dog off the bed. The canine was too quick. Dodging the Miki's wildly flung arm, the dog returned to lave the grumbling man's face. In counterpoint to the slurping, the pounding continued, growing louder, although Miki hadn't thought it was possible.

"Fuck, is it Thursday? Is that the grocery guy?" He sat up suddenly and instantly regretted it when the throb turned into quick, stabbing pains. Gritting his teeth, he reached for the bottle of ibuprofen he'd dropped to the floor the night before and dry-swallowed four of the burnt orange tablets. Bleary-eyed, he tried holding off the dog's enthusiastic greeting and rolled out of the bed he'd set up on the warehouse's lower floor.

The two-storied, narrow brick building had been refurbished while he was out on the road, and he'd slunk back to a home he'd never lived in, hoping to lick his wounds and maybe drink himself to death before anyone noticed he was gone.

So far, he'd only been successful in that no one noticed he'd dropped out of sight. He was still working on the drinking to death part.

Setting up a king-sized bed in a doorless guest room cordoned off from the warehouse's open first floor had initially been for convenience as he healed from his injuries, but it'd been a long time since he gave a damn about the rest of the place. All of the furniture he picked out with the designer languished on the partial second floor, and the studio he'd had built into the farthest two docking bays sat as untouched as the cars in the bays next to it. He couldn't remember the last time he climbed the sweeping metal staircase to go upstairs or walked along the ironwork upper deck that faced the Bay. There'd been talk before of creating a space on the roof for parties.

Before.

He'd wanted to hold barbeques and drink beer on that rooftop. It would have made life feel… real. Like he was finally real. Now the roof just held runoff from rain and fallen leaves from the oak and maple trees nearby.

The terrier mix chewed something out of his light blond hair and grinned a mouthful of teeth at him as Miki hunted for something to tug over his nakedness. The polished wooden floor was cold under Miki's feet, and he cursed when the pounding began again.

"Fucking cut it out! I'm trying to find some clothes!" he shouted over the repeated hammering. A pair of gray cotton drawstring pants peeked out of the pile of laundry he'd done and dumped on the floor. He pulled them on and left them untied, letting the waistband slither down to hug his narrow hips.

Scraping his unruly hair out of his eyes, Miki stood up and immediately sat back down when his nerves screamed and twisted in pain. His mouth filled with blood and he swallowed it, tentatively poking at the shreds of his cheek where he bit through the soft flesh.

"Yeah, laugh it up, furball," Miki growled at the dog. "Find me some socks, Dude."

The terrier went back to chewing on his rump, and Miki grabbed the wooden cane lying next to the bed. The floor's chill moved up from the bottom of his feet into his ankles, and he cursed to himself when his nipples pricked from the cold. The sharp, bitter pain in his leg grabbed him by the balls with each step he took, and after a few feet, the walk to the front door began to seem like a trek across Death Valley.

After shuffling from the guest room into the main area, he used as much of the back of his battered couch as he could to support him while he limped to the front door. The knocking renewed itself just as Miki reached the heavy wooden door. He undid the dead bolts, pulled it open, and stared at the very large, very angry man on his doorstep.

The man had been about to set off on another pounding spree but pulled himself up when the door swung open.

The stranger ate up the air around him. Taller than Miki's near six feet, he looked like a brawler with wide shoulders and lean hips, possibly one that spent his time breaking smaller men in half just to suck out the marrow in their bones. His black hair looked as if he'd been pulling at it in frustration, sticking up at all angles around his temples. His rough, handsome face sported more than a day's growth of scruff along his strong jaw, but the laugh lines at the edges of his blue eyes said he smiled more than frowned. Although, by the scowl on his face, it'd been an eternity since his sensual mouth had seen a grin.

"What?" Miki growled before the intruder on his doorstep could say something.

The cold morning struck him fully and he shivered, wishing he'd taken the time to hunt up a sweatshirt. He wanted to wrap his arms around himself to ward off the biting chill, but he couldn't let go of the cane. Not without falling flat on his ass. His leg was too sore and twisted to support his weight, and there was no way in hell he was going to let go of his hold on the door. If the stranger decided to push his way in, he'd need the leverage to shove the heavy door in the man's face.

But at least the pounding had stopped.

"You live here?" The man definitely had a better growl than Miki's. His voice was darker and deeper. A faint lilt ghosted through the man's words, and the roll of his anger warmed the whiskey tone of his voice to a burbling heat. "That dog yours?"

The man looming over him was huge, and if push came to shove, Miki knew he'd lose more than a few teeth if they got into it. Miki never backed down from a fight, even when he was bleeding out. He'd always been proud of giving as good as he got. Even crippled and half-asleep, that wasn't going to change.

"What. The. Fuck. Do. You. Want?" Miki spat back.

They exchanged glares, and the man took a deep breath, as if to calm his temper. From what Miki could see, it didn't work.

"If you're going to own a dog, you should keep it on a fucking leash."

"I don't own a dog," Miki spat back.

"Then what's that furry thing next to you? A fucking kangaroo?"

Miki glanced down at the terrier sprawled by his feet. The dog's tongue lolled to one side of his open mouth, and his ears perked up as a bird flew by. Looking back up at the furious man on his stoop, Miki shrugged. "Yeah, that's not my dog. He just lives here."

The man closed his eyes and slowly exhaled through his pressed lips. "Who owns him, then?'

"I don't know who owns him," Miki said. "He came by one day. Hasn't left. Why?"

"Because the little thief stole a piece of my koa." The man took a step forward, and Miki's chin rose, a silent challenge, even if he had to look up to meet the man's eyes. "I want it back."

"Your what?" Miki shifted his feet. The cold finally reached his spine, its stiff fingers digging into his bones. His knee, on the other hand, was a searing hot spot, and he gritted his teeth against the pain. "Your cone? Like an ice cream cone? How the hell am I supposed to get that back? Dig around in his stomach?"

"Koa," he said slowly, enunciating each flowing syllable. "It's wood. From Hawai'i. Your dog took a big piece of it. I want it back."

"He's not… screw it. What does it look like?" Miki wasn't going to argue over ownership of the terrier. Not with his brain sending fiery tendrils up and down his spine and leg.

"It's wood. How many damned pieces of wood does the dog have?" The hint of Ireland in his voice thickened. Sighing, he held his hands out in front of Miki's face. "Look, it's about this big, rough, and dark red. Shit! It's nearly the same size as the dog. The damned mutt grabbed it and ran off before I could stop him."

"I'll go look." Miki gritted his teeth when he shifted his weight to turn around, and his bad knee nearly buckled. The rubber tip on the end of the cane squeaked loudly as it caught on the wooden floor, and he recovered his balance, breathing heavily from the spikes of pain.

Throughout the noise and Miki's flailing, the dog lounged back and licked his lower belly.

Miki left the door open. The cold was already deep in his bones, and if he closed it, he couldn't trust himself to open it up again. Bed seemed like a good place to crawl back into, but instead he hobbled through the room and opened the door to the garage.

And stopped to take a breath.

He could face the garage. The steel and glass pink elephant in the space was covered by a drop cloth that obscured most of its shape, but the car's lines were still visible. Averting his eyes, Miki stumbled through the space, using what little light came from the terrier-height gap at the bottom of the garage door

Most of what the dog brought in from outdoors was small, such as a cast-off plastic toy or a sun-bleached bone he found in another dog's yard. Braving the garage every week or so, Miki tossed away nearly all of it, saving only the occasional tennis ball to bring into the house for the mutt to chase after. All of the canine's dubious treasures were piled up in a far corner, and there on the top of a torn, stained towel sat a milk-carton sized piece of wood, its rough bark still moist from the dog's mouth.

Bending over, he nearly lost his balance when he picked up the wood. "Fuck, Dude. How the hell did you carry this? It's a damned brick."

It was heavier than Miki expected, and he grimaced at the twisting pain in his knee when he stood back up. Cradling the wood against his side, he shook his head in both disgust and amazement at the dog's tenacity. The warehouse's open space gave the man a clear view of when Miki came back into the house, and he looked as if he were going to cross the threshold but stopped when Miki's glare dared him to take a step.

"Do you need…," the man started to say.

"I don't need anything," Miki grunted as he slowly walked toward him. The dog was gone, and by the time Miki got to the front door, he had a light sheen of sweat on his face. Holding out the chunk of wood, he said, "Here's your cone."

"Koa," the man corrected. The hardness seeped from his blue eyes, and he reached to take the wood from Miki's hands. "Sorry about the… you know. It's been a really rough day and… damn it, you're turning blue. You should—"

"Yeah, whatever." Miki shivered and his body prickled with goose bumps. The heavy door swung smoothly shut on its balanced hinges, and the world slowly closed behind him. "Take your fucking wood and go."

THE cold never left his bones, or at least that's what Miki felt like. Long, thick curtains and double-paned windows took the chill off of the San Francisco air, but the fire he finally coaxed to life in the narrow fireplace barely seemed to generate enough heat to warm its own hearth, much less the enormous open living space. Even with the central heating turned up to a comfortable seventy-two, the shuddering roils of cold rocked him with every other breath.

His knee throbbed with the fire of a thousand suns, but the memory of the infuriated man on his doorstep a couple of days ago burned Miki more. A tingle resonated in his cock when he thought about the man's deep blue eyes, and the reaction startled him. His dick hadn't shown an interest in anything or anyone since the accident. He wasn't hard, not by a long shot, but the awareness was definitely there.

"Great, now I'm getting a kink for someone who wants to beat me," he muttered, his voice rough with disgust. There'd been no lingering appraisal in the man's eyes, only fury and then a dash of pity. Pity was the last thing Miki wanted or needed. "Like I can't do that to myself. Fuck him."

Curled up on the couch he'd brought from the apartment he'd shared with Damien, Miki drew a thick quilt around his shoulders, tucking the ends in under him. The flames lulled him, and he stared into the flickering heat, his mind drifting from the too-chilled warehouse and the echoes of his thoughts. He didn't feel like gaming, even though he'd turned on the large-screen TV and the game systems. Food was out. His stomach rebelled at the mere suggestion of heading to the kitchen.

Miki caught a fragile tune wrapping through his thoughts and reached a notebook from the pile he kept on the coffee table. Too focused on the page, he almost jumped out of his skin when a chirruping scared the hell out of him. Floundering to free himself from the quilt, Miki nearly knocked himself off the battered couch before realizing it was his phone.

The handset rang again, chittering across the flat storage container he used as a coffee table. He knew the number flashing across the phone's display, and for a long moment, he debated letting the call to go the voice mail he never listened to.

"Hello, Edie," Miki said softly into the phone.

"Hey, kiddo." She exhaled breathily, and Miki wondered if she'd just let go a sigh of relief or if she'd taken up smoking again. "I'm glad you picked up."

"You'd just keep calling back until I did."

"You know me so well, Miki dear."

He did know her and hated that she knew him as well as she did. Grabbing his coffee cup, Miki ruefully discovered it'd gone cold. Disappointed, he set it back down and cradled the phone against his shoulder. The sofa cushions dipped as the dog jumped up and settled down next to him. A spit-damp tennis ball rolled from the dog's mouth, and he snuggled down into the quilt, twisting until he lay on his back with his feet in the air.

"What do you want, Edie?" The dog gave off some heat, and he shifted, sliding his feet under the mutt's body.

He knew why she called. The business end of Sinner's Gin still needed tending to, and she'd held those reins before the accident. It made sense for her to continue managing the group, even if Miki was all that was left. Back then Edie dealt mainly with Damien, but now she was stuck with the band's gutter-raised singer. Every week the phone rang, urging him to pick up some of the pieces of his former life. Often he'd let it go unanswered, ignoring the outside world for another seven days.

"I wanted to see how you—"

"What do you *need*, Edie?" Miki said through gritted teeth.

The woman didn't understand how her voice reminded him of the long weeks he spent on the road, complaining about the bad food, weather, and their bus drivers' aversion to bathing. She shadowed them through the ups and downs, either soothing their nerves or pushing them past their fears. The others griped constantly as they dragged themselves and their equipment from city to city, but Miki had never felt more alive. Living in each other's pockets strained their tempers at times, but they became tighter as a whole. He agonized over the loss of Damien's bossiness or Johnny's cocky, swaggering boasts of his hookups from the night before. Miki longed for a few more minutes of Dave's quiet faith as he murmured thanks to some god before they hit the stage.

Hearing Edie made him miss them all the more, and his heart couldn't take any more breaks in its already fragile shell.

"I *need* you to get out of the house, baby, but I'll settle for a long chat with you on the phone," Edie replied. "Let's get some business out of the way, and you can catch me up on what you're doing."

He listened with half an ear while Edie ran down the finances. European and Asian sales were still increasing, and the band's last album seemed fixed steady on album charts with no sign of dropping. Good news all around, and Miki wondered if he should feel anything other than the numbness inside of him. She continued to rattle off terms and agreements when something jarred him loose from his disinterest.

"Wait, back up." Miki shifted, and the dog opened one eye in reproach. "What did you just say?"

"Damien's parents were approached by a car company. They want permission to use a song for a commercial."

"Did you tell them no?" It wasn't much of a question. Damien hated hearing songs he loved being used to sell things, and the rights to Sinner's Gin's songs were solely Miki's. Every few months, the Mitchells pushed to break his hold, and he shoved back... hard. Fighting with Damien's parents seemed to be all he had left.

"I did. Their lawyer threatened to sue again to gain control of Sinner's Gin's catalogue."

"Last time they did that, they ended up paying the court costs. Why do they keep doing this? We all have enough money. Damien didn't want that shit. Why do they keep pushing?"

The tennis ball suddenly appeared in Miki's outstretched hand with a wet thump. The dog was off the couch in an instant, wagging his stump of a tail as hard as he could. He encouraged Miki to throw the ball with a sharp bark and scrambled after it when Miki whipped the stained tennis ball down the length of the warehouse.

"I don't know, honey," Edie said in a soft whisper. Her Minnesota cadence rolled over him, and Miki rested his forehead against his pulled-up knees.

"You know I don't care, yeah?" He fought a brief struggle with the sniffles, and tears filled his eyes. The ball reappeared at his feet, and Miki picked it up and carelessly tossed it over the shoulder for the dog to chase. "I don't care if they sell everything we ever made to a pork rind company. I don't give a shit, but Damien... he did. Why can't they understand that? Why can't they see that? Why the fuck can't they just leave me alone?"

"We'll let the lawyers handle it, kiddo," she reassured him. "I can't *not* tell you about these things, Miki. I have an obligation to tell you. You know that, right?"

"Yeah, I know. Thanks, Edie. It's... not you. It's them," Miki grumbled. "Let the lawyers deal with them. I'm not going to get into it. I'm too... tired for their shit."

"You getting out more?" She slid her concern into the conversation as skillfully as Johnny had de-panned his famous jalapeño eggs. Like the eggs, Edie's concern burned through Miki, and he blinked, hating his eyes for watering.

"I went for a walk yesterday." He didn't tell her it was to the liquor store to get bread and whiskey. The delivery truck had been in short supply of both, and he wanted a sandwich. He'd fallen asleep before he could get into the whiskey.

"Is the dog still with you?"

"He hasn't moved out yet. Might have to raise the rent." Miki glanced around. The tennis ball was sitting by the doggie flap he had a handyman put into the door to the garage. "Looks like he went out for a minute. Want me to tell him to call you back?"

"It's good you have him. At least he's company." Edie laughed. "Name him yet?"

"He's not my dog. He just lives here." He snorted.

"You feed him."

"Seems like the thing to do. I'd have to feed you if you came up here."

"Would you let me in, Miki?" Edie asked softly. "If I came up there?"

He closed his eyes, but the past flooded him. Memories of Edie haranguing the band, coddling Damien when he was hungover, and the soft voice she used to coax Miki out of his antisocial shell before an interview. She'd been as much of a mother to him as Damien's mom had been, and Miki hated that he couldn't trust the feelings lingering inside of him. The Mitchells turning on him hurt. He cared too much for Edie to shut her out.

"I don't know," he whispered. "Yes?"

The older woman sighed, "I'm here for you, Miki. If and when you let me, okay?"

"Okay." He disconnected the call and lay still under the quilts. Edie's warmth touched the cold inside of him, and he dozed, cradled in the cocoon he'd made for himself.

CHAPTER
TWO

You act like I'm the only sinner you know.
And say I'm someone who sets your skin on fire.
But I know different, little girl.
I know other men who'd call you a liar.

—Empty Promises

THE damned dog was back.

He never seemed to be there when Kane opened his studio, but it was like the dog had radar. He showed up solely to haunt the shop Kane leased from the art co-op.

But then so did the man who owned the damned thing. Well, at least he haunted Kane's mind.

Something about the younger man tugged at Kane's guts. His green-gold eyes were enormous, with a faint slant to them, ringed black with heavy lashes, and there was a heated challenge in them that taunted Kane and pulled him in. Fuck with me and I'll tear you a new asshole, that hazel glare said, but the simmer did nothing to hide the anguish lingering there.

"And I know him from somewhere," Kane swore to himself as he unpacked a set of chisels he'd gotten shipped to him. "Damned if I haven't seen him before."

He was too pretty to forget. Not a delicate face, Kane thought, but vulnerable and beautiful. Those high cheekbones and full lips had been nearly hidden beneath the man's shoulder-length mane, but when his long fingers pushed the dark brown strands out of the way, Kane forgot how to breathe. Now Kane caught himself wondering how the man's wide mouth would taste, or if he could chase away the faint pain lines around the younger man's lips.

The belligerent young man needed at least ten more pounds on him, and the kanji characters inked on his upper arm were splotchy and uneven, more like an old prison tattoo than calligraphy. The tips of his fingers ghosted over the ink, obviously an old habit, and the motion drew Kane's attention to the man's bared chest and the whorl of down around his flat belly button. The faint trail led down, disappearing under the younger man's loosely tied cotton pants, the jut of hip bones barely holding the waistband in place.

"No, last thing I need is that kind of trouble," he scolded his brain, then found himself fretting about the faint blue cast around the man's mouth and his shivering, half-naked body. The guy was definitely trouble and, despite the lean muscles and long legs, much too skinny for Kane's tastes. Too skinny and far too memorable.

The dog was still a menace, and its presence was a constant reminder of the pale, pretty-faced man next door. Sitting right outside of the workshop, the mutt woofed and scratched and panted like a blond, furry harbinger of doom.

It also reeked like it took a dive in the River Styx.

His focus shrunk down to the spinning block he'd set into lathe clamps and the small red-brown curls he coaxed from the wood. The sweet smell of the curled chips seduced him, and Kane quickly lost touch with the rest of the world. He didn't notice the chill biting through the air when the sun dropped behind a wall of clouds, and he didn't hear the dog's ruffling snores as it chased something in its sprawling sleep.

When the cramping in his hands became too much to bear and a bead of sweat tickled his eyebrow, Kane finally pulled back from the burl and took his foot off of the pedal, letting the lathe spin down so he could inspect his work. Running his hand over the carved wood, Kane felt for uneven spots in the grain.

"Look at the cop doing some work." A deep voice much like his own jerked Kane's attention up. "Hey, where'd you get the dog, and why's he eating your lunch?"

Kane glanced at the corner of the studio where he last saw the terrier, only to find it chewing on the remains of the ham sandwich Kane had left on his work bench.

"Fucking dog," Kane swore loudly.

"Nice," Quinn drawled. "You kiss our mother with that damned mouth?"

"Sure I do. She likes me best. 'Zup, Qbert?" Kane returned his younger brother's broad grin. After flicking the lathe off, he began to shake off the curls covering his shirt and thighs. Nodding to the scruffy dog, Kane said with an ironic chuckle, "That's not my dog. He's from next door. So far, he's stolen some koa, a screwdriver, and now my sandwich. Don't leave your wallet out where he can get it."

"Ever thought of... I don't know, rolling the door down... to keep the dog out?"

"Yeah, it crossed my mind," Kane drawled. "But I like the fresh air."

A year separated them, and the second and third Morgan boys spent much of their youth being mistaken for one another. Now that they were older, subtle differences made it easier to tell them apart. Kane's collar-length hair, the tiny scar cutting through Quinn's right eyebrow from a Hot Wheels accident, and the opposite-angled slight breaks in their noses gave their mother something to focus on when she needed to know who she was scolding.

Of all his siblings, Kane was closest to Quinn. They'd spent their boyhood years sharing a room until Connor moved out and Kane claimed the converted attic for his own. A few months later, Kane helped Quinn move his things into the long room, since Quinn spent more time in Kane's new room than he did in his own. The rest of the Morgan children spread out through the remainder of the rooms, quickly establishing their own territories in case their older brothers changed their minds.

It was Quinn whom Kane called the night his girlfriend left him, and it was Kane that urged Quinn to come out of the closet they'd both been hiding in. It was also Kane who helped him weather the storm that hit when Quinn told their traditional Irish Catholic family that he preferred men.

Kane told their family he'd considered the occasional man as well, and if the younger brother was to be damned for it, the older would be damned as well.

Quinn reached up and rattled the guide chains to the bay door over the dog's head. The terrier ignored him to chew on a stray bread crust. "Mom wants to see your ugly face at the dinner table on Sunday. She's a bit pissed off it's been missing of late."

"With you around, I'm surprised she can see past your ugly to miss mine."

"Keep it up, brother mine, and I can take care of what little pretty you have left."

"Yeah, I'd like to see you try," Kane growled. "Sunday. Got it."

Quinn studied the dog again. "Doesn't have a tag. Want me to call Animal Control and ticket the owner?"

"Really?" Kane stopped cleaning the tips of his chisels and looked up at his younger brother. "I'm a cop. You think I need a history teacher to call in a stray dog?"

"Just saying, if the dog's bugging you...."

"Yeah, I don't need my baby brother to take care of it for me." He put away the tools in a work cabinet and locked the doors. "You want some dinner or something? Or are you heading back to the college?"

"Let me check on something, and we can meet up at Leong's later," Quinn said. He retrieved his phone and tapped the screen. "Unless that welding glove the mutt just took isn't all that important."

Kane turned in time to see the terrier trotting off with a long white glove he used while stacking rough woods. Taking a deep breath, he tilted his head back and exhaled slowly. "God, I hate that dog."

"Leong's then?" Quinn asked. "Half an hour?"

"I'll either see you there or I'll call you for bail," Kane muttered. A quick twist of a key opened the gun safe where he kept his badge and Glock. After snapping the holstered gun onto his belt, Kane shrugged on his leather jacket, covering the weapon. "That guy's got to do something about his mutt."

"Offer to run it in still stands," Quinn said. "Or I could shoot it. I'll have to borrow your gun, though. I don't have one."

The younger Morgan chuckled at the poisonous look Kane shot at him. Shrugging, Quinn returned to his phone and stepped aside as his older brother closed and locked the rolling door.

AS HE expected, the dog was gone before Kane circled the building, but unlike the last time, the warehouse's garage bay was open, and a throaty rumbling seduced him into coming closer.

A door that probably led to the warehouse space was closed, but the partially raised dog door cut into it gave Kane some idea of where the mutt went. He barely noticed the small pile of odd items stacked next to the rolled-up bay door or the open half-full trash bag sitting next to it. Kane stepped over his missing welding glove and stood in awe in front of the beauty stretched out before him, a custom cover pooled on the concrete by its grill.

Even in the fading light of a San Francisco twilight, the backed-in 1968 GTO gleamed black and sleek under the garage's single overhead light. Its classic lines were clean, without a hint of a ripple on the metal. Curiously, the car sat up on risers, its wheels a few inches up off the cement floor, but the rims gleamed, and the area beneath the engine was spotless. The driver's side door was slightly open, and the engine rumbled, a low, growling purr that filled the garage.

Kane forgot all about the welding glove and the plans he'd made with his brother to grab Chinese food. He only had eyes for the sleek, gleaming black car.

"Hello, baby," Kane purred back.

He hesitated to touch its gleaming paint but compromised his reluctance with the promise to wipe off any fingerprints he might leave behind. The black sheen was smooth under his hand, obviously done in a high-end paint shop. From what Kane could see, the interior was as pitch black as the exterior, but the dark tint on the side and rear windows made seeing inside the car difficult, especially with the garage light on.

"How come the dome light isn't on?" Kane patted the car. "Your daddy fixing that?"

He walked around to the driver's side door and stopped dead in his tracks. A step forward, then a longer peek into the interior told him all he needed to know, and Kane pulled his gun and moved closer, slowly approaching the car.

"Damn it, I'm supposed to be off today." Kane swore a hot Gaelic curse he learned from his grandmother. "I don't need this kind of shit."

Even in the GTO's glossy black leather interior, Kane knew the wetness on the seats was blood, probably coming from the punctured remains of the naked, elderly Asian man sprawled across the front seat. Years of living already ravaged the man's face, but a knife had helped deepen the thick, wrinkled grooves in his skin. A sluggish glut of yellowish trickle eased from a gaping wound along his abdomen, joining the other drying trails of fluids crisscrossing his flaccid gray skin. One eye stared up at the car's black headliner, but the other was only an empty socket partially filled with black dried blood. The man's mouth was torn open, a mocking echo of the ragged slashes on his torso.

From what Kane could see, someone had taken their time hacking at the dead man's body... a very angry, very determined someone with a jagged knife.

Kane took his phone and dialed Emergency as he kept watch on the dead man's body and the closed door he assumed led to the warehouse.

"Hey, Dispatch? This is Inspector Kane Morgan out of Personal Crimes. I need you to send a couple of cars to...." He glanced out of the garage and read off the cross street to the cul-de-sac. "I've got a DB. Yeah, it's a bad one. I need to check the residence. I'm going to do a welfare check on the guy that lives here."

As if on cue, the door opened and the young man he yelled at a few days ago stepped into the garage. Splashes of water and bubbles turned his thin white T-shirt nearly transparent, and the man's dark nipples peaked from the cold air when it hit the wet fabric. Coming around the car's trunk towards the driver's side, the young man seemed about to tear into Kane when he spotted the slaughter in the GTO's interior and froze in shock.

"What did you do?" He gasped at Kane.

The sight of Kane's gun seemed to shake him up, and he stumbled, still stricken with alarm. His fall was a graceful wreck, as if his body refused to respond as it should, and the young man tumbled, tangled into a broken heap on cold cement.

Kane's gut twisted in response to the young man's horrified mewl. Putting away his gun, he strode across the floor. He bent over the man to help him up, and the younger man flinched, drawing back from Kane's hand. His hazel eyes darted from the dead man's body up to Kane's face, worry and fear flitting over his pretty features before falling away under a fierce glare.

"Did you... do that? Did you kill Shing?" His voice was thick, rough with emotion, as he accused Kane of murder.

"I was about to ask you the same question." Kane held up his badge and offered his hand again. The man's clothes were clean of blood splatter but that didn't mean he didn't change them before coming back outside. It was the horror on his face that partially convinced Kane of the young man's innocence. That and the slightly green flush forming around his cheeks and mouth. To his knowledge, most killers didn't spontaneously throw up when they spotted their handiwork again. "Inspector Kane Morgan, SFPD. Let's get you on your feet. Do I need to call you a medic?"

The young man shook his head and tried standing up, but his right leg gave out and he flailed. Muttering to himself, he attempted it again with little result. "Shit. This is fucking… insane. I can't—"

"Grab my hand," Kane insisted. "We need to get you out of the garage. I called dispatch. You can't be here while Forensics does its work."

The man's fingers were ice cold, more from shock than water, and he trembled as he wrapped his hand around Kane's. Up close, he smelled of cloves and soap with a faint underlying hint of tea and chilies. Kane had thought he was too skinny before, and the light weight of the young man against his arm didn't do anything to change his mind. The trapped, fearful look in the man's wide eyes made Kane want to wrap him up in a blanket to tuck him away before any other cops arrived, but the feral hardness of his full mouth gave Kane pause. The man didn't need protection, certainly not from anyone except maybe himself.

It'd taken him long enough, but Kane finally recognized the dog's owner. The first time he'd seen the man, he'd been plastered up on one of his sister's bedroom walls, wearing leather pants and a come-fuck-me snarl. Several of the man's CDs were in Kane's truck, and he sometimes popped them in when he needed a good kick of bluesy rock to keep him awake after a long night.

"Son of a bitch, you're Miki St. John." Kane whistled. "You're the singer from Sinner's Gin."

From the expression on St. John's face, someone would have thought Kane had kicked him in the balls. The man recoiled, sliding away from Kane. He slid along the wall, still unable to hold himself up on his right leg, but he didn't appear to care. If anything, Kane recognizing him seemed to drive him back into the house.

Not the typical reaction Kane expected from a musician, even one who'd disappeared off the face of the earth. Then St. John turned violently green, and the man's fears were the farthest thing from Kane's mind.

"Don't throw up in here," Kane ordered. "Turn your head. Aim for inside the house if you're going to do it."

Shock bled the man's skin to a deathly white, so the sickness taking him over was a quick wave of cold sweats and ashen pallor. Shaking, St. John bent over and heaved. Kane grabbed at him, trying to drag him out of the garage so he didn't ruin any evidence, but it was too late. He retched, losing everything he had in his stomach.

Which, to Kane's eyes, didn't appear to be anything more than water.

St. John clutched his stomach and retched again, more air than anything else. His eyes were wide with distress and more than a little bloodshot. The heaving didn't appear to help his color any, and Kane kept half an eye on the door, hoping the dog wouldn't decide to trot out and track through the watery vomit.

"Damn it, you're going into shock," Kane grumbled. He quickly shed his jacket, then hissed when a cold wind whipped through the open garage. If he was cold, he couldn't imagine how St. John felt. The man looked barely strong enough to walk, much less ward off a freezing San Francisco wind. He leaned down and wrapped the warm leather jacket around St. John's shoulders and checked his phone again. "I'm going to have Dispatch send out an ambulance. You look like you need one."

"No, I'm... fine. What the...?" St. John didn't finish. Instead he tried to get to his feet again, bracing himself against the wall with one hand. His eyes never left Kane's face, although they shifted once in a while to look at Kane's holstered gun. "Do you know who killed him? How.... Fuck...."

"No, but I want to know who did," Kane replied, tapping the badge he wore on his belt. "How do you know him? How'd he end up here?"

"I don't know. I didn't kill him," the young man said. He shook slightly, a barely perceptible shiver under his skin, and his eyes remained fixed on the carved up remains of the body draped over the car seat. "If you find who did it, I want to thank them something fierce."

OLD Man Shing was dead.

Miki struggled to wrap his brain around the one single thing he knew was a fact. Other than that, his mind whirred from the endless questions and accusations flung at him as he sat in the tiny khaki-painted room.

Still, Shing's death did something to him inside. He wanted time to think, a spare moment to stop his mind from spinning. He wanted to see the body, to touch it. Anything to have some evidence that the old man who'd terrorized his nightmares was gone, but all he got from the police were whispers and accusations.

Bright lights prevented him from seeing past the one-way observation window, and he imagined there was a line of people who came and went in a tag-team interrogation dance. Mute, hard-faced men came to scrape at his fingers and skin then he'd been told to strip. A pair of scratchy blue cotton scrubs they gave him provided little warmth against the cold air blasting down on him from an air conditioning vent, and Miki wondered if that was part of a cunning plan to freeze out answers from a suspect.

Wiggling his toes did nothing to hold off the chill in them, but it gave him something to do while the cops decided who to send in next.

The door opened and the Hispanic detective who brought him to the police station walked in. There'd been some noise about Miki's band and more than a few curious glances as he walked past the blue sea of cops and into the bathroom, where a stone-faced uniformed officer watched him strip off his clothes. They let him keep his underwear but took his battered Vans, giving him a pair of thin flip-flops to wear. Miki almost told the cop he'd kill for some socks, but the cop's tight lips made him think twice.

Mostly, the cop was overly polite. If anything, his good manners made Miki's skin crawl more than the uniforms staring at him when he was walked into the station. The ride to the station was a brief, silent torture. He hadn't been cuffed and was informed he was only there to answer a few questions, but his lack of clothes told him a much different story.

"Mr. St. John? Mieko? Do you remember me? I'm Inspector Kel Sanchez." The detective sat down in the chair across the table. Shivering, Miki leaned back and waited as the detective shuffled through the folder he'd brought in with him.

"Can I go home? I left the bathtub full of water and the car running." Miki eyed the folder's contents from under his lashes. A younger version of himself stared up out of an outdated photo, and a cynical rage flared up in Miki's belly. Leaning forward, he tapped the piece of paper on top. "Isn't that supposed to be... like, sealed? Isn't that the bullshit you're told? That your juvie records are sealed?"

"Juvenile records aren't sealed or expunged unless requested, Mr. St. John." Sanchez's sympathetic look set Miki's teeth on edge. "A lawyer can help you with the process, but for right now, what's in here is relevant to the case. I only have a few questions. Then you can go. Let's start with the last time you saw Tingzhe Shing?"

"I haven't seen Shing in years." Miki closed his eyes, trying to repress the shudder threatening to take over his body. He shoved Shing into a box a long time ago, hammering it shut in the hopes of never seeing the man again. Finding the interior of his car painted with Shing's guts shocked him deeper than he thought possible. Miki looked up at the detective. "I told my cop... the other cop that. The one who... found him. Shing wasn't someone I wanted to keep in touch with."

"But you worked for him when you were younger, about fourteen or fifteen, right? Even lived over the restaurant his family owns when you and your foster father were fighting?" It wasn't really a question but rather a probing, as if the man was searching for a broken tooth or open nerve. He found it, and Miki bit the inside of his cheek to keep from swearing. "Can you tell me about then?"

"Nope."

Sanchez looked up, surprised at Miki's soft whisper. Leaning forward, he placed his hands on the table and relaxed his shoulders, doing everything he could to appear as nonthreatening as possible. Miki wasn't fooled. He'd been a pawn for cop games for as long as he could remember.

"I just need to know what your relationship with Shing was. Was it a good one? Did you have a falling-out? We'll just go over a few things. Then you can leave."

"We didn't have a relationship," Miki replied, leaning back in the uncomfortable metal chair he'd been given to sit in. "There never was a falling in. End of story."

"His son was surprised to find out his father's body was in your garage. He said you and Shing weren't close, but he wasn't sure," Sanchez pressed. "Have you been in touch with anyone from the Shing family? Perhaps to pay them back for giving you a place to live when you had problems with your foster parents?"

"Shing got everything he was ever going to get from me." The sourness returned to Miki's throat, and he swallowed, wishing for a glass of water to wash away the past choking him. "I don't know how he got into my... car. I started it up because I'm supposed to do that every month or the engine goes to shit. I was inside. Then the dog came in, so I grabbed him to give him a bath. I was filling the tub up when your guy came through the garage door."

"Do you have any idea who'd want to kill Shing?"

More papers were shuffled out of the folder, and Miki looked away, not wanting to see his life spilled out onto the table. He didn't know why it bothered him. It wasn't as if he didn't know what was in there. Miki had no delusions of where he came from and who he was. Damien had been the one with the plan to wash the street off of him, but Miki didn't think there was enough soap in the world to get rid of the filth he was born into.

"Maybe he finally ticked someone off who could do something about it." Miki shrugged. "You want to ask someone about Shing?

Start with his son, then work your way around the neighborhood. You'll find a lot of people in Chinatown Shing pissed on."

"No one's talking, Mieko," the detective said softly. "I was hoping you'd be the one who spoke up."

"You'd be wrong. I've got nothing to say." Miki kept his voice flat as he met the cop's steady gaze. "So can I go now?"

CHAPTER THREE

Picked up a piece of silver from the ground,
Used it to end a bit of my strife.
If I'd known I'd need it to get into Heaven,
I'd have carried it with me all of my life.

—Going Over The River

"THAT boy's a mess."

Lt. Mark Casey's booming voice rattled Kane's eardrums, and he grunted a greeting at the man, meeting his lieutenant's eyes in the reflection of the glass. The barrel-chested black man strolled closer to the glass and unwrapped a piece of gum. The senior Inspector folded it into his mouth and chewed at the strip until it was tucked into the corner of his cheek. Within seconds of discarding the foil wrapper, another slice joined the mass in his mouth, its sweet, fruity odor nearly strong enough to cover the stink of Kane's bitter coffee.

Kane couldn't do anything but nod. His lieutenant was right. Miki St. John was a hot mess. Unfortunately, he was all they had at the moment.

"He knew Shing." Kane flipped through the file folder he'd gotten from Sanchez before his partner went into the interview room. "St. John's got to be connected to this somehow. No one just randomly dumps a body into the front seat of a car, even if it's owned by a rock star. There are better ways to say I love you."

"I personally would have gone for chocolates or roses, but then again…." Casey shrugged his massive shoulders. "That's something I've learned from my wife."

"I spoke with the oldest son." Kane refused the gum Casey offered him with a shake of his head. "He was wholly unhelpful. 'Everyone loved Shing. No one had anything bad to say about him.' Someone universally beloved doesn't end up looking like he's been run through a garlic press. Those kind of people die peacefully in their bed."

"You and Sanchez are on this." The smell of fruity gum got stronger when Casey leaned in toward him. "I watched a bit of you with the son. That's a cold son of a bitch."

"Yeah, Bradley Shing." Kane made a face at his coffee. "He was too calm. He didn't ask to see his dad. If it were me, I'd be tearing the place apart until I had proof. You saw him. It was like I was ordering up a bowl of soup. He didn't give me anything to go on but a bad feeling."

"Not everyone's got Donal Morgan for a father," The lieutenant reminded him. "You believe what the son was selling you? That no one hated his old man?"

"I haven't spoken to anyone else yet, but Miki St. John seems to hate him," Kane said, jerking his chin toward the interview room where his partner sat with the singer. "But he's not talking about it. He could have had someone kill Shing for him, but my gut says the guy was really shocked when he saw Shing's body in his car. We'll have to check on his financials to be sure."

"Find out what Shing and St. John had going on between them." Casey popped his gum between his teeth. Kane's partner was still trying to coax more than one-word responses out of the other man in the interview room, and the lieutenant grunted at Miki's obstinacy. "That kid's not giving anything up to Sanchez. He's definitely hiding something."

"I asked the family if we could take a look at Shing's office to see if we could find something to point us to who killed him, but the son shut me down fast." He crossed his arms and quirked a smile.

It was funny to see his smooth-talking partner being outfoxed by a pretty-faced, street-smart asshole for a change. Kel danced as hard as he could with St. John, alternating between sympathetic and nearly aggressive to wedge a crack into the young man's steely façade. So far, Kel was failing miserably, and the corners of his mouth were tight, a barely noticeable sign of his growing impatience with the singer.

"Kel said something about St. John living over the restaurant." Kane grabbed at the stray thought before it got away from him. "I want in that room and the office. Think we can get a warrant for a search?"

"It'll be kind of rough," Casey drawled. "The family just suffered a loss. Judges tend to frown on making the victim's family go through shit like that."

"There's something there," Kane said. "Wish I'd known about it before I let the son go. I'd have asked him just to see how he responded. If he hit on it, I'd have pushed harder."

"St. John had to go through the lab stuff first," the lieutenant reminded him. "So far, they don't like him for anything. No blood on his clothes, and the team we left behind said nothing's in the house but the dog. No blood or anything. Well, except for the spots Lau got on the kitchen floor when the dog bit him."

"No one shot the dog, did they?" Kane turned and gave his boss a suspicious look.

"No, they tossed it in the bathroom with a water dish. The place came up clean." Casey popped his gum again, and from the looks of things, Sanchez's mouth was getting thinner by the minute. "Let me go see about securing a warrant for Shing's place. We'll let the rock star go. Have a uniform run him home with our apologies, but put a car on the place for a bit. If he did pay someone to off the guy, that someone's going to come by."

"Probably," Kane agreed. "The car's registered to him, but he doesn't have a license. It was up on risers, so it wasn't going anywhere. The lab said it'll be a couple of weeks until they release it."

"You better go save Sanchez before he blows," Casey commented as a flush turned Kel's face bright red. "That kid's going to give him a heart attack if he stays in there much longer."

"Deal," he said. "Maybe I'll take St. John home myself. God knows, I can't do worse than Sanchez there."

"Just don't hit on him until after we clear him as a suspect." Casey poked Kane in the chest, glaring at him warningly. "Can you promise me that? Or am I just pissing in the wind?"

"Something about him, Lieutenant," he admitted. There *was* something about Miki St. John. The man had peppered his thoughts ever since he saw him shivering half-naked in the doorway of the warehouse, defending a dog he refused to admit owning. "He grabs at my gut."

"That's not your gut he's grabbing, Kane. Those are your balls." The man chuckled. "I saw the way you were looking at the boy. He's trouble… trouble you don't need, kid."

Kane finished the rest of his coffee with a gulp and balled up the paper cup in his fist. Lobbing it toward the trash can, he made an open-mouthed hissing noise to mimic a crowd. He grinned at the man who taught him how to play basketball and said, "I'm a Morgan, sir. We always need trouble. It's how we survive."

HIS cop was waiting for Miki when he came out of the interrogation room. Miki wasn't sure when the man became *his* cop, but that's how he felt when he spotted the lanky, loose-hipped Irish man leaning against the wall. The detective had shed the leather jacket at some point, and the stretch of T-shirt across his wide chest made Miki wish his dick would respond with more than a tingling lift at the sight. An ancient pair of jeans, complete with frayed rips and bare spots on the man's thighs, hugged the inspector's long legs, but nothing the cop wore unmanned Miki as much as the man's cocky, uneven smile.

"Hey." The cop's deep voice warmed Miki's cold belly. He held up a blue SFPD T-shirt and a pair of black sweats. "Want to change out of that crap they gave you to wear?"

"You going to watch me get naked like that other cop did?" Miki growled, but he limped closer to take the clothes. Stiff from being in the cold cinder block room, his right knee began its familiar salsa of pain and throbbing.

"You offering?" Kane asked with a wider smile. It faded when Miki stared back with an uncomprehending look on his face. "You have no idea what you just said, do you?"

"Look, I just want to go home and get warm," Miki replied. "I've got to feed the Dude."

"Home's off limits for now. Forensics isn't done with the place yet. Might be another hour before the Lieutenant says you can head back, then. Your dog's fine. They put him in the bathroom with some food and water." He shrugged helplessly at Miki's disgusted hiss. "I was thinking you probably needed some food in you. God knows I do. How about if we get something to eat?"

"I don't have my wallet. You guys grabbed me before I could get it. I don't have anything on me."

"I'm buying," the cop offered, falling in behind Miki.

Miki pressed his hand against the wall, using it for support as he limped toward the bathroom. "Fuck this shit. God, I hate cops."

"Hey, I'm one of those cops."

"You can cut the I'm-a-nice-guy shit out. I don't know anything. I keep telling all of you that, but you're not listening," Miki said, wincing as the feeling started to come back into his leg.

"Mieko, stop." Kane came up behind him. The whisper of breath on his neck brought Miki up short. He inhaled deeply, pulling in the rich scent of masculine skin with a hint of coffee and mint. "I'm just trying to help. Let me help you."

The cold in Miki's bones evaporated when Kane touched his arm. The thin cotton of his borrowed scrubs separated their skin, but the heat of Kane's fingers burned through him. He wanted to lean back against Kane, to rest his head against the other man's chest until the chill inside of him whispered away and he fell asleep, safe from the darkness that stalked him.

"Like that's ever going to happen," Miki muttered to himself. He pulled away, working the kinks out of his thigh with a shake of his leg. "Let me get changed, then I'll figure out how to get home."

"Easier if I take you," the cop said. "There are reporters outside waiting for you to come out. Cops find dead body inside of rock star's car. You're a big story, you know. They're outside the station like fleas. I'm parked in the inside garage. My car's windows are tinted, and no one will know you're inside. Go get changed, Mieko. I'll wait for you out here, and we'll grab something to eat before I take you home."

Miki turned and stared up into Kane's unwavering blue gaze. Discomforted, Miki looked away, blinking away the sting of tears in his eyes. Nodding, he started to move forward and sniffed as he reached the bathroom door. "Fine. Just stop calling me Mieko. That's a girl's name."

FRAGILE wasn't a word Kane would have associated with the young man who served him back his attitude a few days ago, but when Mieko St. John came out of the bathroom, he looked like he was made out of glass. Ghostly pale and dressed in Kane's too-large T-shirt and the pair of sweats Kane swiped from his younger brother's locker, the young man struggled to pull on the black hoodie he'd been given.

And looked as fragile and as dangerous as a million shards of broken glass as he did it.

A pair of socks was all the footwear Kane could find to protect Miki's feet from the cold, and the man wore them like tabi with the flip-flops he'd been given. Miki fought with one sleeve, and Kane stepped in, grabbing the material bunched up around his elbow.

"What?" Miki narrowed his eyes. The menacing effect was lost under the swaddle of the hood as it fell over his forehead and smashed his hair into his face.

"Stop." Kane grinned and resisted the urge to brush the hair from Miki's eyes. He straightened the sleeve out and pulled it over the man's arm. "Just let me help you. It's not going to kill you."

"Might one day," he grumbled but let Kane adjust the hoodie on him.

"Yeah, well for right now, it's not."

Kane led Miki down the sterile hallway and into the enormous maze of cubicles and offices that housed the station's Personal Crimes division. The bullpen vibrated with activity, but curious eyes followed their progress toward the far side of the room. One uniformed officer brought up a cell phone, and Kane narrowed his eyes at the man, warning him off with a shake of his head. A trail of murmurs followed them through the low-walled maze, a whispering tide rising and falling as Kane guided Miki.

When Kane turned his head, he could have sworn he heard Miki singing softly to himself, his hooded green eyes hazy from lack of focus. Touching his shoulder jerked Miki's attention back to his surroundings, and he blinked, seemingly surprised to find himself in the middle of a police station.

The late afternoon chill had turned into a brisk, cold evening by the time they left the police station in Kane's SUV. Dark tinted windows protected Miki from prying eyes as they drove past the front of the building, where a gaggle of cameras and equipment had been set up. Suited men and women were isolated into circles of bright lights, tiny theaters where they were the sole stars. Miki snorted as they drove past, pulling Kane's attention from the road.

"What's so funny?" Kane glanced at the pack, worried one of the reporters had spotted them, but the SUV eased by without anyone's notice, lost in the stream of police cars coming in and out of the garage.

"They look like they've each got their own stage," Miki replied. The line of his mouth softened, and his eyes took on a dreamy glaze. The green in his eyes shone through the gold, chopped emerald spun with topaz. "Must be why shit like that's called a three-ring circus. They're all little ringmasters looking for a stage and their own lion to tame."

"Do you miss it?" Kane asked. "The stage? The screams of the crowd?"

"No." The wistfulness of Miki's smile evaporated. "And I don't want to talk about… then."

"Okay. How about something else, then?" The SUV came to a stop beneath a tree of red lights, and Kane bent forward, watching a family of tourists cross the street. "So, Dude, huh?"

"What?" Miki shifted in the seat, trying to get his leg as comfortable as he could. "Who?"

"Dude. You called the dog Dude." Kane mulled. "Does he come when you call him that?"

"Yeah."

"If he comes when you call him that, then that's his name." He chuckled. "If he's got a name, and he comes when you call him, then that's your dog. Just once, I'd like to hear you admit that is your damned dog."

"He's not my dog. He comes and goes when wants. One day, he'll bail," Miki murmured. "Then what?"

"Then you go look for him 'cause he's yours," Kane said. "And he should have a collar on it with his name and your number so the next idiot he suckers can save himself by calling you to come get him."

"I call him a lot of things. Dude's just the one I use the most. Sometimes, I call him Dipshit. He doesn't seem to care so long as he's got food in his bowl." He shrugged off Kane's laughter. "Names are shitty things, sometimes. Look at mine."

"Why'd they name you Mieko if that's a girl's name? I've seen you without a shirt. Not much girl there."

"Seen a lot of girls, then?" Miki's mouth quirked when Kane laughed.

"I've got sisters. Even gay men sometimes see girl parts."

"Some lady found me on the street and called the CPS. Had nothing on but diapers and this damned tattoo." Shifting in his seat, Miki turned to face the window, leaving Kane to stare at the reflection of the man's face in the glass. Miki's breath steamed the window. "One of the cops said it meant Mieko. Found out later it doesn't, but by then it was too late. Don't know what it means, but it sure as shit isn't Mieko."

"What cop?" Kane swore as the car behind him honked, and he looked up, surprised to see the green light. Pulling forward, he let the sedan behind him swerve past. "Where?"

Miki shrugged. "I don't know. Some guy that was there when Social Services got there."

"No, I mean what did you mean; some lady found you?"

"She was taking the trash out or something, and I guess I was wandering around on the sidewalk." He grunted as he shifted his legs. Kane didn't miss the wince when Miki hit his leg on the SUV's side panel. "So CPS came and took me."

"How old were you?"

"I don't know. Two? Maybe three?" Miki wrapped the hoodie tighter around his chest. "Not like they could cut me open and count the rings."

"Shit," Kane whispered under his breath. "And St. John? Was that the family that adopted you?"

"Street I was found on," he replied softly. "I went into the system. No one wants someone else's kids, dude. Especially not some fucked up mongrel kid with shitty undies and a tattoo. Trust me on that."

"It's not like that," Kane objected. "Not everyone's like that."

"Yeah, they are," Miki asserted. "Life might be a magic mushroom ride for some kids, but most of us live in the cow shit it grows in. You just have to do what you can, that's all."

"And you became a rock star."

"No." Even in the watery reflection of the glass, Kane could see Miki's eyes tear up. "The other guys were the rock stars. I was just there when it happened to them."

"I've got some of your stuff, you know. It's good," Kane said, softening his voice. "Even Kel says you're a big deal."

"Kel was that guy in the room with me?"

"Yep, that's Kel. Kel Sanchez. He's my partner."

"Yeah, he's an asshole," Miki said, turning around to face Kane. "Where are we going?"

"Small Mexican food place I know. They've got some seating outside and heaters," Kane said. "Give me a few minutes to get there. It'll be fast."

One thing Kane learned as he drove was that Miki St. John was never really quiet. The man hummed. Constantly. The snippets of song were barely audible, but they rose and fell without stopping. At times, whispers would slip in, melodic drops of words following some tune Miki had in his head. Sitting in Kane's SUV and staring out the window at San Francisco, Miki St. John sang to himself, building a soundtrack for a life he seemed to live behind brick and glass with only a mutt to keep him company.

Kane turned the SUV into a parking lot next to a brightly painted faux-adobe building. Despite the late hour, the place was busy, and the smell of carnitas and carne asada permeated the air. Kane got out first and waited as Miki grabbed at the passenger side door to maintain his balance.

The stiffness in the younger man's knee was obvious, and it clicked loudly when he took his first step. It was difficult not to reach for Miki. Even when he stumbled, Kane was held back by the piercing glare Miki gave him. Beyond the stubbornness and pride in the man's set mouth and hazel stare, Kane still saw the pain and hurt Miki fought to hide. The brittleness he'd hoped to coax from Miki was back, his spirit as tenuous as a pane of thin glass riddled with spiderweb cracks.

"You warm enough?" Kane asked.

Miki nodded. "Yeah, I'm fine."

"You can talk to someone, you know," Kane said softly. He gave in to the temptation to touch Miki, and his fingers glided over the man's shoulder blades, rubbing at the jut of bone he found hidden under the thick fleece. "About Shing, I mean. I can help you find someone to talk with. Someone discreet and private. We... the police... don't need to know what you spoke about, but it might... help you heal, Miki. I can tell there's something there you need to heal from."

"I... can't. I won't." Miki stopped walking, and Kane wondered if the young man would pull away from him, but instead, Miki leaned back, resting his slight weight against the flat of Kane's hand. "Not about Shing. I'd sooner talk to you about the band, and I think we both know that's not going to happen any time soon."

"Okay, no rush." Kane led Miki to an empty wooden picnic table. "Have a seat. What do you want to eat?"

"Tacos? A burrito?" Miki eased onto the seat and stretched his leg out. "No beans. I don't like beans."

Kane strolled up to the counter and placed a hefty order of carne asada burritos and quesadillas. Leaning on the tiled shelf, he watched Miki as he scanned the crowd. The singer kept his head down, with his face nearly buried in the fleece hood.

"Salsa? Spicy carrots?" the young woman behind the counter asked. Kane nodded and grinned at sight of the red peppers poking out amid the carrot and onion chunks.

He carried the overloaded tray back to the table. "The carrots look deadly tonight. Don't choke on one. I come here a lot. Don't embarrass me."

"Are you talking to me or yourself?" Miki lowered the hood, exposing his face.

"You," Kane replied, setting a burrito and a quesadilla in front of Miki. "Horchata okay? I should have asked. I can grab something else if you want."

"No, it's good," Miki said, taking a sip of the cold spiced rice milk.

"You eat meat, right?" Kane glanced up and caught the smirk on Miki's face. "Yeah, okay. Right now, I'm going to assume that's a yes."

Miki picked at his food at first. Then Kane nudged his foot under the table and nodded at the burrito. A few tentative nibbles, then Miki dug in. Chewing around his mouthful, he said, "It's good. How's yours?"

"Not as good as what's across the table, but it'll do." Kane smiled as innocently as he could as Miki choked. "Don't die on me just yet. I've got plans for you later. Especially teaching you a thing or two about dogs."

CHAPTER FOUR

The poison inside of me kills what I touch,
So why should I love, when I know it'll die?

—Arsenic Kiss

THE cop ate like he was performing surgery. Every motion was controlled and precise, from the dipping of a piece of quesadilla into tomatillo sauce to the selection of a hot pickled carrot slice out of the plastic bag. Kane fished out a tiny pepper from the baggie and popped it into his mouth, chewing through it before picking up his burrito.

Miki watched Kane from under his lashes. The tangerine glimmer from the street lights turned the hair on Kane's forearms to a deep mahogany, with splashes of gold where the sun had bleached a few strands. A battered gold ring sat on Kane's left pinky, the metal dinged and matte from wear, the only piece of jewelry Kane wore besides the thick-banded watch on his wrist.

There was a tiny chip missing from the tooth between his front tooth and incisor, a triangular imperfection that caught the eye when Kane grinned. From what Miki'd seen, the man did not smile softly. Instead, he threw his whole mouth into it, a slightly off-kilter, masculine expression that had more in common with Dude's mischievous appearance than Kane probably would want to admit.

It was a grin that tugged at Miki's belly and had his body tingling in all the right places. If only it did more than tingle.

It wasn't that Miki wasn't willing. Kane definitely had his interest. The man's hands were strong, and Miki could almost feel them on him. It didn't take a stretch of the imagination to feel Kane's fingers digging into his hips or the heat of the man's breath on his mouth if they ever kissed. A coiled power lay in Kane's broad shoulders, his strength a casual confidence he wore as easily as he breathed.

Definitely more than a tingle, Miki realized as his cock thickened slightly for the first time since he woke up from his coma. And all for a cop who'd found his worst nightmare slaughtered and left on display in his car.

"You doing okay?" Kane looked up from his food and caught Miki's eyes on him. "Kind of seem out of it. Tired?"

"Yeah, a little bit," Miki mumbled, studying his food. "I want to go home and crash."

"Any friends you need to call?" Kane asked, folding a piece of cheesy tortilla into his mouth.

"Nope." Miki took a breath and blinked, willing away the sound of torn metal and cries he held inside of him. "Not anymore."

The pain inside him grew, and Miki inhaled deeply, hoping the chill in the air would cut through him. Kane studied him, dark lashes hooding his bright blue eyes. It was disconcerting being under that stare, and Miki shifted on his seat, torn between walking off or staring the man down.

Kane threw a curveball. "Tell me what music *you* like."

"You serious?" Miki looked away, thinking. "Um, different stuff, I guess. What do you like?"

"I like Metallica," Kane ventured.

"I like them." Miki paused. "Well, the *Black* album and anything before that. Things kind of went to shit after they hooked up with someone who told them the bass has to be in line with drums. It changed their sound. Yeah, that's technically right, but it changed how they worked. *Black's* more marketable, more approachable to mainstream listeners. You can definitely see that."

"Who else?" Kane gave a small smile and leaned forward to listen.

"Tool," he said, thinking for a second. "*Ænima*, and anything before that. After that, it's too much Zomb, and I don't like Perfect Circle. Love VAST's *Video Audio Sensory Theatre*. That's a *perfect* album. BRMC's *Howl* is pretty good. I like to listen to it when I just want to drift a bit. Dave and Johnny used to argue about Lynyrd Skynyrd, but I only like some of their stuff. Anything by Stevie Ray Vaughan. *Anything*."

"Mostly blues stuff, then?"

"Nah, depends on my mood," Miki said, shrugging. "Hyde, I love Hyde. I like him solo or under VAMPS but only some of L'Arc-en-Ciel. Love X Japan's trance album. That's something else to listen to when I want to drift."

Kane chuckled, and Miki gave him a hard sidelong glance. He sniffed, then picked at his food again. "What?"

"You sound like my brother when he talks about books. Quinn deconstructs what he reads. He just can't *read*." Kane reached for another carrot. "Can I be honest?"

"That'll be different coming from a cop," Miki snorted. "Sure."

"I'm worried about you," he admitted. "And fuck me if I know why."

"I can take care of myself," Miki huffed. "I've been at it a while."

"You're as skinny as shit and look like you haven't been out in the sun since you were hatched. So excuse me if I don't believe you," Kane drawled and leaned against his elbows, cradling the remains of his burrito in his hands. He took a bite and chewed, then swallowed. "And God, you pissed me off when I first met you."

"Dude pissed you off," Miki pointed out. "I just answered the door."

"No, you pissed me off too," Kane said, waving the last bit of burrito at Miki. "You should've kept your dog inside or leashed. I only just found out you know jack shit about owning a dog."

"He didn't come with a how-to book, you know." Miki helped himself to one of the carrots and tentatively took a bite. He spit out into a napkin and reached for the horchata to cool off his tongue. "Fuck, that's hot."

"I think you kind of need someone to have your back." The cop reached over and took Miki's bag of carrots. "Don't take this wrong, but you're kind of in a shitty situation. They've found a dead body in your garage—"

"*You* found a dead body in my garage."

"What did you think I was going to do? Help you get rid of it? Walk away?" Kane lifted his eyebrows. "I'm a cop… what did you think was going to happen?"

"Dunno. Shing wasn't there when I went out to start the car. Wasn't like I planned *anything*." Miki shrugged. "Like I told Sanchez, the car was running for about fifteen minutes before Dude came in and I grabbed him. He was being an asshole about the tub, so I thought I would turn it off. That's when I found you all Malcolm Reynolds in my garage."

"Someone put him there," Kane said. "Someone went specifically to where you lived and dumped a dead man into your car. Doesn't that bother you?"

"Yeah," Miki replied softly. "But what am I going to do? Crawl under my bed? I can ask Edie if she'll find a security company, I guess, but I don't want some guy I don't know lurking over me."

"I don't like you being there alone, and I don't know why I give a shit. You've been nothing but a pain in the ass since I've met you," he grumbled at the singer. "I don't want you going back there without taking some precautions."

"Luckily, you're not my mother," Miki shot back. "Or fucking me, 'cause then you'd have something to say."

The scrutiny went from guarded to hot, and Miki met Kane's gaze straight on.

"Who's Edie?" Kane finally asked.

"My manager…." Miki paused. "Ex-manager. I don't know. She's… she deals with all the big life shit I can't figure out. Taxes, music rights… that kind of stuff. She used to be on the road with us. Now she's handling other bands, but she still… does Sinner's Gin's crap too. We talk every once in a while. If there's something I've got to make a decision on, she calls. Sometimes she just calls to nag."

"I've *got* to get this woman's number," Kane muttered under his breath. "Maybe she can get you to get some help."

"She's tried. I just want to be left alone."

"Excuse me, Greta, but someone needs to watch your ass since you don't seem to be doing such a good job of it."

"You offering to?" Miki smirked, then wrinkled his nose. "Who's Greta?"

"Jesus, it's like you were raised by wolves. Greta Garbo. Never mind, we'll catch you up to the real world later." Kane sighed heavily. "And yeah, that's what I'm offering, Miki. There's something shitty going on around you, and if you're not going to keep an eye on that skinny ass of yours, then I'll do it for you."

"My ass isn't that skinny," he grumbled. "And I'm fine. I don't need—"

"You *do* need." Kane cut him off. "That dog of yours only seems good for biting cops, and there was a fucking dead body left in your car. If you're not careful, Miki, the next dead body is going to be yours."

IT TOOK Kane five minutes of sitting in his car and staring at the front of the warehouse before he felt comfortable driving away from Miki St. John's place. He knew it was silly. Someone from Forensics was still inside the garage doing last minute lab-monkey stuff, and Casey promised to have someone on patrol lurk nearby. Still, when the front door closed behind the singer's pert ass, Kane wanted to pound on the door until he could see those hazel eyes again.

"Like it's his door you want to pound, Morgan," Kane muttered to himself as he turned the key in the SUV's ignition. His phone started singing about being sexy and knowing it, and he sighed heavily before putting the car into gear. Kane thumbed on his earpiece and barked into the phone, "What's up, Sanchez?"

"Got a small situation over here in Chinatown. Feel up to hanging out with a gorgeous Puerto Rican for a couple of hours?"

"Why? You know one?"

"Funny," Sanchez snapped back. "Get your ass over to Shing's restaurant. We got some strange things going on, partner mine. Figured you'd want in on the action…." He paused, then Kane heard him guffaw. "Unless you got some of your own action going on over there with the rock star."

"Fuck off, Kel," Kane replied without heat. "I left him at the door with orders to crawl into bed. I'll be right there. Don't start anything without me."

The admonishment obviously came too late. By the time Kane pulled up to the alley behind the restaurant, the back door was open and clogged with uniforms standing guard over several overstuffed black trash bags. A few feet away, a skinny, middle-aged Chinese man Kane recognized as Bradley Shing stood, arguing heatedly with a placid Sanchez and Connie Lau, another inspector from their station. His partner looked serene, a far cry from the taut face he'd had on when trying to breach Miki's defenses. From the looks of things, Shing wasn't getting his way.

Kane parked behind Sanchez's black Porsche Boxster, angling the SUV so he blocked any traffic from coming down the alleyway. A couple of patrol cars were across the other side of the alley, boxing in the restaurant. After activating the blue light flashers tucked up on the seam of his rear windows, Kane climbed out and headed over to inspect the bags. Sanchez broke off from the tirade and tucked his hands into the waistband of his gray trousers, pulling his jacket back to expose the badge he wore on his belt.

"Funny time to be cleaning house," Kane said, toeing one of the bags. "Anyone take a peek to see what's in it?"

"Not yet," Sanchez admitted. "There's a transport coming to take them in. I want some space to spread out what Mr. Shing there thought he couldn't wait until morning to toss out."

"Who saw him toss the stuff?" Kane spotted someone he knew from his brother's class, and he smiled, nodding to one of the uniforms standing by the open door.

"I did." Sanchez shrugged when Kane shot him a look. "I discovered, after a long night of tracking down a murderer, I was hungry for some Chinese food. So while I sat behind the restaurant for an hour or so, deciding what I wanted to order, Mr. Shing came out and threw some trash bags into the dumpster over there."

"Which you had to retrieve, of course."

"Of course." Sanchez had the good grace to look embarrassed. "Actually, I caught a patrol coming by and snagged one of them to climb in."

"Dude, abuse of authority." Kane clucked at him, grinning.

"These are new pants." Sanchez tugged at his trousers' pockets. "If you think I was going to get *gau yuk* all over a pair of new Pradas, you're fucking insane."

"You're an embarrassment to cops everywhere, Sanchez," Kane drawled. "Casey come across with the warrant yet?"

"Yeah, right after I called you. I was about to head in, but I thought I'd wait for your sorry ass. I'm tired of showing you up to the Loo." Sanchez nodded briefly at Shing, who was trying to get around Lau. She maneuvered in, blocking him off. "There's a couple of guys in the front closing the place down. Place is open until two in the morning, so there's some stragglers. Martinez is in there. He said he'd take the kitchen staff's statements. I already jotted down what Shing wanted to share with me."

"Let me guess." Kane eyed the irate man pacing off a circle as Lau warned him to calm down. "Fuck you and oh… fuck you?"

"Spot on," Sanchez agreed. "Funny behavior for a grieving son."

"It's all clear, sir." A fresh-faced blonde woman dressed in SFPD blues popped out the back door and nodded at Sanchez. "I'll wait for the transport."

"Thanks," Sanchez said, flashing the young woman a brilliant smile. "Good job."

Kane shook his head and entered the restaurant, ducking to avoid the clusters of garlic strings dangling near the door. A strong wave of spices assailed him as soon as he cleared the doorway. Mingled in with anise and curries, an undertone of cabbage, onions, and garlic lingered alongside dishwashing liquid and fresh meats. Martinez, a beefy man recently transferred in from another station, waved absently at Kane and turned back to the loosely gathered line of men clustered near the sinks.

Another detective, a junior who'd pulled the midnight shift, said a quick hello when they peeked into a cramped office near the back of the kitchen. The woman gave them a harried look as she packed up the contents of the elder Shing's desk. From the piles of loose papers and ledgers scattered about everywhere, it looked like someone had beat them to the office and tossed the place. Sanchez gave the woman a quick nod and pushed his partner past a bank of metal shelves stacked high with dry noodles and bags of rice. There, tucked into a corner of the kitchen, a narrow flight led upstairs.

"How's Martinez's Cantonese?" Kane asked Sanchez as they climbed the tight stairs.

"Passable. Better than Lau's, but Kelly's is nonexistent. Lau's got better Spanish, so she's going to take a crack at the two dishwashers. They're from El Salvador. I talked them up a bit. Seems like no one shares our boy Bradley's opinion of dad. They hated the man's guts, but hey," Sanchez said, shrugging as he reached a door at the top of the stairs, "you gotta work where you find it."

"You got gloves on you?" Kane asked and smiled when Sanchez handed him a pair of black latex gloves, then fitted a pair on his own hands. "Not exactly department issue."

"So I dated a tattoo artist. They're sexier than those blue ones they give us, and they fit." Kel broke the seal one of the uniforms had put on the door. The knob looked grimy from being printed, and it slid a bit in Sanchez's hand when he turned it. "Okay, let's see what fresh hell we've got waiting for us behind door number one."

Sanchez took a slim camera out of his inside jacket pocket and stepped in first. Kane stopped at the door, working the air in the gloves out from between his fingers. He reached up and tapped the dead bolt set into the door above the knob. "Grab a pic of this too. Locks from the outside. The inside's flat."

"So, locking people out of the place?" Kel cocked his head.

"Or locking them in," Kane responded flatly.

The room was narrow and airless, running only twelve feet in against the cinder block wall. A full-sized bed was wedged into the far end of the room, its simple rail frame set low to the ground. Bare shelves took up most of one wall. A layer of dust ran along the front edges, marking where boxes once sat. Those boxes were now empty and lying on the floor, tossed haphazardly into the corner near the door. A few were still full, and Kane nudged one with his foot, surprised at its lack of heft.

Bending over, Kane carefully lifted the open flaps of the box and inspected its contents. Kel walked over with the camera to record what Kane found.

"It's ties." Kel frowned. "Who the hell has a box of ties? And ugly ties at that."

"They're knotted together tight," Kane said, glancing at the bed. "Look at the bed frame. There's one looped over the end, and you can see another one on the other side."

"Some kind of BDSM thing going on up here?" Kel snapped a few pictures of the metal shelves, pacing off the room. "Far cry from some place to crash when you're not getting along with your foster father."

Kane didn't need the reminder, not when he walked over to the bed and caught a whiff of the rank, musky sheets. Reminding himself he was on the job, he crouched next to the mattress and examined the frame. "Paint's worn off near the ties, and this one's abraded. So either the players are really hardcore, or the person being tied down really didn't want to be here."

He didn't like thinking of a young, teenaged Miki spending nights up in the room, especially not on the worn-out, sagging mattress in front of him. Kane had to shove away the images crawling up from his darkest thoughts, and he shook his head, focusing on the job. Behind him, Kel's camera continued to pop off flashes as the other inspector went about the room.

Kane stood up and stretched his legs. The long day was beginning to wear on him, and it'd been hours since he had his last cup of burnt cop coffee. Rubbing at the fatigue lingering on his eyes, Kane stifled a yawn when Kel turned the camera on him.

Kel gave Kane an exaggerated pout. "Smile for me, pretty boy."

"I'll kick your scrawny ass if you take that picture, Sanchez." Kane flipped his partner off and stepped forward. "Did you take a peek at the rest of the boxes?"

"Not yet," Sanchez admitted. "I was making sure I got pictures of all the empty boxes. Most of them are marked 'clothes', but it makes me wonder what's in those trash bags downstairs. Think Bradley boy was just grabbing things and tossing them away before anyone came to find out what Daddy was doing up here?"

"Kind of makes him an accessory if there was anything illegal going on," Kane pointed out. "Let's have Lau wrap him up into one of the cars and take him down. Let him sweat it out there. If he lawyers up, then we know we've got something to go on."

Sanchez nodded and shifted one of the smaller boxes with his foot. "Wanna pop this one open? I'll grab some shots, and we'll have the lab guys up here to print stuff for us. I want to see if Bradley's fingers were all over the contents too. It'll be easier to talk him down from his holier-than-the-cops attitude if we've got something on him."

Kane flipped open the cardboard flaps, then pulled back when the camera's flash went bright and he saw what the box held. From the looks of things, Shing had emptied a sex shop of its toys during a half-off sale. His stomach rolled, and Kane inhaled sharply through his mouth, not wanting to pull the room's scents into his nose. In some part of his brain, he suspected what Shing did in his closed up little hidey hole, and Kane didn't want to think about it, not when Bradley Shing was still downstairs and within choking distance.

When Kel leaned forward to get a better angle, Kane spotted the camera's white burst reflecting on something shiny wedged far beneath the bed frame. Leaving his partner to document the contents of the box, Kane kneeled down and reached under the bed. A squat metal box was long and buried deep behind an ocean of dust bunnies. Hooking his shoulder under the frame, Kane stretched his arm and snagged the box's corner with his fingers, dragging it forward an inch. After working the box loose from the shadows, Kane pulled it free with a triumphant smile, only to see Kel standing there with a disapproving look on his face.

"Why the hell didn't you just lift the mattress?" Sanchez sniped. "Aren't you the brains of the outfit?"

"I'm tired." Kane shrugged bashfully. "Okay, and I didn't think about it. Sue me. I got it out."

The case was heavy, resembling a vintage safety deposit box more than anything else. More than half of its long, flat side was lid, and a worn, battered hinge bisected the case's top. Bright yellow and scored from years of use, the latch was broken, rattling loudly when Kane lifted it up onto the bed. A scrawl of Chinese characters was lettered across the top of the box, the bold black characters chipped in places from being shoved under the metal frame. Kane adjusted the case so it was straight on the mattress, then stood back, letting Kel document the outside of the box.

"Okay, let's open it up," Kel said softly, and Kane braced himself for what he'd find as he flipped the case's lid up.

It was a scene out of Kane's worst nightmare.

Most of the photos were turning spotty from being in the damp, suffocating room, but the scenes they captured were enough to turn Kane's stomach. He counted at least three young teenaged boys in the photos, their faces wet with tears and contorted into masks of pain and fear. They were shot posed on the same dirty linens on the bed, or against the surrounding putty colored cinder block walls. All were naked or in various stages of undress. None of them looked like they wanted to be there.

At the bottom of the pile were stacks of glossy photos wrapped with wax paper and tied up with red ribbon bows. His fingers trembled as Kane reached for them, the black latex of his gloves slick on the shiny paper.

These photos weren't throwaways for Shing. No, he'd packaged these carefully, almost lovingly, documenting a sickness he clearly enjoyed exploring. Kane didn't need to unwrap the wax paper from the first stack to know the face he'd find in Shing's treasure pile, but he did it anyway, needing to confirm the crawling suspicions vomiting up ill thoughts in his brain.

It was still a shock to see those haunting hazel eyes staring up at him from the first photo. Miki's face was rounder and blushed with youth, but there was not a hint of innocence in the boy's wide-eyed stare. Caught on film at an age when his world should have revolved around sports and dodging homework, Miki's face was contorted with anguish, and his lashes were spiked with his tears. Even wrapped in Shing's perversion and beaten down with bruises marking most of his pale body, Miki stared up at Shing's camera and defied the man with a snarl on his young mouth.

"Fuck," Kel whispered as he peered around Kane's arm. "Looks like we've got a motive for St. John murdering Shing."

"Looks like," Kane agreed reluctantly. "Good thing he's already dead or I'd kill the fucking bastard myself. Let's go see what his son has to say about this shit. Suddenly, I'm not so tired anymore."

CHAPTER
FIVE

Hey, Damie, this song sucks.
You wrote it, Sinjun.
Yeah, I know. It still sucks.
Tell you what? How about if we finish it up? Then take the master
tape and the sheet music and set them on fire in the alley. That way,
no one'll ever know this shit ever existed.

—Unknown song, never released. Burnt in a dumpster.

MIKI was back in the khaki colored room again, staring at the one-way mirror and wondering if there was anyone behind it. He'd been separated pretty quickly from Kane once they got to the station. The cop went one way, past a pair of swinging doors, while a woman in uniform dragged Miki down a hallway and into an interview room before he could object.

Sitting in the cold and staring at the walls was growing old, but short of throwing a chair through the glass, Miki didn't think he had much of a choice.

Then Sanchez walked in, and Miki's evening went to shit.

"Hey. How are you doing?" The casual manner Sanchez showed him the other day was gone, replaced by a patented used-car-salesman charm designed to squeeze something out of a conversation. Sanchez set a thick folder down on the table and placed a paper cup of milky coffee in front of Miki. "Here, I brought you something hot to drink while we talk."

The coffee was bitter under the sweet, but Miki took another sip, focusing on the bright yellow pattern on the paper cup. Sanchez pulled out the chair across the table from him and sat down. He flicked one last look up at the mirror, resigned to seeing his own bruised expression in the reflection and not the faces of the maybe-people behind the glass.

"The only one there is Morgan. Is that okay?" Sanchez glanced behind him, following Miki's gaze. Miki nodded once and watched Sanchez take out a small recorder, put it down on the table, then turn it on.

"We're going to record this. I'm going to ask some sensitive questions, and I understand if you need to stop at some point in this to get yourself together, but unless you ask for a lawyer, I'm going to try to get through this as quick as possible, okay?"

"Okay," Miki said, nodding. He picked at the cup's cover, lifting the edge with his thumbnail. "*Do* I need a lawyer?"

"I can't tell you that," the cop admitted. "I'm only asking questions. You're not being charged with anything, but I need to talk to you. If you refuse, then we can bring lawyers into this, but I don't want to. Do you?"

"No, I'm good." He leaned back in the chair, his shoulders rolled in. A burning feeling began in Miki's gut, overriding the ache in his knee. "Is Kane in trouble or something? Is that why he's not in here?"

"No, Morgan and I thought it would be better if I were the one to talk to you," Sanchez replied softly. "He'll be waiting for you after we're done."

"Okay." Miki nodded. "Go ahead then."

Sanchez started. "I really need to talk to you about Shing and how you're connected to him. Do you understand?"

"I don't know anything about how Shing ended up in the car," Miki replied. "I was in the house washing the dog—"

"I know." The cop opened the folder and took out a large envelope, folding open the clasp so he could pull out the contents. "I've got to ask you some questions... and understand you don't have to answer them without having a lawyer present, but they have to be asked. It's your choice how you do this."

"I've got nothing to hide." Miki's chin tilted up, his mouth set into a hard, straight line.

"We found some evidence at Shing's restaurant that shows he hurt you when you were younger. Now, we have to ask you, did you have Shing killed? Because of what he did to you? Or do you know someone who would kill him because of what he did?"

Miki hissed in disgust. "No, I swear to God, I haven't seen Shing in years. Not since…."

"Not since when, Miki?" Sanchez pressed.

"Not since I was a kid," he replied. The talk of Shing and the bad coffee was doing a number on Miki's stomach, and his belly gurgled, threatening to return Kane's dinner up onto the table. "I… fucking hell, what do you want from me?"

"I know Shing hurt you," the cop said, softening his voice to a whisper. "Did you tell anyone about that? Anyone at all?"

"Shing…. Look, I just crashed in the storeroom at the restaurant…." Miki bit the inside of his cheek, forcing the bile back down his throat. "I don't know…. I didn't kill Shing. I don't know anything. God, just let me go home."

Miki turned his head, willing himself back to adulthood. Sanchez's gentle tones and soft voice were too much like the coaxing whispers he'd heard when he was a kid. Miki shook out his arms, then shook his head, needing to feel his body respond. Kneading his fingers into his thighs, Miki fought the agitation rising inside of him, and he searched for something to bring him back to the now of the room.

Grabbing his knee, he pressed into the damaged tissue, riding the sharp rip of pain as it tore up his leg and into the base of his spine. Panting slightly, he rocked forward, digging in again until he couldn't see through the red haze. A scream lingered on the back of his tongue, driven more by the memories of the nights he spent waiting for footsteps in the darkness than his self-inflicted torture.

The taste of blood on his tongue stilled Miki's rocking, and he swallowed, chasing the cop-house coffee down with a wash of metallic copper.

"I need to show you what I found in the storeroom. It's not pretty, but I need your help," Sanchez said calmly. "If you didn't kill Shing... and no one here really thinks you did... we need to know if you recognize anyone else he hurt. They might have killed him and now think you should pay them for doing it. Do you know someone like that?"

"I didn't pay anyone to kill him," Miki protested. "I wouldn't even know where to go looking for someone to do that."

"We ran your financials, Miki. Hell, I spend more on gas and coffee than you spend in a month, so I know you didn't dump a few thousand dollars to have him killed. I had to ask. It's my job. But someone in these photos *might* have killed Shing. Can you look for me? Just to see if you know someone. Anyone."

"You... fuck, you don't know what you're asking," Miki whispered tightly.

The pain from his gouging no longer touched him, and he was left floating on the eeriness of his past rising up from where he'd buried it. He pushed the chair back from the table and leaned over, trying to breathe. His lungs seemed caught on his ribs, and no amount of pulling seemed to undo the pinch in his chest. Reaching up, Miki grabbed at the table, willing the room to stop spinning.

"I know it's hard, Miki," Sanchez said. He picked up his chair and moved it over to the side where Miki sat. Perching on the edge of the seat, the cop touched Miki's shoulder lightly. "Do you want me to have someone else come in to talk to you? A counselor maybe?"

Miki sucked in some air, shuddering as he exhaled. The linoleum was beige with tiny specks of bronze and gold scattered through it. Laid down in tiles, the joints were beveled in, and bits of grayish glue poked up between the pieces.

That's what my stomach feels like right now, Miki thought, like I'm being shoved in between two hard things.

"You doing okay?" Sanchez sounded far away, an echoing whisper in Miki's ears.

No, I'm not fucking doing okay, Miki screamed in the frozen wasteland of his mind. I don't want to fucking go there again. Not to Shing. Not to Carl. I just want to go home. Why the hell are you asking me to do this?

His body had his memories. Foul things rising up from under the surface to claw at his mind. His skin remembered the slime of tongues moving over his belly and hips and then the horror of pain moving out from the deepest, most intimate places inside of him. Miki hiccupped and pressed his knuckles to his lips, looking for some escape from the craziness closing in.

Miki found that sibilant tendril and grabbed hold of it to drag himself back to a sane world where a cop screamed at him because his dog was a thief and had a mouth that promised to rip him apart when they finally kissed.

A quick eternity passed before Sanchez leaned in again and touched Miki's shoulder. Somehow, a bottle of water appeared under Miki's face, and he blinked, startled by the sudden intrusion of blue plastic and white lettering.

"Here, drink some water, okay?" Sanchez said as the room's door closed with a whispering click. "I need you to talk to me, Miki. I need you to tell me something. Anything at all that will help."

"I don't know if I can do this." A strangled sob escaped with his words, and Miki choked it back, refusing to let loose the nightmares he kept inside of him. Everything he ever gained lay in ash around him, burnt up by the fiery disgust he held inside. "I just wanted to forget it happened. I just wanted to be normal, you know? Fuckers made me... not normal. I'm not sorry he's dead. Fucking hell, I'm not, but I didn't kill him."

"I know," Sanchez assured him. "But I need you to do this for me. I don't have anywhere else to go with this. I wouldn't ask you if I had a choice, okay? I've cropped in as much as I could so there's only faces. There's a few of you only because there's someone else in the picture, a couple of boys that I'm hoping you know something about, but that's all. Nothing else, okay?"

"Why?" The word broke into pieces as Miki spoke, scattering out like the glass from his front window.

"Because we think Shing's death is somehow related to what he did in that storeroom... to you," Sanchez replied, his voice low and quiet. "And because I don't want the next person Kane calls in dead to be you, because that's what I'm afraid's going to happen if you're connected to this in any way."

Kane.

Miki hissed between his teeth. The cop had gotten to him. He couldn't shake the man loose from his brain, and worse, he wanted to feel Kane on his skin.

"Fucking Kane," Miki spat. He *felt* again. The numbness somehow leeched off, and the feelings he'd bricked up behind it were now exposed and raw. He didn't like it. It *felt* too much... way too much for Miki's liking, but he didn't know how to put everything back away, especially since it looked like Kane had dismantled all of the walls he built up.

"Yeah, I say that a lot too," Sanchez said with a chuckle. "Probably for different reasons, though."

"I can do this," Miki muttered to himself. "Just faces, right?"

"As much of their faces as I could get in," the cop reassured him. "And if it gets to be too much, we can take a break. Okay?"

"Okay." He took a breath and steadied himself. "Okay, let me see."

The faces were shadows at best, only a glimmer of recognition striking Miki as he shuffled through them. More surprising was to see his own tearstained and terrified face, a much younger and innocent version, staring back at him. The boys arranged with him were unfamiliar to him, a distant nothingness submerged in his childhood fugue.

"You doing all right there, Miki?" Sanchez finally asked.

"I don't know any of them," Miki whispered. "I don't remember anyone's names. I don't know if I ever knew them."

"It's okay. Just take your time."

Miki pulled out a page and slid it across the table to the cop next to him. "I think he was one of the kids who used to live with Carl."

"Carl Vega, your foster father?"

"Yeah," Miki said, nodding. "I don't remember the kid's name. He wasn't there long. Just a couple of months, maybe?"

"How old were you then? In this picture. Do you know?" Sanchez's whisper was soft, a pleading tone meant to soothe, but it rankled Miki's skin.

Shoving down his irrational distaste, Miki stared at the photo of himself and another boy. Their eyes were glazed, nearly bleached out from the flash, and their faces were ghostly pale, floating against a brown-patterned background. "These here, they're not from Shing's place. They're from Carl's house. I remember that bedspread. I got really sick on it, so Carl threw it out. So, maybe I was twelve? Thirteen? I don't remember exactly when."

"How did Carl know Shing?" Again, the softness irritated Miki, but he focused instead on trying to parse out his memories.

"I don't know. I ran once, but Carl came home early and caught me. After that, he made sure I wasn't alone," Miki said, turning the pages over. He couldn't stare at the faces anymore. There were too many things coming to the surface in the reflections of their eyes, and Miki's mind crawled with the horrors he'd left behind. "If Carl had to work at night, Shing'd take me with him to the restaurant. During the day, he'd make sure I was at school."

"Did you talk to someone there? Tell anyone what Carl was doing? Carl's wife, maybe? The school?"

"The school?" Miki snorted, a sharp cut of derision on Sanchez's soft words. "Nobody there gave a shit. I'd come to school with a black eye or a bloody lip, and they wouldn't say a damned thing. Why would they? Carl's like a big shot with them. No one's going to touch him. Same reason the CPS lady told me I was full of shit when I tried talking to her. Told me I was making shit up to get him into trouble. After that, I figured if I just survived it, it would be okay."

"Someone should have helped you, Miki." Sanchez sounded angry, and Miki pulled back a bit. Sanchez softened his voice and touched Miki's chilled fingers. "You were a kid. It wasn't even ten damned years ago. They should have known better. Someone should have listened to you."

"Who the hell's going to listen to some kid they found on the street, Sanchez?" His mouth twisted into a sour pout. "Like people even give a shit about their own kids? You think they're going to care about me? It doesn't matter anymore. I got out of it. It's done."

"What about the kids fostered after you?" he asked. "What about them? Do you know if any of them said something?"

"I don't know." Miki turned his head, struggling to breathe again when Sanchez hissed with frustration. "So it's on me? That shit's my fault now? Don't put that on me. Don't you fucking—"

"No, it's not on you. That's not what I meant," Sanchez replied. He gripped Miki's shoulder and turned him until the cop could see Miki's face. "It's on me. I'm a cop. Kane's a cop. It's on us. Your foster father's a monster, and he fed on you. It's our job to take him down. Our job to stop him, okay? Look at me, man. Okay?"

Miki opened his eyes and stared into Sanchez's steady brown gaze. Nodding, he mumbled, "Okay."

KANE pressed his hand against the glass. It was cold, nearly freezing on his palm, but it did nothing to numb the anguish building inside of him. If he could have, Kane would have crawled through the glass and held Miki close. Even if the cold turned his soul to ice, he'd risk it to take the terror away from Miki's expressive face.

The door to the room opened, and Kane shut his eyes, forbidding the tears on his lashes from falling. He dropped his hand, clenching his fingers against his palm until his knuckles ached. A thick-fingered hand gripped his shoulder, and Kane turned his head to look up at his Lieutenant standing next to him.

"He'll be okay, Morgan." Casey's reflection in the glass was stern, but his voice was gentle. "You okay listening to this?"

"Yeah, 'cause no one listened to him before," Kane replied. "Because the someone listening to him now is me... and Sanchez. This is fucked up. This kind of shit happens to him, and we're putting it out in front of him like it's nothing."

"This isn't *nothing*, Morgan," Casey snapped back. "Sanchez is damned good at what he does. He knows how this goes down. He's doing well with the kid. You said it yourself. There's no way you can sit across of St. John and ask him these questions. Where does that leave me when I've got a cop that can't do what needs to be done because he's got a thing for a suspect?"

"He didn't do this," Kane said, shaking his head. "He didn't kill Shing. I don't know who did, but it wasn't Miki St. John."

"Willing to risk your badge over that? Because from where I'm standing, that's what you're doing." The man stabbed his finger at Kane's chest. "You're letting your dick lead you around, Morgan. I don't like it."

"It's not my dick, Loo." He tightened his mouth and stared at the men sitting behind the one-way glass. Miki was trembling but holding his own, almost robotically going through the pictures, but there was a gleam of something insane lurking at the edges of his eyes. "This is fucking killing him. Whoever murdered Shing was *angry*. You saw the body. St. John doesn't have that kind of rage inside of him. And there's no fucking way he could have lifted up Shing's body and dumped it in his own car."

"People do strange things," Casey said, shrugging. "Maybe Shing came over to his house to shake him down for money. 'Give me a million dollars or I'll tell the tabloids you were a whore?'"

"Shing couldn't have done that without implicating himself," Kane pointed out. "Miki was underage. Hell, he was barely into puberty. What Shing did was wrong, and someone he did it to probably killed him for it, but that someone wasn't Miki."

"You're going to have to shake out the foster father," the lieutenant rumbled. "Tried to have the uniforms pick him up, but he went to ground."

"I've got people looking for him." He shifted on his feet and leaned against the glass again. "I'm wondering if Vega didn't do

Shing and leave him in Miki's car as a warning. That could be the money angle. 'This could be you if I don't get my cash.'"

"Any sign of a blackmail threat?"

"No, but that doesn't mean it didn't happen," Kane replied. "He's good at keeping secrets. He might have kept that one. I'll work on him."

"You do that," Casey agreed. "In the meantime, get your arms around Vega. He might become a victim in this like Shing did. He might not be the murderer. We have to work that angle too."

"Last thing that guy is now is a victim," Kane growled. "We hunt down Carl Vega and do what? Protect him from whoever's doing this shit? I've got to put Miki in front of him and say what? 'Yeah, sorry about your screwed up childhood, but we need to take care of the man who hurt you because someone might kill him too?' If whoever got Shing came for Vega, if I wasn't a cop, I'd say we let the guy finish the job."

"You're better than that, Morgan. You know that." The Lieutenant nudged Kane around until the man faced him. "You're too close to St. John. I'm tempted to yank you from this case."

"It's not like that—"

"Damned if it's not," Casey cut him off. "You start something with St. John and it compromises this case, I'll have your ass. Do you understand me, Morgan?"

The lieutenant didn't wait for him to answer. Casey grunted and quit the room, leaving the door open behind him. Kane rocked back on his heels, his hands shoved into the pockets of his jeans, and watched Sanchez gather up the printouts he'd shown Miki. The singer remained seated, his arms tense from gripping the chair's sides.

He looked shell-shocked, his hazel eyes open wide enough to dominate the rest of his face. The lips Kane lusted for were now bleeding from Miki's teeth worrying at them, and his tongue dabbed at the chap, playing at the raw spots. His damp hair had dried to a tousle around his face, falling down in a straight line to his jaw, and Miki tucked a length behind his ear to get it out of his eyes.

Sanchez whispered something to the young man that Kane couldn't hear, but Miki nodded and stood, nearly stumbling back down to the ground when his weight shifted to his right leg. Sanchez reached for him, but Miki yanked his arm away, holding up a hand to ward off the cop while using the other to brace himself against the table.

Kane was waiting for him by the interview room's door when Miki came out. Sanchez spotted his partner first and glanced back behind him, a worried expression drawing his dark eyebrows together into a point. The singer emerged slowly, and he turned slightly when he saw Kane, glancing at the open door nearby.

They stood staring at one another. Kane held himself as still as he could, trying to read the complicated mix of emotions playing across the other man's face. Miki splayed his hand against the wall for support, keeping his knee bent to ease the pain Kane could see resonating in Miki's taut mouth. Canted forward, the singer said nothing, only breathing as he stared up at the cop who was pushing his way into his life.

Then Miki took a step toward him, and Kane closed the distance between them in a single stride.

CHAPTER
SIX

I can feel you breaking my skin.
My bones shatter when you walk by.
The blood I taste is from my tongue.
You say you love me but I know it's a lie.

—Shattered Lies

Kane caught the man up in his arms, sliding his hands around Miki's slender waist to support his back. Miki fought him, pushing him away, but Kane held him tighter.

"You're a damned cop, for Christ's sake," Miki grumbled. "You can't just grab people in the middle of the place. They think I killed Shing."

"We don't. Well, Sanchez and I don't," Kane said. "Right now, how about if I'm just the guy who took you out for dinner and let you ramble on about music. I'll be a cop again when I let you go, but right now, I'm a guy who's worried about you. No one will see. Sanchez will keep people out of the hallway."

"You don't even know me," he whispered.

"Yeah, I think I kind of do," Kane replied and pulled Miki in. "Let's face it. You need a friend right now. I'll be that friend, Miki. Let me."

"I've never wanted to fuck a friend before." Miki's whisper was almost lost in Kane's shirt. The singer's hands came up, slowly finding purchase around Kane's chest, then around his neck when the cop buried his face into Miki's soft, long hair. "God, this fucking sucks."

Kane's insides churned, as if he'd truly gone through the glass to put his arms around the trembling man. He tightened his embrace and sighed in relief when Miki let himself go. Catching up Miki's slack weight, Kane held the man up, stroking the small of his back. Kane heard a sob catch in Miki's throat, but the sound was muffled when he buried his face into Kane's chest.

They became the eye in the center of a wicked storm. Kane rested his chin on Miki's shoulder and simply listened to the man breathe, stroking his fingertips up and down Miki's spine. The singer dug his hands into Kane's shirt, tightly fisting the fabric as if afraid to let go… afraid he'd fall into something he couldn't crawl out of if he didn't have Kane to hold on to.

Kane couldn't count the minutes they stood together, but eventually Miki looked up from the safety of Kane's embrace. His face was bare of tears, but the specks of skin on his lips were nearly chewed through to blood. Taking a deep breath, Miki took a small step away from Kane, only enough so he could meet Kane's gaze.

"I can't believe I'm fucking crying in the middle of a police station," Miki whispered. "Did you hear… all of it? Behind that damned glass? God, I want to throw something through it. Creeps me the fuck out."

"You're not the first person to cry in a cop house." Kane kissed his forehead, then leaned back to cup Miki's chin in his palm. "I don't think you know how fucking strong you are. I couldn't have done that. There's no way in hell I could have stayed through that."

Miki's scoffing snort brought a smile to Kane's lips. He hugged the singer tightly, then gently released him, keeping one arm around his waist to support Miki's damaged leg.

"I don't feel strong," he complained under his breath. "I feel like a whiny bitch."

"Yeah, well, trust me," Kane said. "Not a lot of guys could have dealt with that shit. Makes me want to kill someone."

"Like I had a choice," Miki muttered. "Can I go home? Or am I stuck here for a bit?"

"Nah, I'll take you home," Kane replied. "Just promise me that hellhound you've got isn't going to eat me alive when I get you there."

"No promises. Dude usually likes everyone. I don't know why that guy pissed him off. And why the fuck did I leave that damned cane behind?" Miki took a few tentative steps, using Kane's arm to lean on. "God, I'm an idiot. Aren't they going to kick you off the case for hitting on a suspect... or whatever the hell I am?"

"Only if you really killed Shing. Then, I'm up to my neck in shit," Kane teased. "We'll stop someplace, and I'll grab you some ice cream. My mom always says ice cream can solve everything. Well, that and a cup of tea, but I'm going to disagree with her on that one."

"Thanks," Miki murmured. "For everything. For this. For the ice cream."

"Not a problem," he replied, gently squeezing Miki's waist. "Let's get you home. Sanchez and I will figure it out. He's a good guy... a good cop. Almost as good as me."

"Yeah, you guys better be," Miki grumbled with a soft purr. "I want this shit to go away."

"Do I have to go away when the shit goes too?" Kane prodded as they walked.

"No," Miki mumbled, ducking his head. "Maybe you can stay. Even if you're a cop, you're okay. Especially if you're buying me ice cream."

SANCHEZ was waiting for him in an unmarked when Kane got back to the station an hour later. He slid into the sedan and passed Sanchez one of the two Mexican mochas he'd grabbed on the way. The smell of the coffee did little to mask the sour smell of vomit coming from the backseat, and Kel hit the button to raise the bullet-proof partition, hoping it would help.

It didn't.

"Don't look at me," Kel warned Kane off before he could say something. "This was all they had."

"God, I hate the motor pool," Kane muttered. "Why do they have to punish me because they can't stand you?"

"The dog shit wasn't my fault," Sanchez protested as he pulled into traffic. "I was doing the old lady a solid. It was pouring out, and she had five fucking poodles. How was I supposed to know they all had the runs?"

"I hate your guts right now." He shook his head and reached for the touchscreen tablet on the seat between them. "Roll down the back windows. Maybe that'll help some."

Sanchez turned the heat on and lowered the back windows. The rattling wheeze from the air vents wasn't promising, and when the lukewarm air finally hit them, it reeked of motor oil and cat pee. Resigned to being a victim of Kel's ongoing feud with the department's motor pool, he turned on the tablet and hooked it into the car's network system.

"You didn't tell me no one's seen Vega in three days," Kane said accusingly. "When'd you find that out?"

"Like an hour and a half ago," Sanchez shot back. "You were busy cuddling your rock star and ferrying him home. I stayed back, remember? Working on this shit. He was supposed to go camping with some of his buddies, but he never showed up. They figured he flaked, so they didn't call it in. I guess at some point someone realized he'd left home but never showed up at the campsite, so someone notified us."

"He could have been grabbed before Shing, then," Kane murmured, sweeping through the reports on the screen. "We don't have time of death on Shing yet. The family wasn't sure about the last time he was seen. He wasn't working the restaurant as much. Bradley pretty much has taken that over."

"Our boy Bradley, who's cooling his heels in lockup right now," Kel responded. "He's none too happy about that. We've got enough to pop a warrant on the house too. Martinez and Lau are going to shake that down, but I don't know how much they'll find. I'm guessing old man Shing only used that upstairs room for his fucking sick games. Too many people at home, unless they turned a blind eye to it."

"Sounds like Vega's wife did." He stopped at a screen and maximized the text. "The uniform who responded to the call said she was out of it when he got there. One of Vega's coworkers... um... one Daniel Bassor, was there to answer questions. Valens, the uniform, said the wife wasn't fully there. He was going to call in a medical, but Bassor responded that Cynthia... Mrs. Vega... has behavioral issues and is usually drugged up to the gills."

"Is that a technical term?" Kel asked caustically.

"Must be." Kane grinned. "That's how it was written in the report. Very professional, our boy Valens. No listing of Cynthia's medications. That would have been helpful. We could have chased down her doctor and seen if there's any evidence of physical violence."

"Surprised they let them foster kids if she's like that. Any domestics called to the home?"

"Her medical issues apparently escalated." Kane skimmed through an amended attachment. "Some domestics were called in over the last six years, all on her. Vega declined their foster parent status eight years ago, stating his wife's mental issues and increase of his workload at his law firm."

"So she's crazy?" Kel whistled under his breath.

"Not everyone with issues is crazy. My brother Quinn's wired a bit funny, and he's done just fine," Kane pointed out. "I don't see you teaching college history."

"Your brother's hot. That goes a long way." Sanchez winced at the look Kane threw him. "Hey, just stating the obvious."

"Q's worked hard to get where he is," he said, going through the rest of the reports to hunt for more information. "Don't know if being hot's helped him any."

Coming up empty on Cynthia Vega, Kane turned his attention to Vega himself. There was little to nothing on the man, mostly public citations of cases he'd worked on. Kane frowned at the lack of information, then called up the Vegas' fostering records.

"They only took in boys, usually between the ages of eight and fourteen. He had Miki the longest. Some only stayed for a few weeks before being placed out elsewhere." Kane looked up. "Shit. Why the fuck didn't anyone see what this guy was doing? He had a total of eleven boys placed with him. Out of the eleven, seven tried to kill themselves. Four succeeded. This guy's a walking time bomb."

"From the sounds of things, I'm going to guess he split because he heard about Shing, or he's not walking anymore," Kel replied as he turned up a hill toward the Presidio. "I'm not going to cry over that either."

"How far out are we?"

"Another minute. Why?"

"'Cause Casey's coming across with a warrant for Vega's house. Just got the clearance. Let's hope the printer in this unit works, or I'm going to set some asses on fire in motor pool. I can deal with puke and cat piss, but if those fuckers cost me search time on this, then we're going to have some words."

DESPITE the high-end zip code, the Vega house straddled the edge of a middle-class neighborhood and a lower rent district. The residence itself was an unassuming, small adobe-style ranch set far back on its elevated tiny lot. Its front lawn was clipped down to a brutal half inch and thick, prickly hedges ran along either side of the house, effectively cutting off the view to the neighbors' homes. There was nothing to soften its harsh lines, no flowers or bright colors to ease the sandy adobe or browning grass. To Kane, the place shouted temporary, even though their records said the Vegas lived there for years.

Sanchez parked the car on the slight incline in front of the house and waited as Kane fought with the printer controls in their car. After a phone call to a computer tech and a few choice swear words, Kane finally got the printer to spit out the warrant. Spreading the accordioned paper on his thigh, Kane worked out the creases and shook his head in disgust.

"You talk to them when we get back," Kel said, getting out of the car. He adjusted his tie and flicked off a piece of hair from his sleeve. Stealthily sniffing at his arm to see if he carried the car's odors with him, Sanchez was satisfied he'd been spared at least some of the motor pool's revenge and nodded.

"Fuck talking to them," Kane growled. "I'm going to find a baseball bat and threaten the shit out of someone if we get that car again."

Sanchez stepped around a plastic three-wheeler left on the sidewalk and waited for his partner to join him. "Let's go talk to Mrs. Vega and see what she's got to say."

It was hard to imagine Miki's horrific childhood amid the rambling rose bushes and tall juniper trees, but they both knew some of the prettiest wrappers hid the foulest packages. Kane studied the house, wondering what other nightmares were forged inside of its walls.

Turning to Kel, he nodded, "Yeah, let's do this."

The door was newly painted, an earthy red that still smelled fresh. Sanchez rang the bell and they waited, listening to the chimes echo through the house. After a few moments, there was no sign of anyone coming to answer the door.

"She knew we were coming, right?" Kane asked as Kel rang the bell for the third time.

"Yeah, I had dispatch call ahead. She said she'd be waiting for us but that was over an hour ago." Sanchez nodded. "Think we should do a welfare check?"

"Yeah, I think that's a good idea." Sanchez ducked his shoulder down and Kane grabbed him before Sanchez shoved at door. Reaching over, he took hold of the knob and turned it. The door swung open. "Always check the door, Kel. We went over that."

They drew their guns, holding them down as they entered the house. Kane took point, stepping to the right. Kel followed, sniffing at the air as he stepped in. The overpowering paint smell from the door did little to mask the dankness of the shadowy interior. Slivers of light came through the living room curtains where they did not meet, catching on dust motes stirred up as they moved through the house.

The front room was an empty shell, a formal parlor of rose-patterned settee and wingchairs covered in a fine layer of dust. Across the hall, the kitchen echoed the house's desolate feel. A bowl of wax fruit took up most of the banquette in the breakfast nook by the back door, and a single line of tumblers sat sentry on a rubber dish tray.

"Cynthia?" Kane called out. "I'm Inspector Kane Morgan from SFPD. If you can hear me, come out, please."

"Valens, our uniform, said she wasn't lucid. Maybe she passed out since she talked to Dispatch?"

They stood, poised and silent, but no one answered. Kel nodded toward the narrow hallway leading off of the living room. With all of the doors closed, it was pitch black, and Kane stepped forward, searching for a light switch. The bulb flared bright, and Kel blinked, chasing away the spots in his eyes. Hastily checking the house, they came to the one closed door off the main hallway.

"Ready?" Kane motioned with his gun toward the door.

"Yeah," Kel grunted. "Kick or knob?"

"Kick. Hard."

The hollow-core door splintered under Kel's foot, and Kane ducked, taking one of the splinters in his cheek. He spat out a mouthful of grit and wood dust, then went in, covering Sanchez as the other cop went low. Sweeping the room carefully, Kane raked his gaze over the space, looking for any threat.

What they found was the remains of Cynthia Vega, swinging from a rope noose she'd tied around the broken light fixture.

The room was tiny, nearly as small as the storeroom in Shing's restaurant, but unlike its cinder-block counterpart, it was furnished as if awaiting a guest. A daybed sat under a long window, its wrought-iron frame curling up and around the back, the white paint girlishly embellished with metallic pink flourishes. The floor was a wood laminate, cheap and easy to clean, but someone—probably Cynthia—had laid down a square floral rug to soften the room.

Death had not come quickly to Cynthia Vega. Instead, it flirted with her, tantalizing her with promises of a numb forever as she kicked and struggled before losing consciousness. Without enough space and momentum to snap her neck, the frail-bodied woman instead choked slowly, her neck's waxy skin bearing a scrabble of long, bloody grooves where she clawed at the rope with her broken nails.

Those hands now swung freely at her sides, her body twisting slowly as the hot air from the room's vent poured in. Kane stepped closer, careful to avoid touching the body. She wasn't pretty in life, and the bloat to her dead face did little to soften the pinch to her sharp features. Deep grooves dug themselves in between her eyebrows and around her mouth, engraving a lifelong bitterness into her skin. The flowing white dress she'd put on as her final shroud was stained black from blood splatter and vomit, the eyelet at its hem yellowed from her body's purge. Her legs were skinny and marked with blue veins, the blood drawn down to purple her bare feet in death.

"How long was it they called her?" Sanchez asked. "Half an hour, maybe?"

"Yeah," Kane agreed. "For this much livor mortis, she must have done this right after she spoke to Dispatch. Fucking hell. Shit, Kel, look at her arms and legs. She was a cutter."

Cynthia's bore signs of old cutting, small nicks allowed to heal over, then sliced open again. She'd taken a blade to herself one final time. Before she tied off the noose, she gouged out furrows from her bare arms, opening up the flesh to bleed out enough to pen her final words to the world she obviously fought to escape.

The shock of her body was nothing compared to the horrors stapled to the walls.

There were literally hundreds of photos, each more depraved than the one next to it. He recognized Miki's face first. How could he not? The defiant, beautiful man he knew was laid out in front of him, younger and fearful. His face figured prominently among the others. Pictures of a young Miki were the most plentiful... and the most horrific in what Vega chose to do to the innocent boy he'd been given to raise.

And all were smeared over with hateful words using Cynthia Vega's blood.

"Whore" seemed to be Cynthia's favorite, but others were used as liberally, filthy accusations made against the young men in the images but none for the man who'd put the pain in their eyes.

"I'm going to call it in," Kel said finally. "The rest of the house is empty. This is the only room like this."

"Yeah, okay," Kane murmured, putting his gun back into his holster. He needed to shove his feelings for Miki aside, at least long enough to finish up the job laid out before them. But as he turned, he caught a glimpse of bright hazel eyes, and his heart skipped a beat. Nodding at the carnage of lives splattered on the room's walls, Kane stiffened his shoulders and reached for his phone. "Let's see if we can't get CPS to shake out the names of the kids who survived this asshole Vega. One of them murdered Shing and maybe even Vega by now. We just have to find out which one."

"What's his beef with St. John, then?" Kel stopped dialing.

"Maybe Miki was Vega's favorite. I don't know, Kel, but he's all over this room. He means something to Vega," Kane replied. "We're not going to know anything until we find either that kid or Vega. My bet's that Vega's gone. Our only hope is to find the monster he made."

CHAPTER SEVEN

When Death took you, I didn't notice.
You left me behind you.
In the rain.
Tossed aside without looking back.
Now you're back in my dreams, telling me you're sorry.
I need Death to come and take you back again.

—Letter to My Mother

THE dog was back. Again.

This time, however, he was on a leash, with a lanky, pretty-faced singer skulking in behind him, humming an old rock song that tickled Kane's memory.

He'd spent the rest of the afternoon chasing down Vega's foster kids and writing reports. When the lab technicians showed up to catalogue the walls and remove Cynthia Vega's body, Kel waited in the living room while Kane walked the remains out to the curb. They were silent on the way back to the police station, but once they sat down across from each other at their desks, they both breathed a soft sigh and forged ahead, scrambling to find answers in the muck Vega made of so many lives.

When he finally got free, Kane headed for his workshop. A quick text to Miki, and he picked up his tools, needing to lose himself in the wood. A single chirp on his phone made him look up, and he smiled for the first time since stepping out of the unmarked police car and finding Cynthia's body swinging from the light fixture. Miki was promising him company and some food. Kane replied, asking for a little time to shake off the day. Miki's vow to bend over and kiss it better gave him his second smile... as well as a quick erection he needed to lose before stepping up to a power tool.

Kane almost didn't hear them approach. The lathe wasn't loud, but the constant hum and the sound of the wood peeling away from the chisel often masked everything but a cacophony. He finished the pass he'd started, then switched the power tool off, taking his foot off of the pedal to let it wind down to a standstill. Shoving the safety glasses up onto the top of his head, Kane grinned and nodded a hello at the young man hovering at the threshold of his studio.

Kane was surprised at the time when he glanced at the clock. He'd gotten over to the art co-op after work, intending only to put in a couple of hours, then see if Miki wanted to grab something to eat. Somehow, ten o'clock crept up on him and smacked him unawares. Or at least he was unaware until he moved, and then the strain of working the hard wood became apparent, and his shoulders whined in protest.

Miki rattled the brown paper bag he brought with him. "Hungry?"

"You cooked?" Kane grinned at Miki's derisive expression.

"You crazy? I poison a cop and they'll shoot me," he sniped playfully. Dude trotted in behind Miki as he made his way through the studio's shotgun layout. Sprawling out in a metal folding chairs Kane brought in for him, Miki dug out a couple of sandwiches from the bag and held them out for the other man. "Pastrami or roast beef?"

"Sauerkraut on the pastrami?" Washing his hands in a work sink, he dried off and used a shop towel to dust off his shirt and jeans.

"Doesn't that make it a different type of sandwich?" Miki curled his lip at the idea. "And why would you put that shit on a sandwich? Kim chee, maybe, but sauerkraut?"

"With kraut, it's a Reuben," Kane replied. He was okay with pretending they'd not spent ten minutes of their lives with Miki holding onto the cop for dear life, but his body burned with the memory of Miki's lithe body pressed into his. "Well, and it would have some Russian dressing on it too."

"Then no, this is a pastrami sandwich," he said, waving it at Kane. "Take it or leave it."

Kane took the pastrami, opened it up, and grabbed a few packets of brown mustard from the bag. He spread the mustard, then stopped to watch Miki as he arranged barbeque chips on his sandwich. One of the kettle-fried potatoes made it into Miki's mouth, and he chewed noisily while he placed the sourdough slice back on top.

The young man caught Kane watching him and visibly moved the chip to the side of his mouth, speaking out of the side of his lips. "What?"

"Do you eat Captain-Crunch-and-sugar sandwiches too?" Kane chuckled when Miki gave him a quizzical look. "You are one strange kid."

"Not much of a kid," Miki pointed out. "I'm twenty-six. Maybe. Pretty sure. Whatevers."

"You know what 'whatevers' means, don't you?" The cop bit into a pickle spear, enjoying the garlicky snap. Miki shook his head, and he waved the end of the pickle at the man. "It means 'fuck you'."

"Nuh-uh." Miki shoved Kane lightly with his hand, barely nudging him. "Christ, you're like trying to move a tree."

"Genetics," he replied. "That, and in our family, the strongest survive."

"Even the girls?"

"Especially the Morgan girls," Kane teased. He liked coaxing Miki's skeptical glances into the barest of smiles. "Ryan's the youngest, and even Con's scared of her. She bites."

"Ryan's a girl? Shit, and I thought my name was fucked up." He made short work of half of the sandwich, then picked out the tomatoes from the rest. "How many kids did your mom have?"

"Eight," Kane said, counting them off in his head. "Six boys and two girls. They were thinking about only having one after Quinn, but that one turned out to be twins. Mom was ready to get Dad clipped after Ian snuck up on her after Braeden and Riley. She made the appointment when she started throwing up because of Ryan."

"Aren't you guys Catholic? Irish or something?" Miki nodded to the gold cross at Kane's neck. "Isn't that against the rules or something?"

"Yeah, but so is murder, and that's pretty much where it was heading if Dad didn't go in." Kane grinned. "Only fair. Mom went through the pain of childbirth. Dad could sit on frozen peas because his nuts got trimmed."

"You guys talk about stuff like that?" He handed Kane the other half of his sandwich when the man finished off the last bit of the pastrami. "Don't give me any shit about the chips. You don't like 'em, don't eat them."

"I'll give it a go." He nodded. "And yeah, we talk about everything in our family. Nothing's sacred."

"Do they know?" Miki hesitated, then waded in carefully. "About you liking other guys. Like that, I mean."

"Yeah, eventually," Kane admitted. "Quinn... he's the runt... came out to me first. He was scared a little bit, so he thought he'd try it out on me. I thought he knew I'd been with both... guys and girls... but he didn't. So, Q had a bit of a shock. Then I told him if he wanted me to talk to the family with him, I would."

"You weren't going to?"

"Never really thought about it, I guess." He shrugged and bit into Miki's leftover half sandwich. The chips were weird, a sweet onion-spice taste on top of the roast beef, but it was doable. "I figured if ever I found that *one* person to introduce to the rest of the asylum, they'd figure it out then if he was a guy."

"How'd they take it?" Miki leaned back in his chair. He tossed a piece of crust over to Dude. The dog caught it in midair and fell down over it, rolling the bread into crumbs.

"That dog's fucked in the head," Kane remarked. "How'd my family take it? Dad was… it was hard for him, I think, but he took it pretty good. He kind of adjusts in midstream and keeps paddling. But Mom… she started crying. I think she was… angry."

"Angry? How come?" Miki leaned forward to tug on the dog's ears and pursed his lips to make noises at Dude.

"Don't know." Kane concentrated on eating the sandwich as slowly as he could. "But then Ian spouted off some shit about Mom blowing the ten percent rule for homos, and she flew across the table to beat him with the wooden spoon she had in the veggies. Peas were flying everywhere, Ian was screaming blue bloody murder, and Mom was yelling at him that I was his brother, and he better get his shite together or she'd get it together for him."

"Fucking hell," Miki muttered.

Kane waved the remainder of the roast beef at Miki and grinned easily. "Never piss off an Irishwoman when she's made a Sunday roast and two of her sons have just told her they're gay."

"I'll try to remember," Miki drawled. "Maybe you shouldn't have done it on a Sunday."

"Seemed like the best time. Most of us are there then."

"You guys were older though, right? Like out of the house?"

"Yeah," Kane said, nodding. "I'd been with someone for a bit, but it wasn't going anywhere. Quinn was solo. He just needed it out there."

"What did your dad say? Afterwards, I mean."

"Honestly? Right then at the table? Nothing." Kane leaned over and fed the dog the last of the bread. "Later, he asked me if I was being safe. He was worried more about that than anything else. Dad doesn't… it's not like he goes out and starts giving you a piece of his mind. He's one of those stone-faced guys you go to when your life's gone to shit, and then he says a couple of sentences and *boom*, things are all good."

"He wanted you to use condoms?" Miki laughed. "That's kind of funny."

"More like he wanted me to take care of myself. To fall in love or at least give a shit about who I was going to bed with. A lot of gay guys he knew something about were sluts." He shrugged. "Dad always said we needed to at least like the person we were with. He doesn't care if we weren't married before we had sex or if we fucked a guy. That's not important to him. He wants his kids to be happy. Unless we're doing a sheep, in which case he'll disown us, 'cause you know, we're Irish, not some Scot come down from the hills."

Miki snorted. "Is that supposed to be funny?"

"Dad thought it was." Kane nudged him, and Miki bent sideways to avoid his sharp elbow. "What about you? Tell anyone?"

For a moment, Kane wondered if Miki even heard him. The singer stared out of the open dock door, watching the boat lights move on the water. At his feet, Dude snored loudly, twisted partially around the chair's metal legs. Miki shifted in his seat and rested his hands on his knees, seemingly enraptured by the flickers of life going on outside of the studio's rolling door. Somewhere out in the darkness, a horn blew, a low and mournful sound carrying over the water.

"Just Damien, really," he finally said. "I... wasn't sure I was gay. Not after... you know. I used to wonder if I was just fucked up and didn't know what I wanted because of Carl and Shing...."

Kane didn't say anything when Miki's voice trailed off, but he reached over and touched Miki's thigh. "Dude, if you want to talk about anything, you can. *Anything*, okay?"

"Dog can't talk. You know that, right?" Miki gave Kane a sly, mischievous glance. "I don't think he'll cough up anything to you. He doesn't normally like cops. You... he might make an exception."

"Asshole." Kane chuckled. "I'm serious."

"Yeah, I know." He ran his fingers over Kane's, tracing the man's knuckles. "This thing... you and me...."

"What the hell is it?" Kane finished.

"Yeah, kind of." Miki squeezed Kane's hand once, then let go. "A week ago, you were screaming at my head. Now, we're sitting here having dinner while you're making salad bowls. It's kind of weird. Not bad... but weird."

"Salad bowls?" Kane clutched at his chest and gasped. "Ah, 'the tongue like a sharp knife, kills without drawing blood.'"

"You sound like Yoda."

"You don't know Garbo or Buddha? God, we're going to have to get you some schooling." Kane threw his head back and laughed.

"Hey, public school," Miki said, making a face. "Well, when I went."

Hooking his arm over the back of Miki's chair, Kane leaned over, brushing his fingers on the man's shoulder. "What did Damien say when you told him?"

"He told me I was stupid if I thought he didn't know, and that I was a fucking idiot who should get as much cock and ass while I could." Miki tilted into the crook of Kane's arm. "Damien could be a dick sometimes."

"Yeah?" Kane made a face. "But you guys were close. He couldn't have been a dick all the time."

"Actually, no. He always was a dick," Miki replied. "But he made me feel safe, you know? Like I could depend on him to take care of any crap that came along. D was good like that. He was a cocky, arrogant shit but never to me. Never to the other guys either. We were... tight."

Kane was about to respond when he heard Miki whisper, nearly too soft to hear.

"I miss them."

"Yeah, Miki," Kane bent closer and pressed his lips to the man's temple. "I know, man. I know."

"You had a shitty day too, huh?"

Kane was going to say that Miki had no idea, but it hit him that it'd been Miki's face in those photos, those scraps of time captured for a couple of sick men's pleasure. Truth was, his shitty day was nothing compared to all of those shitty days the other man had lived through.

"Yeah, I did," he admitted. "But it got to be a damned sight better once you got here."

MIKI opened the refrigerator door and stared at its echoing whiteness. Except for a few bottles of beer and some questionable condiments, his icebox was dead empty.

Over the past week and a half, he and Kane had fallen into a routine. The cop would get off shift and head over to his workshop for a few hours to detox San Francisco out of his system, then Miki would amble over with Dude and takeout. Last night, they ate Chinese, picking at each other's food while arguing about science fiction movies. Miki's deep love for *Bladerunner* took a pounding from Kane's opinion of the movie, and he scoffed at the cop's fondness for *Empire Strikes Back*.

"Well, shit, I forgot to order groceries," Miki growled and slammed the fridge door shut. "Fucking Kane. All of this shit with Shing and Carl is making me nuts, and you're not helping."

The cop was taking up too much of his thoughts, especially in the middle of the night when Miki's suddenly aware dick twitched and throbbed at the thought of Kane's cocky grin and deep blue eyes. He tried palming himself for the first time since he woke up in the hospital, but his skin was too sensitive. The tingling nerves short-circuited, and the soft velvet head ached when he brushed it lightly with his fingers.

In the shower that morning, the washcloth became a rough caress, and Miki could nearly feel Kane's callused hand on his cock.

He shot off without even so much as a few strokes, splattering the shower wall with enough come to clog the drain.

And his dick still ached when he thought about Kane.

"Stop thinking about him. Food, Miki, it's not going to just walk through the door. Get some stuff for sandwiches. That's easy." He stopped and tried to think of what one of his foster mothers tried to pound into his head about her religion. "Isn't that what Jesus made? Sandwiches? Tuna fish and bread, right, Dude? Fuck, I'll ask Kane. He's got that God thing down."

Dude had no opinion other than to flip over to the other side of the couch. Flopping down on the cushions, Miki reached for his Vans and tugged them over his heels. His wallet was missing, then found again, buried underneath the notebook Miki'd been scribbling thoughts down in. There were beaten-up notepads all over the living room, some neatly arranged in a milk crate while others were left to fend for themselves. Only a few were dog-chewed, their corners indented and marked from Dude's sharp teeth.

All held pieces of Miki's pain, and now one held whispers of something more… of wanting to be touched and kissed.

Miki flipped through the pages of his newest book. He'd started the first page off with how he felt being alone without the others shadowing behind him. In truth, he'd been their echo, reflecting out into the audience what the three wanted him to be. They understood Miki loved the music and words but hated the noise of being in a band. Having so many eyes on him made him nervous, and he was glad when the lights blurred out the audience and the only thing he could see was the stage and the men who stood by him.

He missed writing songs with Damien. The words that seemed to tear free from his brain were often tinted with how he was feeling, and his best friend had taken his meanderings to turn them into pieces of art Miki didn't even recognize. The sweet ache of Damien's guitar created something out of the nothings Miki found inside of himself. He *missed* spending the hours hunched over a guitar and piano, arguing about how something sounded in his heart compared to the tones Damien's sharp mind crafted.

They got drunk over words and music, sometimes talking about stupid things until the wee hours of the morning when the moon was no longer visible from the narrow windows of the band's shared loft. He woke up on egg-crate foam they eventually used for soundproofing, sometimes more hungover from the music than the whiskey they drank the night before. But Damien had always been there, even when the sun was hidden behind the clouds; a brash, self-confident soul mate willing to do battle with the shadows curdling Miki's life.

"You'd hate him, Damie," Miki whispered, clutching the notebook in his hands until it was nearly bent in half. "Or you'd both bully the shit out of me. He likes the car you bought me. The cops still have it. Fuckers. I used to hate walking by it, but now I hate them for keeping it so long. It's mine. Fuckers need to give it back. I'm going to have to ask Kane about that."

The tears came, as hot as when he'd shot off thinking about Kane's mouth kissing his neck. Ducking his head, Miki laughed when Dude swam across the couch on his belly and shoved his tongue up Miki's nose, licking furiously. After shoving the canine lightly aside, Miki ruffled the dog's back and wiped his face.

He rode the wave of sorrow, letting it wash over him. There wasn't a need to sink into its darkness, and Miki breathed a sigh of relief, emerging from his memories of Damien and the others with a smile. He made a promise to call Edie later to check on how she was doing, and opened the notebook to a blank page and scribbled down a quick list of things he wanted to eat over the next few days.

"Okay, Dude." He sniffed, shaking off his melancholy. "I'm going to hunt and gather. Guard the house. Don't let anybody in."

The dog was already asleep before Miki grabbed his keys off of the table. Wiping at the tightness in his nose, Miki opened the front door and nearly stepped into the mess left on his stoop.

He was good about keeping Dude inside, taking the dog out for walks every few hours, so he was pretty sure the terrier had nothing to do with what looked like chewed-up meat on his sidewalk. Wrinkling his nose, he looked down again, trying to make some sense of what he was staring at.

The plastic bag it'd been in was from an Asian grocery store down the road. His jaunts with Dude had strengthened his leg enough that Miki'd been debating going over the few extra blocks to grab some things, figuring he could catch a cab back. Something had torn apart the handles of the bag, more than likely another dog or one of the cats roaming the neighborhood. A bright pink, bulbous object was seeping out of a hole in the side, its precarious balance on the sidewalk edge losing to the pull of gravity.

It plopped out of the bag before Miki could head back in to grab something to clean the mess up with, bouncing slightly against the cement before coming to rest in the damp greenscape. Light stretches of fibrous tissue clouded the oval chunk, and curled swirls of darker pink were visible through the filmy patches.

"What the fucking hell is that? A gizzard?" Miki curled his lip in disgust when a darker crimson mass slithered free of the back, oozing out in a sticky rush. It fell apart when its tissue caught on the rough cement, exposing the crushed remains of a man's fingers it'd been wrapped around.

They looked like they'd been chewed off. He could count at least six pieces, each nearly bleached white from blood loss, but Miki couldn't be sure how many there actually were. The skin at each joint was frayed, exposing pink-tinged bone, and the three tips that had nail beds were empty of the actual fingernails, bits of torn cuticle clinging to the depressed, pale surfaces.

Choking back the bile hitting the roof of his mouth, Miki gritted his teeth and made it as far as the garage before losing his coffee on the sidewalk. In the time it took him to dial Kane's cell, he threw up twice more, his stomach twisting on nothing as he gagged. Panting through his mouth, he listened to Kane's phone ring, and then sighed in relief when the cop's deep, Irish-soft voice murmured hello.

"Kane." Miki swallowed, tasting nothing but bitter and horror on his tongue. "I... um... need some help, man. I think that asshole left pieces of someone on my porch."

CHAPTER EIGHT

Hey baby girl, smiling at me so wide.
Much too young for what you have in mind.
Come see me in a few years, and then we can talk.
I'll show you how to scream, scream yourself blind.

—Keep Walking

THERE were only so many ways Miki could say he didn't know, and after talking to at least five cops, he was pretty sure he was done. The first one to respond had been a walrus-mustached man who looked more like he'd belong to Jim Rose's Freak Show, swallowing swords, than wearing a uniform.

He wasn't amused when Miki pointed that little fact out to him.

By the time Kane got there, he'd already been chewed up and spit out by four more officers, each more suspicious than the one who'd questioned him before. The final cop was another detective, a skinny Asian woman who flared her nostrils at Miki when he admitted he tossed his cookies before calling Kane.

Explaining why he didn't dial 911 but instead called his own detective earned him all kinds of filthy looks, and refusing to let them go into his house, where Dude was slamming himself against the glass to get at the cops outside, didn't gain him any friends either.

Miki practically threw up again in relief when Kane's SUV pulled down the long asphalt drive in front.

He'd never really seen the man in full cop mode. Wearing faded jeans and a black leather jacket over a white button-up shirt he left open at his throat, Kane still screamed cop when he got out of the car. His boots crunched on the specks of gravel the pavers left behind at the edges of the asphalt. His badge glinted when his jacket moved to his stride, broadcasting his Inspector rank to the cops around him. Nodding once at Miki, Kane then barked out a few questions, hammering at the uniforms in succession until it appeared one of them gave him what he asked for.

Fuck, the man was sexy. Even his wayward dick knew it, and Miki was more than willing to agree with it.

Kane's face didn't betray a single shred of emotion as he inspected the contents of the plastic bag. Instead, he queried the man documenting the evidence. The only time Miki could see Kane losing any bit of his stern countenance was when one of the cops asked him about Miki having his cell phone number.

"That's personal," Kane responded smoothly, but his eyes sought Miki out when he said it, and they burned through him, a sizzling blue heat that promised more than hand-holding and whispers if ever he got the chance. "See if we can get some prints off the digits. Mark off the homeowner's purge, and see if there's any other trace in the area. I'm going to talk to St. John."

Miki stood to the far side of the garage, hugging himself as Kane approached him. The cop's fingers ghosted over his bare forearm, and he ducked his head, smiling at the touch. "Don't kiss me. I puked. Apparently I throw up when people leave dead bodies or parts of dead bodies near my house."

"I'd kiss you anyway, but I'm on duty," Kane said solemnly. "Okay, that and you puked. How are you doing?"

"Okay, I guess." Miki waved at the battalion of cops that seemed to be cluttering up his sidewalk. "I'm thinking of opening up a doughnut shop. It seems like I'd get steady business."

"Your sense of humor's still crap," he replied dryly. "So I guess that's good, since nothing's changed."

"Were there really... um... you know... in the bag?" He'd heard one of the techs whispering about what Miki had thought was a gizzard. "The guy said it was—"

"They're kidneys. I know what they looked like, but the tech said they're cow kidneys," Kane cut him off with a shake of his head. "Don't throw up on me again. You're going green."

"Dude, they looked like someone's balls," Miki muttered. "I'm kind of freaked out. The fingers... I could sort of handle... okay, I didn't, but the other shit? That's too fucking much. Do you think they're Carl's? The fingers, I mean?"

"We'll see," Kane promised. "Where were you going when you found them?"

"The grocery store. I've got nothing in the house." He shrugged. "There's dog food and ramen, but that's about it."

"Okay, tell you what." Kane reached for the piece of paper Miki still had clenched in his fist. "I'm going to leave them here and go grab what's on your list. You go inside and wait."

"And do what?" Miki pursed his lips. "I feel like I'm in some damned slasher flick, man. I'm sure as fuck not going into the shower. I've seen that movie. It did not end well for that chick."

"First, go brush your teeth," Kane advised. "I won't be long. I'll come back and cook you dinner. We'll figure out what to do after that. If you don't give the cops any shit, I'll even bring you cake or something."

Miki let Kane lead him to the door connecting the garage to the warehouse, but he got one last mutter in before closing the door behind him. "Better be good fucking cake, because I'm getting sick of all the extra cops showing up when I only wanted you."

HE WAS still grinning at Miki's words as he unloaded the groceries from the back of the SUV. The garage was still open and empty. The GTO would probably be gone another week or so, and only Dude's stolen treasure remained, a forlorn pile of nonsense spread out and picked through by technicians looking for any clues to Shing's murder.

Even though he'd spent nearly two weeks with Miki at his shop, Kane had never been inside the converted warehouse. Instead, they talked either in the garage or on the front stoop, sometimes not realizing they'd been outside for a couple of hours until Miki tried to take a step and his leg refused to bend. They talked about ordinary things, even Miki's band mates, but never about Shing or Carl. There was too much pain in Miki's voice when he said their names. It was the one tender, raw spot Kane avoided poking at.

Coming through the garage, Kane spotted the chamois he lost to the dog a while back. Shaking his head, he walked through the garage and tried the door to the house. It swung open when he turned the knob, and Kane sighed heavily.

"Why don't you lock the door, you fricking idiot?" he grumbled, and shouldered his way in, clutching the bags in his arms and shutting the door with his foot. Taking a look around, Kane was dumbstruck by the high-ceilinged living room.

"Spartan" seemed like too fancy of a word to describe the place. "Empty" came closer, but Kane still didn't think it captured the echoing desolation of the large space.

A big-screen television dominated one wall, a tangle of wires hanging down from connections to lead to an array of gaming systems and players. Sitting a few feet opposite of the screen was an enormous, battered sectional Kane would have tossed out to the curb years before it reached its current state. Bed pillows and a quilt lay piled up on one end of the L, and a metal storage locker between the TV and the couch was mostly clean except for a couple of game controllers, remotes, and a bunch of dog-eared spiral notebooks. Sprawled out upside down on the other end of the couch, Dude snored loudly, his furry body twisted into a pretzel and his feet twitching as he slept.

"You are the shittiest watch dog ever," Kane said to the sleeping dog. "Of course, your master should lock his damned doors."

An archway separated the living area from an equally barren kitchen. A hallway led to the rest of the warehouse, and Kane peeked through an opening in the wall, expecting to find a dining room, but discovered a mattress set sitting on the floor and tucked into a corner. A mound of pillows were scattered around into a nest on the bed, and the linens were in a twisted pile at the foot end of the mattress. An upended milk crate did duty as a night stand, its faced-out interior stacked with books and more beaten-up notepads.

Kane found Miki in the bathroom, sitting partially submerged in a half-full large marble tub. The cop didn't recognize the music coming out of the sound system set up into the ceiling, but the oddly constructed melody seemed to soothe Miki, who'd laid his head back against a rolled up towel and closed his eyes.

He studied the unaware man, letting his eyes roam over Miki's exposed slender body. Soap bubbles hid anything below Miki's hips, but a hint of fine hair ran from Miki's navel to the cloudy water. His muscled arms were stretched out to anchor himself against the tub's rim. The tattoos on Miki's arm were uneven splotches on his ivory skin, the edges faded and almost transparent in places where the ink had run thin.

The man's nipples were a startling plum on his slightly developed chest, splashes of color compared to Miki's pallor. A dip under his sternum formed a deep shadow on Miki's belly, and his torso was lightly scored with two old scars, one running straight down his ribcage from below his left armpit. His Asian blood showed in his near-hairless skin. Miki's arms were bare, and his pits held only a ghost of fine strands in their hollows.

His face was fully exposed, his dark hair falling back from his cheeks and jaw to rest on his shoulders and the towels. The man's strong, triangular chin was as baby smooth as the last time Kane saw him, without even a hint of a beard. Miki's mouth was slightly chapped, either from the pervasive San Francisco chill or his bad habit of chewing on his lips.

Either way, Kane wanted to feel their slight roughness on his skin. Barring that, he settled for clearing his throat and scaring the hell of out of the dozing singer.

"What the fuck?" Miki flailed and caught himself before he slid into the water.

"Door was open," Kane said innocently. "I let myself in."

"Fucking hell," Miki swore again. "You trying to kill me?"

"If I was trying to kill you, I would have shoved you under the water, but I don't think there's enough in there for you to drown in." Jerking his thumb back toward the main room, Kane said, "I brought some steaks. How do you like yours?"

"Cooked." Miki frowned and scrubbed at his face with a handful of water. "I'm not picky. Whatever."

"I'll be in the kitchen." Kane paused in the doorway. "You have pots and pans, right?"

"Yeah, I think so," he said with a shrug. "I don't cook a lot. There's some shit in the cupboards. I don't know what. I only use the rice cooker and a couple of saucepans."

"Didn't you used to work at a couple of Chinese restaurants?"

"I washed dishes," Miki replied. "And I know how to soak noodles before they get cooked. So unless you want to eat soapy water soup or need chow fun prepped, you're shit out of luck for anything fancier than ramen and scrambled eggs."

Kane whistled as he headed out, taking the memory of a soapy, naked Miki with him. The kitchen had been designed by someone who knew how to cook. Unfortunately, it was being used by someone who had little need for the restaurant-grade stove and oven. A set of Henckels knives sat pristine in a block next to a large wood-fiber cutting board. A smaller plastic board sitting by the microwave showed signs of use with light gouges in its white surface. A clean serrated steak knife lay next to it. From the looks of the scratches, Kane guessed it was the only knife Miki used.

Opening a large cabinet was enough of a culinary horror to give Kane nightmares. Stocked with what looked like a year's supply of calrose rice, ramen noodles, and iconic blue boxes of macaroni and cheese, Kane could only stand in front of the carbohydrate cornucopia and gape. A couple cans of chili—sans beans—stood as quiet sentinels of protein with a lone can of devilled ham. The refrigerator held even less promise. Mostly, condiments and tubs of butter kept close company with takeout containers Kane wasn't brave enough to open.

He refused to look in the freezer. There was only so much horror Kane could take in one evening.

The dog trotted into the kitchen and looked up expectantly at Kane after nosing an empty dog bowl on the floor. A thick-walled plastic water dish sat next to the metal dish, filled to the brim and set on a towel. Dude stuck his head into the water and nearly submerged himself up to his ears, drinking noisily before coming up drenched down to his neck. He shook off the excess water, then nudged the bowl again and barked impatiently at Kane.

Dangling from the dog's new collar was a silver tag with "Dude" written on it in block letters and Miki's cell-phone number underneath it.

"Guess you officially live here now, Dude." Kane didn't fight his grin as he hunted for the dog's food. The tag sang a bright chime against the metal ring attaching it to the collar when the dog jumped in place to beg. "Now let's see if we can get you some dinner."

A small can of wet dog food and some kibble seemed to satisfy the terrier, and Kane returned to shuffling food from plastic bags to the icebox. Miki padded in as Kane was lifting the metal cover off of the grill on the stove, his bare feet making light shuffling noises on the tile as he walked.

"Shit, I didn't know that was there." Miki peered around Kane's shoulder. "That's like a hibachi, right? Where does the coal stuff go?"

"The briquettes?" Kane shook his head. "This is a gas stove. You don't put... are you trolling me?"

"No," Miki said, making a face. "I didn't know. Dude, I told you. I don't cook. I boil water on the stove and make scrambled eggs. I've got a rice cooker, a coffee machine that makes me hot water, and a microwave. What else do I need?"

"No wonder you're scrawny." Kane put his hands on Miki's waist and moved him out of the way. The young man's thin cotton pants and loose T-shirt did nothing to mask the heat coming up from Miki's skin, and Kane's hands burned from the contact. "Go sit down someplace."

Miki nodded and hitched himself up onto the counter, leaning back on his hands to watch Kane cook. "Okay."

"Really? On the counter?" Kane gave him an annoyed look. "Your ass is on a place you're going to put food."

"My ass. My counter," Miki replied, shrugging. "And I've never put food here. Too far away from the stove and everything."

"Raised by fucking wolves," the cop muttered. "Stay there, and keep out of the way."

Miki was quiet as Kane heated the grill for the steaks, but his hazel eyes watched the cop's every move. Once in a while, Kane looked up to find the young man studying him intently, especially when Kane pulled a few potatoes out of the microwave and began to mash them with butter and milk.

"I was wondering what that thing was," Miki said softly. "I knew what the egg beater was, but that thing was all kinds of fucked up."

"You can mash parsnips with it too," Kane replied.

"What's a parsnip?" Miki cocked his head, his wet hair falling to the side. "Is that like a vegetable? Don't like those much."

"You don't like beans or vegetables?" Kane tsked. "What the hell do you eat? Never mind. Don't answer that. I've seen what you eat. I'm surprised you're still alive."

"I eat." Miki pointed to the pantry. "There's food in there."

"There's a salt lick and artificial preservatives in there," Kane shot back. "I'm surprised you're not a giant, salty Cheeto. Here, taste this and tell me what you think."

Kane held out a spoonful of potatoes for Miki to taste. The man closed his eyes and leaned forward, opening his mouth into an O and waiting for Kane to slide the spoon in. Swallowing at the erotic sight, Kane braced his trembling hand by the wrist, then slid the potatoes through Miki's parted lips and into his mouth.

"Tastes good. Like KFC's." Miki opened his eyes and mumbled around the mouthful. "It's really good."

"Really? Kentucky Fried Chicken?" Kane scoffed. "Fucking hell."

"What? KFC makes the best potatoes. Better than Denny's. I like their gravy too. Lots of pepper." Miki nodded. "Their coleslaw rocks. It's like the only salad I like."

"I don't even... don't say shit like that around my mother. You'll give her a heart attack," he said, checking on the steaks. "Then she'll beat the crap out of me for not feeding you actual food."

"Yeah, don't think that'll happen. I don't do so good with parents." Miki leaned forward. "Most of them think I'm crap. Johnny and Dave's parents are okay. They e-mail once in a while, but Damien's probably wouldn't piss on me if I was on fire."

"You don't get along with them?" Kane tested the steaks with his finger, feeling the meat bounce back.

"They hate my guts." Another shrug, but Miki's voice dropped to a whisper. "It's okay, really. I mean, now it is. I guess I figured since Damien and I were close, we'd... have a connection or something. They just don't feel that way."

"Were they assholes to you?" Kane flipped the steaks on the grill.

"They're still assholes," Miki replied. "I lost him too. Fuckers keep coming after me for shit like merchandising rights and stuff. Last week, they wanted to use *Blind Crossing* for a car commercial. I told them no... well, I told Edie no. I don't talk to them directly. Lawyers think it's better that way."

"So no commercials?" Kane grinned. "Don't want to sell instant coffee?"

"Hey, I don't care." He wrinkled his nose. "It'd pay the rent, but Damien hated that kind of shit. Said it would be over his dead body. So now... even over his dead body, I'm going to say no."

"You and he ever…." Kane refused to look over his shoulder at the singer. "You know, ever hook up?"

"With Damie? Hell no," Miki said, shuddering. His heels set a beat against the cabinet door as he swung his legs. "It'd be like you hooking up with… what's your older brother's name? Connor? D was the one who… I don't know… it was like he got me. I never had to explain what I was thinking or what I wanted to do. He just knew. We could write stuff together, and it was easy. Everything just was… easy. Now, everything's kind of fucked up, and I don't know what to do without him. Especially with the band stuff. He took care of all of that. I only had to write music and sing."

"How'd you guys meet?" He turned around and leaned against the counter, watching Miki's expressive face as the man gave him a gentle smile.

"I was on a break over at the Golden Phoenix Palace. I used to grab some food and go out onto the fire escape to listen to music. I think it was like two in the morning when he was leaving a club and coming down the alleyway. I guess I was singing to Joplin with my headphones on, and he stopped and listened to me."

"And asked you to be part of his band? Just like that?"

"Yeah. I thought he was fucking crazy. Well, okay, first I thought he was hitting on me, and *then* I thought he was fucking crazy." Miki grinned. "But I said sure. It seemed like free money from what he said. They were doing covers then, so I didn't have to worry about learning new songs. He and I started writing stuff together after that."

"How old were you?" Kane tried counting back Sinner's Gin history from what he remembered, but it seemed off in his head.

"Almost fifteen." Miki laughed at Kane's horrified expression. "I'd just shaken loose of Carl and Shing, so anything I could bring in was good. Damien used to tell the club guys I was eighteen but short because I was Asian, so they'd let me in to play. Caught some shit when we started making CDs a couple of years later, but the record company took care of that."

"I would have loved to see them trying to figure out how to get you a passport." The meat gave slightly when he poked at it with the tongs, and Kane said, "Hey, these are almost done. Grab some plates, and we can dish up some food. I take it the living room couch is where you eat."

"Pretty much." He shrugged. "I kind of took the dining room over as my bedroom. Climbing those fucking stairs with my knee was not on my list of things to do every day."

Miki found a box of plates stacked up in the kitchen's unused walk-in pantry. The forks were mismatched, rescued from a thrift store back when Sinner's Gin lived together in a two-bedroom apartment, and a pair of jelly glasses were the best Miki could find to hold the red wine Kane brought with him, their crisscross pattern sparkling from the scrubbing Kane ordered Miki to give them.

Miki's lone steak knife had cousins, and Kane excised the thick bone from his porterhouse to hand over to Dude. The dog accepted the offering with a delicate bite, then pranced off into Miki's bedroom with his prize.

"He's not going to eat that on the bed, is he?" Kane leaned back to see if he could spot the dog. "You don't sleep enough as it is. If any bone's going to poke you, it's going to be mine, not the dog's."

"You're…." Miki shook his head. "For a cop, you're kind of a whore."

"So long as he's not eating that in your bed." Kane smirked. "Okay?"

"Nah, he's got a blanket in there he hides stuff in. He'll eat it there. I give him dog cookies, and that's where he takes them." Miki took a sip of the wine and swallowed. His mouth twisted slightly, but his expression remained the same as he murmured something desultory at Kane.

"Want me to get you some Gatorade?" he drawled at Miki.

"No, it's um…." Miki tried another sip. "God, yeah. This is bad."

They ate slowly, with Kane talking about the people he'd run into while investigating a teenaged girl's disappearance. Dude came out from the bedroom and gnawed loudly on his stripped-clean bone, perking up when Kane laughed at something Miki said.

Miki slid back into the couch, his plate still half full. Kane glanced at the leftover food, then drifted his gaze up to Miki's face. The man reached over and nudged the plate toward Kane. Falling back in a slump, he waved negligently at the cop. "Go ahead. You look like Dude when I'm eating hot dogs."

"Now that's something I'd like to see," Kane murmured as he stabbed the remainder of Miki's steak and lifted it to his own plate. The thought of Miki's full mouth wrapped around a length of sausage got him hard. Of course, seeing the man laid out on display bare to the waist under bubbles was a hard memory to shake.

He leaned back over to steal a forkful of potatoes, solely to tease, but Miki's mock frown was too delectable to pass up. His fork clattered onto the plate, and Kane ran his fingertips under Miki's chin, capturing the man's jaw in his palm. Miki's eyes widened, deepening in color when his pupils dilated. His lips parted, and Miki sat stone-still, transfixed as Kane lowered his mouth down on his.

It wasn't fair, Kane decided. In that sweet moment when he first tasted Miki in his mouth, there should have been something sexy playing on the stereo and the promise of something hot and chocolate to pour on the man's body for Kane to lick off.

Instead, they were being serenaded by a terrier chewing through a steak bone, but Kane savored the moment anyway. Especially when Miki moaned into his open mouth and their tongues touched briefly, sharing the heat building between them.

Then the sound of the front window's glass shattering into a million pieces broke them apart.

Kane came up off the couch and reached for his leather jacket, where he'd stashed his gun. After shoving Miki down against the sofa, he came up with his weapon held steady and slid around the storage locker, using front wall as cover. Reaching the switch, Kane doused the overhead lights and waited by the door for something else to hit. He could hear Miki breathing hard on the couch and the concerned whimpers coming from the dog somewhere in a corner of the room.

Nothing happened. Nothing moved, and nothing more came through the windows. Keeping his weapon down, Kane turned on one of the switches, and light flared in the far side of the living space.

"Stay there," Kane ordered Miki. "Keep Dude with you. If you can reach your phone, call 911 and tell them I need backup."

He was barefoot, having shed his sneakers earlier, but Kane didn't want to approach the remains of the window. Even from a few feet away, he could smell the rancid pungency of death and rot coming from the dog's stiff body. The canine's fur was a patchy ashen blond, running darker in places where mange ate at its skin. Its belly was slit open and stuffed with what looked like rocks to give it enough weight to break the window.

At first glance, he would have assumed the dog was Miki's, so Kane reasoned that was what the intruder intended. A neon-green piece of paper was partially stuffed into the dog's slack mouth, and Kane craned his head around to see if he could read the writing on it. The black marker bled through, and the letters were a childish block scrawl, but the words were clear enough.

"*Your next?*" Kane snorted. "Damn dickwad fucks up my night and can't even spell."

CHAPTER NINE

The sweet smell of you stayed when the sun came up.
I needed you there, in the flesh not in dreams.
And on the nights when I cry, so deep from inside.
The sheets are cold and filled with my screams.

—Untitled song, Hidden Track 34

A ROUGHER, larger version of Kane was waiting for them when they came back from another round of questions at the police station.

Connor stood by the curb, his thick arms crossed over his wide chest. His hair was shorter than Kane's, a black thistle following the lines of his skull, and his bright blue eyes were warier than his brother's. The younger Morgan definitely shouted cop to Miki, but Connor's stern face and tightly sculpted bulk screamed danger, even when he shot his brother a welcoming smile as Kane got out of the car.

Kane jerked his chin up at his older brother in passing and walked around to the car's passenger side where Miki was struggling to get out of the cab. "Hey, hold up."

"I can do this, you know," Miki said, waving Kane off. "I did fine without you."

He grabbed the doorframe, easing himself down onto the pavement, and held on tight as his leg threatened to face-plant him before he could take a single step. Gritting his teeth, Miki took short, skipping breaths to ride out the pain, then shuffled back to close the door.

He couldn't trust himself to touch Kane. There was too much going on in his head. Torn between needing to lick his wounds and wanting Kane to spread him open and pierce him through with his hard, long dick, Miki knew he'd come apart if Kane ran his hands over him. Everything he'd been through was too close to the surface, and it scared him. The monsters haunting him in his nightmares were suddenly walking around in the daylight, and Miki didn't know where else he could hide.

"Would you just fucking wait until I can help you walk to the door?" Kane muttered as he came up behind him. "You are so damned stubborn."

"If this was you, would you let someone help?" Miki sniped as he dug his fingers into Kane's arm.

"I know you've had a shit day," Kane grumbled back. "Don't be crappy to me too."

"See you've got your hands full," Connor rumbled, opening the door. "Need some assistance there, little brother?"

Miki tensed up, and Kane gave his brother a filthy look. "You're not helping, Con."

"He might be more willing if you weren't growling at him." Connor strolled up to Miki and lowered his shoulder. "Here, lean on me. My brother can lock up the car."

Good. Connor was safe. Miki didn't get the rush of tingles along his spine like he did when Kane was near. Reaching out for the older Morgan, Miki heard Kane mutter a few choice words at his brother and then swear when Miki slid his arm around Connor's waist for support. It was like hugging a tree trunk, a large, shambling tree trunk that smelled almost like Kane. Miki looked back over his shoulder, meeting Kane's gaze, then bit his lip when the cop winked at him.

Flustered, Miki hobbled toward the door, stopping to look at the plywood covering the broken window. "Thanks for doing that for me. You'll have to let me know how much I owe you."

"We've played baseball in my parents' backyard for years." Connor said, helping Miki into the warehouse. "You think this is the first time these sheets have been used to board up a window?"

The floor was spotless, without a speck of broken glass or gore. Dude was snoring peacefully on the couch, his back legs twitching in the air. From the looks of his puffed-out belly, Connor had gone with bribery to curry the dog's favor. Miki whistled once to get the dog's attention, but Dude's eyes remained shut, giving Miki a couple of thumps of his tail on the couch to welcome him home.

"Yeah, vicious attack dog," Kane said, shaking his head.

"I was expecting Cerberus or something from how the guys at the station were talking." Connor led Miki to the couch and eased him into the pillows. "I brought a couple of In-N-Out burgers to soften him up. No onions, though. Didn't want him to get sick."

"Onions are bad for dogs?" Miki tilted his head quizzically. "I thought it was just chocolate."

"First time he's had a dog," Kane answered Connor's frown. "He needs a manual or something."

"Or something," Connor agreed. "I'm going to head out. I had company when you called. Going to see if she's still up."

"Oh, dude, you should have said something," Kane said, walking his brother to the door.

"What? Like Quinn was going to come over here and do this?" The older Morgan snorted. "You'd be lucky if he didn't nail the door shut."

"Thanks." Kane laughed, slapping Connor on the shoulder. "I owe you."

"Not a problem, K." Connor gave his brother a quick one-armed hug and tossed a wave off in Miki's direction. "Get some rest. If you have any problems and Kane's not around, give me a call. Get my number from K, all right?"

"Here, I'll walk you out," Kane said, and followed Connor outside.

They left the door open, and their laughter carried into the warehouse. Miki closed his eyes and pulled a pillow up against his chest. Listening to the brothers talk was too intimate, nearly as intimate as unexpectedly overhearing lovers having sex. Someplace deep and dark inside of Miki's chest began to hurt, pounding with an envy he'd thought long dead.

An envy that died when he found himself in front of three men he loved as brothers and then resurrected when their laughter and bonds unraveled under a twist of metal and pain.

"Yeah, it's not fair, but fuck that, we had good times." He only had the band for a few years, scarcely long enough to wash away the stains Shing and Carl left in him, but they'd been damned good years. Miki cradled the pillow as tight as he could and waited for his cop to come back inside.

"YOU doing all right, K?" Connor unlocked his Suburban, leaning on the hood to talk to his brother.

"Yeah, I'm okay," Kane murmured. They left the living room door open, so Kane had a clear view of the couch where Miki was curled up into a ball. "He's had a real rough day. There's a lot of ghosts he's got to deal with."

"Been a long time since I've seen you this… invested." His older brother clapped a hand on Kane's shoulder. "He comes with a lot of problems…."

"Yeah, so everyone keeps telling me," Kane replied wryly. He turned to smile at Connor, punching his brother lightly on the shoulder. "It'll be okay."

"Do you remember when we were kids and you found that hawk or falcon… whatever the fuck it was… when we were out at the Presidio?"

"Yeah, it had a broken wing." Kane chuckled. "Man, it was pissed off."

"You picked it up. You didn't want to wait for someone who knew what the hell they were doing to come. No, you had to wrap it with your shirt and take care of it." Connor sobered. "It tore the shit out of you, K, but you still wouldn't let it go. Not until the Wildlife Rescue people came."

"Why does everyone bring that up whenever they think I'm jousting windmills?" Kane leaned against the fender and crossed his arms. "It was out in the sun, cooking. The ranger said it would have died if I hadn't dragged it into the shade and given it water. Why doesn't anyone remember that part of it?"

"Because we had to take you to the hospital to get stitches down your arms, and Mom wanted to beat the shit out of me for letting you pick it up," Connor reminded him.

"Dad understood," he replied.

"Dad's known for jousting windmills too, you know." Connor's laugh echoed against the warehouse's brick exterior. "I'm just saying be careful."

"You're just saying that 'cause you listen to country music," Kane said. "If he was a shitkicker, you'd be pushing me at him and planning a shotgun wedding."

"Only if he got you pregnant," Connor countered. "Then, all bets are off. You bringing him to dinner tomorrow?"

"And the conversation takes a left turn." Kane shook his head. "I don't know. It's kind of late to spring it on Mom, and I don't know if he's in any shape to be dragged in front of the Morgans to get his tires kicked. I don't know who I'd be more scared of. Ryan, 'cause she's got him and his band on the walls, or Mom because he'd be the first guy I'd ever brought home, even if we're just friends."

"K, if you look at your friends like I saw you look at him, you're getting laid a lot more than I thought," Connor rumbled.

"He says he doesn't do parents well." He shrugged and rocked back on his heels, shivering slightly as the breeze kicked up. "I get that his best friend's mom and dad have been assholes after the accident."

"A lot of parents are assholes to their kids' friends," Connor pointed out. "Look at how Dad was to Riley's friends."

"Only those with dicks," Kane said. "That's kind of what I'm afraid they're going to do if I bring Miki around. I'd like him to be around an actual family thing, you know, so he can see what it's like, but not if everyone's going to tear him apart."

"I'll tell Mom you won't be around tomorrow." Connor got into his SUV and started the engine. He rolled down the window and leaned out to talk to his brother. "Don't bring him around if you're not going to keep him, K. If he's as broken as you think he is, don't let him get attached to the family if you're going to jerk them away from him. That's fucked up."

"Like meeting the rest of us is going to make him fall instantly in love with me?" Kane snorted. "If anything, that'll guarantee him running off."

"Only if he wasn't already in love with you," Connor said, lightly smacking his brother on the side of the head. "Why don't the two of you take it slow and see where it goes? He likes you, Kane. He doesn't trust himself with you, and sometimes that's a good thing. Don't screw it up, little brother. If you're going to keep him, hold onto him, even if he tears you up. Stitches heal. Your heart won't if you walk away and leave him dying out in the sun."

MIKI heard the living room door close and then Kane's footsteps approaching the couch. Dude grumbled as Kane moved him to the floor. Then the sofa cushions gave slightly under the cop's weight. He held his breath, hugging the pillow he'd buried his face into. The couch shifted when Kane leaned forward, and Miki trembled when the man's large hands stroked his arm and hair.

"Come here," Kane whispered.

Miki let himself be gathered up, not resisting when Kane pulled the pillow out of his arms. He shuddered as he breathed, caught up in the tremors racking his spine. Kane peeled off Miki's jacket and tossed it over the back of the couch. Spreading his hands over the singer's hips, he lifted Miki up and moved him back. The couch was barely wide enough for them to fit side by side and Kane used the stuffed couch arm for support, maneuvering between Miki and the seat back. With one arm under Miki's shoulders, Kane stroked at the man's face with his free hand, running his fingertips over Miki's ripe mouth.

Miki parted his lips when Kane's thumb skimmed them. Kane's fingers were gentle on his chapped skin, rubbing gently as he traced the fullness of Miki's pout. When Kane's touch moved to his cheekbone, Miki closed his eyes, sighing and relaxing into Kane's arm.

"You are so pretty," Kane whispered. "Sometimes it hurts to look at you."

"Yeah?" Miki opened his eyes and stared up into Kane's face.

Kane's black hair looked as if he'd rolled out of bed and dragged his fingers through it to get out most of the tangles. Faint fatigue lines framed his eyes, their deep blue a shade Miki'd only seen off the reef in Australia. The cop's face wasn't perfect. Someone or something had taken care of his nose's straight line, and at some point Kane lost a minor skirmish with something that left a thin curve on his cheekbone. Another small scar, barely noticeable until Miki was close up, slightly creased Kane's upper lip.

Kane was a guy Damien would call someone to keep instead of just fuck. Miki was inclined to agree. If only he was someone Kane could keep in return.

"You doing okay?" Kane whispered. His hand was large, big enough to cover Miki's face, but every pass of his fingers was a velvety whisper over Miki's skin.

"Yeah, I've had worse days." He tried laughing it off, but Kane placed his thumb against the side of his mouth and stilled the fake smile Miki tried to conjure up.

"I hate that you've had worse than this," Kane murmured. "I hate that you had this."

It was a moment where a kiss would happen.

And Kane did not disappoint.

Stretched out over Miki's body, Kane balanced his greater weight so he didn't crush the lanky singer. Moving slightly, he turned and slid his knee between Miki's legs, supporting himself as he moved over Miki. The heat of Kane's body turned Miki to a spongy mess, and he sighed, reaching up with quivering hands to press his fingers against Kane's broad chest. It felt like steel under the rumpled cotton of his T-shirt, and the harsh rasp of their jeans rubbing denim to denim turned Miki on like nothing he ever felt before.

The accident left his cock nearly inert since the coma so it was still a shock for Miki to feel it thicken and grow heavy between his legs. He nearly lost himself when Kane's thigh brushed over his dick. His boxers left him with enough room for his sex to snake down against his leg, and now, trapped against the silken material, it twitched and churned, trying to reach the man lying over Miki's length.

Miki met Kane's mouth, eager to take the man's taste into him. The fatigue bearing him down left him weak, and the anguish pouring out of his knee turned numb when Kane's lips touched his. Kane's hand rose up to press against Miki's cheek, his thumb coaxing Miki to open up further for him. When Miki sighed, Kane dove in, fiercely possessing the singer's mouth.

Kane's tongue invaded him, but unlike… the others… the man felt like he wanted *Miki*, not just some warm body to empty his seed into. Their tongues curled, teasing guttural sighs out of Miki. He could feel Kane smiling against his mouth, and Miki worked his hand into Kane's hair and pulled him closer with a sharp tug. He needed it rough, far rougher than what Kane was giving him, and Miki pressed into the cop, working his other hand up the back of Kane's shirt to rake his nails across the man's muscular back. The cop hissed and growled, lowering himself down on Miki until the singer was fully pinned against the couch.

There, Miki thought, that feels… right.

Then it all stopped when Kane pushed himself up on his hands and stared down at him.

Kane studied Miki's face, a serious expression easing away the fiery lust Miki had stoked in him. His eyes, darkened with desire, ran back to their brilliant hue, and the flush in Kane's cheeks faded.

Miki squirmed under Kane's scrutiny, uneasy and laid bare. Miki curled his shoulders in slightly, suddenly feeling vulnerable. Looking down, Miki tried to break off the man's intense eye contact, but Kane's fingers on his jaw kept him still.

"I'm not going to hurt you," Kane murmured, rubbing his thumb over Miki's chin. "Don't ask me to. Don't expect it. Hasn't anyone just made love to you, honey? Hasn't anyone just held you and told you how gorgeous you are?"

He needed to cry, to shove Kane away and hide someplace the man couldn't see into him. Biting his lip hard, Miki tasted blood and turned his head, refusing to let Kane see the tears burning his eyes.

"Talk to me, Mick," Kane coaxed. "Let me take some of that pain you've got, hon."

"Get off of me," Miki grumbled. He tried pushing at Kane's chest, but it was like shoving a wall. "Get the fuck off of me."

It sounded weak, even to his own ears. He would have been humiliated if Kane laughed at him, but the man merely brushed his mouth down Miki's nose.

"Yeah, I'm not going anywhere," Kane didn't even have the good grace to pretend Miki nudged him.

It wasn't fair that Kane kissed him again. He couldn't think when the cop's mouth was on him, even more so when Kane's tongue licked briefly at the skin on his cheek, tasting him before kissing him again. Their mouths brushed, and every curse word Miki wanted to fling at Kane fled under the scorching fire of Kane's tongue touching the curve of his upper lip.

"Tell me what happened," Kane said, then shrugged ruefully when Miki recoiled in shock. "Well, not exactly what happened, but how you felt. How you feel now."

"I don't know where to start," Miki whispered. It was too hard to look at Kane. Not with the taste of the man on his mouth. It was too difficult to have Kane on his tongue while his mind wandered to darker, more painful places.

"Start anywhere you want," he replied. Moving to the side of Miki's body, Kane kept one arm around Miki's waist and looped the other under the singer's neck. Nuzzling in closer, Miki turned onto his side, crooking his right leg to take the strain off of his knee. "Anything you say… it's between us. Just you and me. No one else."

"Not even Sanchez?"

"Especially not Sanchez," Kane promised. "This isn't a cop thing, Mick. This is an… *us* thing. Talk to me. Tell me about your last boyfriend. Anything."

"I don't have a last boyfriend," Miki snorted. "Fuck, I've never had a first boyfriend. Kind of the only sex I've had was… them. Everything else was pretty much blowjobs in a back room someplace."

"Thought you were supposed to have rock star sex," he teased, lightly brushing Miki's cheek with the back of his hand. "Isn't that what bands are supposed to do?"

"Hah!" Miki mockingly pursed his lips. "Maybe if you're Damien or Johnny. They're whores. We had a no sex on the bus rule. The carpet was getting disgusting."

"How long did you stay? With Vega?" Kane brought Miki back to his nightmares, gently circling him back around.

He dropped his eyes, staring at the stretch of skin and sinew on Kane's neck. It was a safe place to look. There was a small dark beauty spot where his throat and shoulder met, and Miki studied it intently, hoping to keep the horrors at bay.

Carl's touch still crawled under skin, and Shing's viscous spit clung to the back of his neck. Nothing Miki did could erase the feel of their hands on him, digging deep into him until he'd felt like he'd burst apart. Kane's weight on him felt different. The cop didn't suffocate him. As massive as Kane was, he *fit* against Miki, filling in the spaces where Mike felt the most empty.

"I was… in school when CPS picked me up to take me over to Carl's. I don't know what happened at the other house… the family I was living with. They were… okay, I guess. The guy was an asshole, but the woman was all right. I can't remember their names. Funny, huh? I lived with them for a year, and I don't remember them." Miki rested his head against Kane's arm, burrowing into the man's side.

"The first few weeks were okay. He wasn't home a lot, and Mrs. Vega was kind of spacey. They didn't have any kids, just me. But then he started coming into my room, and... stuff changed."

Kane didn't say anything but moved his arm over Miki's body, draping it over his stomach. Miki clutched at Kane's forearm, playing with the soft hair crinkling his skin.

"I tried telling the CPS lady when she came over. He'd told me not to, you know. They always do," Miki murmured thoughtfully. "I mean, Carl wasn't the first time that kind of shit was done to me, but usually it was quick, and then I'd be kicked out of the house. He was different. He'd stay. Like for a really long time, and his wife, it was like she didn't care he did it, or maybe she was happy about it. I don't know. She wouldn't talk to me when he was home. She'd make me dinner and stuff, but it was like I wasn't there. Like she was setting food out for a ghost or something."

"Did he hit her?" Kane asked quietly. "Was she scared of him?"

"She was scared of everything." Miki's laugh was bitter. "She'd have dinner ready, then go to her room to eat. I never saw her. Only time I ate at the table was when he was home. Then she'd put everything out like it was Thanksgiving dinner, tablecloth and all. Rest of the time, I ate in the living room."

"What did the CPS rep say when you told her?"

"That he was touching me?" Miki snorted. "That I was making shit up because I was someplace I had to follow the rules. She told Carl what I said, right in front of me like she was going to prove I was a liar. He acted all concerned and made these noises like he was going to help me, but I could see he was going to beat the shit out of me as soon as she left. He has these small little black eyes, and they'd get all evil looking when he was planning something. So when he went out with her to her car, I grabbed some stuff and bailed out the back. I think Mrs. Vega saw me because I heard him yelling for me about a minute later, but I was already over the fence."

"Where were you going to go?"

"No idea. Didn't matter. I'd jumped the fence, but the neighbor heard Carl yelling and grabbed me. I didn't even get to the street." Miki swallowed, leaning his head back to breathe through his mouth. The cold air calmed him, nearly as much as the heat coming off of Kane as it seeped into his skin to warm his belly. "He had to work that night. That's when he dragged me over to Shing's. To the restaurant. I never went to his house."

"To that storage room. Above the kitchen?" Kane asked and Miki nodded.

"When I got older, he'd make me work in the kitchen, but after the place closed, he took me up there." Miki licked his mouth. "Carl... he was always angry. He'd hit when he did... *that*. With his fists or his belt. He was always pissed off, and he'd say shit like I was making him do this to me. That it was my fault."

"It wasn't your fault, Miki," Kane reassured him. He spread his fingers over Miki's chest, pressing against the spot where Miki's heart was threatening to pound its way out to freedom. "You were a kid."

"Yeah, I know that now. It's just that, Carl was so... mad. All the time," he murmured. The tears were coming, full force and hot, and Miki sniffed, trying to keep his nose from clogging. "But see, Shing... he was worse. With Carl, I'd get bruises or he'd bloody my nose, but at least he saw me."

Kane tried to pull Miki closer, but he wouldn't let him. He needed space if he was going to tell Kane how he felt. Miki knew he needed air between them if he was going to hold it together long enough to finish ripping himself open for Kane to wade through.

"But Shing? He acted like it was just something he had to do, like brushing his teeth or eating dinner. He wouldn't say anything, not really. He'd just make noises and take. He'd take what he wanted. He'd do it for hours, and then he'd get up and go. He'd lock the door behind him and just leave me there. Like I was nothing. At least with Carl, I wasn't nothing, Kane. At least Carl saw me enough to hate me."

CHAPTER
TEN

Sinjun, I swear to God we're almost done.
D, why the hell am I doing this again?
For the chicks, man.
I don't like chicks.
I do. Okay I like both dick and chick
but do it for me so I can get laid.
Give me one good reason I should worry about you getting laid?
Fuck, I don't know. Finish this up and I'll buy you a car. A nice one.
Old Detroit steel.
I don't drive, D. I can't drive.
I'll teach you. Just finish the damned song.

—Negotiations at four thirty in the morning

HE POURED Miki into bed.

It was more of a bare mattress with a fitted sheet stretched over it and a nest of pillows and linens, but to Kane, it looked like a shelter against Miki's storms. They'd stayed on the couch until Kane's back creaked in discomfort, and when he tried to get comfortable, Miki let go of his sorrow, choking out sobs hard enough to rip Kane's soul from its roots. He let the singer cry himself out, gently rocking Miki in his arms until there was nothing left inside of Miki to give.

Miki grumbled a bit but let himself be carried to bed. Boneless, he slid over the mattress, barely cognizant of anything around him. Kane worked Miki's shirt off and then stared at the other man's jeans. Resigned to the stiffness in his own dick, Kane undid the buttons on Miki's waistband and tugged his pants off, working them off quickly. The dog jumped up on the mattress and curled into the curve of Miki's back before Kane could spread the covers.

Kane knew it was wrong to look at the exhausted man, but he was too tired... too tempted... to ignore the sprawled out body in front of him. The long-limbed singer was a stretch of pale skin and sinew on the merlot-hued sheets. His knees were up, and he was twisted slightly so one of his shoulders lay against the bed. He shifted and murmured in his sleep, throwing one arm over his face to block out the light coming from the living room. Miki's breathing was steady and slow, but tiny shuddering hiccups punched through his sleep, remains of his crying jag coming back to haunt him.

"God, baby. What the fuck did they do to you?" Kane sat on the edge of the bed and brushed Miki's hair out of his face.

The knee was the worst of it. Angry red scars wrapped around Miki's leg, looking like barbed wire rising up out of his skin. Even without touching the man's leg, Kane could feel the heat coming off of it. Frowning, he wondered if he could wake Miki up long enough to take an anti-inflammatory, but the mumbled sighs of comfort from Miki's parted lips threw that plan out the window.

Echoes of older pain lingered on Miki's skin. Several light parallel stripes marked the curve of his ribs and across his back, ending in a curious curved T. The scars were faint, barely visible, but one in particular stood out. Slightly darker than the rest, the stripes ran down the line of Miki's side, ending in a tiny puckered keloid. Unthinkingly, Kane skimmed his fingertips over the scar at the end of the lines, trying to reason out its cause. Too small for a bullet wound and too round for a knife tip, it took Kane a moment to realize he was looking at the remnants of a beating Miki took from a thick belt. The starry depression at the small of his back had been formed by the belt's prong puncturing Miki's tender skin.

"I'd kill them if I thought it would help," Kane whispered, shocked by the well of emotions rising up in him. He meant it. There was no doubting his desire to rid the world of the men who took a lost little boy and made him into a broken young man. "Is that who killed Shing? Someone who knew what he did to you? But why now? After all these years?"

He covered them, dog and man both, figuring the terrier could worm his way out if he wanted.

Kane risked a kiss to the corner of Miki's lips, then stepped back, forcing himself to walk out of the bedroom.

It was a long way to the living room, and the archway back to Miki's bedroom loomed behind Kane, a haunting space beckoning him to the man's bed. He was tired, worn down to the bone from the day, but his mind whirred, unsettled by the waves of anguish racking Miki's body when Kane held him.

He popped the cap off a beer and took a deep pull from the dark, yeasty brew. Their dinner dishes sat on the counter, crusted with food. Kane left them to soak in soapy dishwater along with the utensils, hoping they'd scrape clean later. He returned to the living room, flopped onto the couch, and took another sip of his beer, finally letting the fatigue plaguing him seep down into his bones. His cell phone chirped out a cheery salsa, and Kane sighed, wondering what his partner was up to after the long night they all had.

"Hey," Kane grunted into the phone. Surprisingly, the ancient couch was comfortable, and he squirmed into its cushions. "What's up, Kel?"

"Where are you?" Sanchez barked back. "At St. John's?"

"Yeah, I thought it would be a good idea since he found a bag of severed fingers and cow parts on his porch this afternoon," Kane said, sitting up quickly. "What's going on?"

"Some asshole somehow got ahold of one of the photos from the crime scene… one with your boyfriend in it. This same asshole posted a piece about St. John being a prostitute before hooking up with his band." Sanchez swore, a blistering Spanish curse on the reporter's mother. "It hit the rag's website about an hour ago. The chief's fucking pissed off, and Internal's looking to cut off someone's head."

Kane's stomach sank down. A sickening feeling spread through him, and he glanced toward the bedroom where Miki slept. "Any picture they got would be when he was a kid. What the fuck?"

"There's a cease and desist out. The District Attorney's got a flamethrower going and looking to make some s'mores. Casey's right behind her. Someone's going to get his nuts cut off." Sanchez was running hot, and Kane couldn't blame him. "Problem is, shit's already out there. It was out there before we could do anything. God knows what sick fuck's already downloaded it."

"Damn it, Kel." Kane ground his teeth. "Who the hell did this?"

"I don't know, man. Kane, this shit's from *our* files... *our* evidence room. I can't fucking believe this crap. I'm going to beat the shit out of the guy who let this out. I swear to fucking God, just give me one minute in a room with him."

"Shit." Kane rubbed at his face. "This is crap, Sanchez."

"Some lawyer called...." Sanchez's words were lost when Miki's cell phone sang, vibrating across the table.

"Hold on, let me call you back. Someone's on Miki's cell," Kane said, reaching for Miki's phone. "If it's a reporter, I want to chew them a new one."

"Nah, don't bother. I'm going to go crash," Sanchez grumbled. "I'll talk to you in the morning. Maybe I'll be able to see straight by then. Have fun chewing."

"Deal." Kane hung up on his partner, then debated waking the singer, but, remembering the dark circles under Miki's eyes, he gritted his teeth and unlocked the phone with a slide of his thumb. "Hello?"

"Who is this?" The woman on the line was angry. Her voice reverberated with it, a tingling, molten fury ready to be unleashed on the unfamiliar voice she found on the other end of the singer's phone. "Where's Miki?"

"He's asleep," Kane said softly. "I'm a friend of his, Kane."

"The detective? *That* friend?" The woman's tone softened. "This is Edie. Has he told you about me?"

"Said you were a manager or something? I had you down as a cross of Godzilla and Mary Poppins. And that's a compliment." Kane tried to recall what Miki said as he poured himself out into Kane's heart. "He likes you."

"I like him too," Edie replied. "You're a detective. Do you know what's going on there?"

Kane closed his eyes and tried to rub away the sleep creeping over him. He listened as she repeated Kel pretty much word for word with the exception of the swearing. "How much more is there to know, Edie? I haven't checked the news or anything."

"We've gotten the site to pull the photos and the story, but other places have picked it up." A small dog barked in the distance on the line, and Edie shushed it with a tsk. "Of course, we're going to sue. What does he think?"

"He doesn't know yet," Kane said. "My partner just told me. I'll tell him when he gets up."

"I can try to be up there in the morning," Edie promised. "They're going to be after him... those damned vultures. He'll need to find some place else to stay."

"You've met him, right?" He quirked his mouth, laughing at what he imagined Miki's response would be to Edie's high-handed order. "I found a murdered child molester in his garage, then probably the same asshole threw a dead dog through his window. And let's not forget the bag of fingers and cow parts on his front porch, but that didn't convince him not to come back here. Believe me, he's not going to go anywhere, ma'am."

"In the words of another woman, 'ma'am' is just another way to say 'bitch'." Edie let loose a smoky chuckle. "I don't want to leave him alone...."

"He's not alone," Kane said softly. "He has me."

The silence on the other end of the phone would have been deafening if not for Dude's snores coming from the other room. Kane glanced over his shoulder, taking another look at the man sprawled out on the mattress. Miki's foot was exposed, and from what Kane could see of it, his pinky toe seemed to curl under his other toe. A black nose poked out of the sheets, the linens ruffling as the dog breathed heavily outward.

"You'll have to excuse me, Detective Morgan, but I don't know you. How can I trust you with him?"

"Yeah, I don't know you either," Kane shot back. "But of the two of us, who the hell's sitting in his living room at fucking three o'clock in the morning?"

Another length of silence passed, shorter than the last. Then Edie said, "Point taken, but to be fair, Detective Morgan, he's not let me into his living room... at any time of the morning."

"Do you need to be down there?" he asked. "To deal with the shit that's going to hit? Or can you come to hover over him and do what you have to do up here?"

"It would be better for me to stay down here. It's harder to break heads long distance," she admitted slowly. "But I don't want to leave him alone."

"I've already told you." His reply was gentle but firm. "He's *not* alone, and if there are any heads to be broken up here, I'll deal with them."

"Does he know that?" Edie asked. "About you... willing to break heads open for him?"

"Yeah, pretty sure he does." He cut her off. "And if he doesn't, he will soon. Look, he feels safe here. From what I can see, there aren't too many places he feels safe at. I'm not going to let some asshole take this one from him."

"Let me give you my number. I'll take yours." She rattled off her information and made Kane repeat his twice. "If anything happens... anything at all, I want you to call me."

"You think he's going to like me running to you every time he stubs his toe?" Kane laughed. "I'll let you know if something hardcore is up."

"Will you make sure he eats, at least?" It wasn't hard to hear the worry in her voice, and Kane smiled, almost hearing his mother in Edie's words. "And something other than ramen."

"I promise. He had steak tonight. And vegetables."

"Now I know the world's going to end," she muttered. "I'll call you both when I know more. Thanks for taking care of him, Detective. I owe you one."

"I'm not doing this for you, ma'am," Kane replied. "I'm doing this for him."

HIS beer went warm before Kane could finish it. After dumping the rest in the sink, he prowled through the lower level of the warehouse looking for linens to put on the couch. Not surprisingly, he came up empty. Glancing up at the staircase winding up to the second floor, Kane was debating searching there when he heard Miki murmur his name.

He shed his sneakers an hour or so ago, so Kane's bare feet made little noise as he padded over the wood floors to Miki's bedroom. The light from the lamp he left on in the living room barely reached the bedroom's interior, but it was bright enough to catch the gold specks in Miki's hooded eyes. Kane spotted Dude, snoring and buried in a stolen pillow on the floor. The singer lay on his side, facing the archway, and he watched Kane intently.

"Didn't mean to wake you up." Kane sat on the edge of the bed. "I was looking for sheets I could use on the couch."

Miki blinked, sleep dragging down his eyelids. Nestling his chin into the pillow he clutched to his chest, he mumbled. "Bed's big enough. Just sleep here."

"Mick, even as dead tired as I am right now, I don't think that's a good idea." Kane eyed the enormous bed. "I was thinking of crashing on the couch."

"It's just to sleep. Get in bed. You're making too much noise stomping around for me to crash." Miki grumbled. "And the couch isn't long enough for your ginormous body."

Compared to the too-short couch, the comfort of the feather-topped bed was tempting, but not half as tempting as the young man already lying in it.

"Turn off the goddamned light," Miki grumbled. "And go to sleep."

"God, this is a bad idea," he muttered. "Big fucking bad idea."

After a quick trip to the living room to flick off the lamp, Kane stripped off his jeans and climbed onto the bed. Pulling at the edge of a sheet, he covered himself and reached for one of the stray pillows. Miki slid back to give him room, edging nearly to the wall he'd placed the bed against. Kane let his eyes adjust to the darkness and was surprised to find Miki still awake and staring at him.

"What?" Kane growled.

The singer yawned and squeaked a little kittenish noise. "Thanks for... everything. For being here. Shit, for making me dinner. It was a good dinner."

Neither one of them mentioned their interrupted kiss, but the memory of Miki's tongue lapping at his mouth simmered in Kane's brain.

"You're welcome." He reached up to tangle his fingers into Miki's thick hair, drawing the strands away from the man's sharp cheekbones. "You're supposed to be asleep, remember?"

"It's kind of weird. You being in bed. I've never slept with anyone," Miki rasped. "Well, Damie when we were first touring, but that doesn't count. We didn't have money for separate rooms, so we'd rent one with two queen beds. Johnny kicks in his sleep. Dave lost the rock-paper-scissors, so he got stuck with him."

Kane sighed and edged forward, wishing he could somehow take away the bruises in Miki's heart. The man sighed and laid his hand over Kane's, shuffling his body away from the wall and closer to Kane's heat. It wasn't the time to tell Miki about the fallout from the leaked photos, not when he was wrapped up and sleepy. Kane stroked Miki's face with his thumb and the singer practically purred under his touch. The kitten noises coming from Miki's parted lips made Kane's cock stand up and take notice and when Miki's knee edged against Kane's thigh, he had to close his eyes briefly and take a deep breath to calm his dick down.

"I'm not sure I won anything. D talked in his sleep." Miki grimaced. "He mumbled some nasty things I didn't think anyone could do in bed."

"It was always you and Damien then?" Losing Damien probably drove Miki to the edge of his sanity, and Kane still wasn't sure the singer hadn't fallen off that particular cliff.

"Yeah, always me and D." Miki laughed. "Dave called us the Prince and the Pauper. I didn't know it was a book until he said something. I always thought it was a Mickey Mouse cartoon."

"Mark Twain wrote it." Kane chuckled. "You guys didn't look anything alike."

"Never said we were the sharpest spoons in the drawer. It's 'cause he was rich and, well, I was shit Chinatown ghetto," he replied. "Damie was the smart one between the four of us. I never graduated high school. He went to college when he was like fourteen and got some degree in music."

"But you wrote a lot of Sinner's Gin's songs."

"He liked what I had to say." Miki's shrug was barely discernible in the faint light. "D used to say I wrote good music because I didn't know what the rules were when I started. What's the saying? Put a thousand monkeys in front of typewriters and eventually one of them writes Shakespeare? That's what I told him."

"Did he tell you to shut up?"

"Yeah. Kind of. Mostly it was, 'suck my dick, Sinjun, and fucking take the compliment.'" A grumbling, soft woof came from the floor near the foot of the bed. "He let me get stoned out on music. I'd want to listen to things and pick them apart. Damie was good like that. He'd let me talk everything out until I was too tired to go anymore."

Kane didn't need Miki to say he missed his best friend. The heartbreaking loss in the man's voice was evident.

"Johnny and Dave, they were my friends, but Damie, he was my brother. Tonight, when you and Connor were together, I thought 'that's what me and D were like.'" Miki smiled. "Except Damie was more of a smartass than Connor. Johnny used to say God gave Damien a big dick to balance out how big of an asshole he was."

"Well, that theory explains Connor's dick." Kane chuckled. "Horses are jealous of him."

They lay there, simply breathing, and for a moment, Kane thought Miki had fallen back asleep. Then the man looked up and sighed. "I miss D. You'd miss your brothers, wouldn't you?"

"Hell yeah." He nodded. "Quinn for sure. He's younger than me. We're close. Connor's always been the big badass in the family, but I'd miss him. He used to kick the shit out of me when I stepped out of line when we were kids. I think Braeden and Ian are scared to death of him."

"He's a cop too, right? Connor?"

"Yeah, he's SWAT, 'cause being a regular cop wasn't hardcore enough for him." Kane's fingers stilled, resting on the curve of Miki's face. "The twins just made junior inspector now, and Ian's in the academy. He'll graduate probably next year. Braeden's the freak. He's a fireman. Ryan's the baby. Mom's hoping she goes out and gets a real job like Quinn."

"Way too many kids." Miki wrinkled his nose.

"Sometimes." Kane laughed heartily. "Usually when I needed to pee and the bathrooms were all taken. But now, it's all good. I like most of them. Ian's an ass, but I think it's because he's pissed off Ryan came along and he wasn't the baby anymore."

Miki yawned and rubbed at his eye with the heel of his hand. Kane moved his hand when Miki brushed against his wrist, but the singer shook his head and shifted forward until they touched again.

"You should get some sleep," Kane whispered. "It's going to be a long day tomorrow."

"Yeah, I know," he mumbled under his breath. "I heard you talking to Kel and Edie. I'm guessing she's pissed off."

Kane's face burned a bit under Miki's scrutiny. "I was going to tell you about that crap when you woke up."

"It's okay. I'm kind of used to it. I'm kind of mad about the photos, but those guys have said all kinds of shit about me over the years. At least this time, it's sort of true."

"You were never a whore. You were a kid. There's a big difference there."

"I was never a kid, Kane," Miki whispered, his breath hot on Kane's palm. "He wouldn't let me go. Neither would Shing. I stayed with Carl because I had no where else to go, and at least he fed me. If that doesn't make me a whore, then I don't know what does."

"You did what you had to in order to survive." Kane stroked Miki's mouth once with his fingertips, then leaned in to steal a brief kiss. "That doesn't make you a whore. It made you a survivor."

"A kid shouldn't have to survive his childhood." Miki lightly bit Kane's lower lip, then nuzzled in closer. "I don't mind being called a whore. At least it makes it sound like I had a choice."

CHAPTER ELEVEN

Butterflies and whiskey, catching fire to the moon.
Death's calling to me but I tell him it's too soon.
Songs to sing, places to see.
I don't want to go but Death sure wants me.

—Death Calling

DESPITE the chill on his skin, Kane's cock ached from spending the night against Miki's lithe body. He'd woken up when Miki got up to let the dog out and then again when Dude came back in. The dog's weight dipped the mattress slightly as he turned around a few times near Kane's feet, but Dude settled down quickly, falling off into a snoring heap before Miki shed the sweats he'd worn to hold off the morning cold.

Shivering, the young man crawled back under the blankets and shuffled in close to Kane's body, leeching as much of Kane's warmth as he could. Miki's nose was a sharp bite of ice on Kane's nipple and he bit back a yelp when Miki rested his cheek on his chest, his breath as hot as his face was cold. Kane's cock, already hard from its morning drowsiness, stirred and thrust up, reaching out in vain to pierce his boxers. Scolding his libido, Kane shifted, working his hand down to adjust his dick, then wrapped his arms around the sleepy man curled into his torso.

If Kane could have slept a few more hours cuddled up against Miki, he would have easily traded his left nut to do so. His bladder began to complain, pressing down on the *hurry up* button in his groin. Groaning, he extracted himself from the man's arms and stumbled to the bathroom to piss. A quick search through the bathroom turned up unopened packages of toothbrushes, and he scrubbed the scum off his teeth until he foamed over like a rabid dog.

The night left its stink on his body, and Kane did a mental inventory of the spare clothes he had left in his SUV. Connor had thrown in a backpack of T-shirts, underwear, and sweats he had in his truck, but Kane wanted his own jeans, not his brother's too-big hand-me-downs. He ran the shower as hot as he could stand it, then switched over to an icy cold pour from the waterfall spout set into the tile overhead.

His cock apparently still held a grudge at being told to shut up and go back to sleep, because it flared when he began to lather up with Miki's soap.

A flick of the hot water knob turned the pour lukewarm, and Kane leaned against the stone-tiled shower wall. The glass-enclosed space was large enough for five people, and Kane wondered what exactly the interior designer was thinking Miki would be up to in such a big shower.

Looking at the long sauna bench built against one wall, Kane's dick sent a ripple of ideas toward his brain about what he could do to Miki if given the chance.

His hand was a poor substitute for Miki's mouth, but Kane wasn't going to go begging for affection from the young man he'd left alone in bed. Despite his emotional and physical exhaustion, Miki fought his way out of sleep for the first few hours after Kane lay down next to him. He'd wake, tense and short of breath, his hazel eyes wild with fear. Kane held Miki loosely, rubbing at the small of his back with a gentle brush of his fingers. The frenzied fits and starts slowed. Then Miki's limbs finally went slack, and Kane wrapped them up in a soft cocoon of blankets, cradling Miki against him when sleep took them both.

His dick, however, had an excellent memory of the man Kane left in bed, and it wept a single pearly drop when Kane's palm moved over its head.

He pulled on his cock, circling his fingers around the base, then lifting it up to heft it in his hand. His balls were tight, and Kane could feel them rolling, tightening, and falling down with each stroke he gave his shaft. Pressing his shoulders to the tile, Kane bent his knees, letting his back take his weight, and he leaned his head back, thinking of the hot body he had pressed against him in the early morning.

There was something sensual about a man as he slept. Secret, tender noises were shared, swallowed up in the night before anyone could even admit they'd been made, but Kane caught every sigh and murmur Miki's succulent mouth made. He'd buried his face into the crook of Miki's neck, inhaling the sweetness of male sweat and green-tea soap. Just a whiff of the lather he'd built up on the washcloth, and Kane found himself nearly ready to burst, remembering the length of Miki's back against his chest and the press of his round ass on Kane's cock, the soft cotton of their underwear whispering between them as they shifted in their sleep.

Kane closed his fist over his cock, pulling up hard and slow until his clenched fingers reached the glans. The flare caught the rush of warm water pouring down from the cascade showerhead, parting to splatter down on Kane's thighs and heavy balls. He spread his fingers over his stomach, stroking at the hair around his belly button as he ran his fingers down his shaft. Closing his eyes, he imagined the tightness around his cock was Miki's mouth and the press of his thumb lapping at the wet underside the man's flexible tongue exploring the length of him.

His hand drew him faster, rolling what little loose skin he had on his cock until it grew taut in his grasp. Thumbing his head, Kane peeled back his slit, using the edge of his nail to score the soft flesh at the head of his penis. Miki's sharp teeth would leave their mark, Kane was sure of it. He'd nibble and bite, making Kane jerk and jump even as he slid his cock down Miki's tight throat.

Miki's full lips would fold over his head when Kane pulled out, suckling him tightly before running the edges of his bite over Kane's velvety glans. Tightening his grip, he played with himself hard, pulling his palm over his head, then back down to his root, squeezing lightly when he reached the top. His fingers kissed the pout of his cock, pinching him in until the slight tingle along his shaft grew. His nipples ached nearly as much as his sex, and Kane skimmed his free hand over them, rubbing the flat of his palm over the rough nubs.

Kane kept the rhythm of his strokes slightly off, pulling up slowly, then plunging back down his shaft in a stuttering slowness. He imagined Miki would take his time at first, then devour him whole. The water was a poor substitute for the wet of Miki's mouth, but Kane took what he could get.

Skimming his fingers over his sac, he searched out the skin under his balls. Fluttering his fingertips over the delicate stretch there, he teased his hole, then tugged at the heaviness dangling beneath his cock. A few tugs was all he needed, and Kane sagged, sliding a few inches down the stone wall. The grout dug into his skin, scoring him as lightly as Miki's nails might, and it was enough to take him to the edge.

Grabbing his shaft, Kane tightened his hold and picked up his pace, pulling his palm up and over his weeping head with quick, short jerks. The rush hit him hard, strong enough to bring down a dark haze over his eyes, and Kane rode it out, biting down hard so he wouldn't shout Miki's name as he came.

He pinched at the tight swirls on his chest, echoing the press of his fingers on his head. Another swipe down his cock, and his balls tightened, nearly too soon for Kane to do anything but let the climax hit. It slammed into him, rising up from his curled up sac and pouring electric shockwaves through his dick. The wave of his seed nearly scorched the skin from his hand, and he barely had time to take a gasping breath when another followed, as intense and as hot as the first.

His cock danced, spilling and gasping its climax as his balls emptied themselves of his desire. It was too much to take, and Kane sagged, buckling from the darkness threatening to overtake him. It seemed like an eternity of pleasure to the point of being pain when finally his cock gave up its writhing and sagged under the weight of its release.

The water continued to pour in a rush over Kane's shoulders, tepid and comfortable, but if he didn't move soon, his legs wouldn't hold him up much longer. The slick stone was hard against his spine, and a creaking ache in his back and knees warned him of an impending, vicious muscle cramp. His hands shook as he reached for the hot water knob, but it twisted easily in his grasp, and a moment later, steam fogged up the shower glass, obscuring the rest of the bathroom from him.

He lathered up again, snorting when his dick responded feebly to the green-tea soap as it foamed on the washcloth. Carefully washing his cock and balls, Kane used one hand to lean against the wall, needing it to support his trembling muscles as he rinsed off his release.

"Jesus, Miki," Kane mumbled, bending his head forward under the pour until the water ran through his hair. "What the hell have I gotten myself into with you?"

It was too soon for them. Kane knew that in his gut. Miki was riding a wave of nightmares and old pain. Something lingered in Miki's psyche, something rotting so deep inside of him it made the man question who he was even as he clung to Kane for support. It'd risen when Miki's silent tears succumbed to a whispering keen, and the man rocked slightly as Kane stroked his shoulders and sides.

They fucked me up so much. I don't even know if I really like guys. Suppose it's just 'cause of what they did to me? he'd murmured, nearly low enough for Kane to miss hearing. *That why no one really wants anything but a fuck? You think that's why no one sticks around? 'Cause that's all they made me good for? Fucking?*

It stung to hear those words. Kane's stomach clenched when Miki bared his raw soul. Nothing Kane said would take away those doubts. They both knew that anything Kane *could* say to him would be fleeting and hollow. Instead, they just held one another, first in the soft light of the living room, then in the comforting darkness of a bed linen cocoon as they were serenaded by a snoring dog.

"Damn it, I just want to kill someone for putting this shit on him," Kane swore. "Or go in there and fuck him, like that would do any good. I can't do jack shit right now, and now I'm talking to myself like some fricking crazy person."

He turned off the water and stepped out of the shower, letting the steam pour out into the room. His muscles were still tight, even with the stroking off, and Kane hunted through the cabinets for anything resembling aspirin. Coming up with a nearly full bottle of ibuprofen, he shook out a few and gulped them down dry, leaving the bottle out so he could force two or three down Miki's throat.

"Well, not like I didn't wear enough of Connor's shit growing up." Rooting through what Connor left him, Kane frowned at his choices. He leaned over to roll the borrowed sweats up enough so he didn't drag them on the ground. "Great, and they fucking say SWAT all over them. Egotistical bastard."

The sweats were too soft from years of washing, and the hems unfolded when Kane walked to the kitchen. Digging out a package of Kona coffee from the squillions of bags Miki had stashed in his industrial-sized freezer, he tapped out a heap of grounds into the steel coffee filter and stepped back—falling flat on his ass when his heel caught the back of Connor's sweats, and he slid forward, unable to catch himself before he slammed into the kitchen floor.

"To hell with this," Kane growled, getting up slowly from the floor. "I've got to have something in the car. At least something to wear that won't try to kill me until I can find the washing machine in this place."

A quick glance toward the open archway reassured him that Miki was still asleep. Yawning, the terrier stretched and groggily stumbled off of the edge of the bed, shaking out his blond fur before trotting up to sniff at Kane's ankle.

"I'm just going to the car," Kane promised the dog. Grabbing his keys off of the table, he held his hand up to Dude. "Stay here. I'm going to be right back."

Still barefoot, he opened the front door—and reeled back when the screaming started.

"FUCKING hell," Miki swore as he tripped over a sneaker.

His leg hurt, and the throb in his knee was nearly seismic as it thumped its displeasure. The Nike was too large for his foot, and he blinked, trying to make sense of the size eleven shoe in the middle of his bedroom floor. His answer came to him in a rush of memory:

disheveled black hair, a sinful Irish whiskey voice, and delectably large hands cradling him as he unsuccessfully tried not to cry. He sniffed, catching a whiff of Kane on his clothes, and yawned again, padding out to the living room to find out what all the yelling was about.

The front door was open, and Miki scrubbed at his eyes when the watery afternoon sun hit his face. Taking a few steps from the threshold was a mistake. When his bare feet hit the long swatch of damp grass separating the warehouse from the cement walk, a crowd of people swarmed toward him.

Miki turned his head, ignoring the crowd. He spotted his dog and limped over to where Dude stood, furiously ravaging a man's pants leg. Further down the walk, Kane shoved a beefy-faced photographer to the ground, shattering the man's camera when he threw it onto the asphalt.

Amid all of it, nearly every single person clamoring in on him was shouting his name, trying to get his attention.

"Miki! Is it true you murdered your own dog and blamed it on a stalker?"

He didn't spare the man a second glance. Dude was done chewing up the tabloid reporter's pants and was beginning to nip at the tender flesh he found under the fabric. The man's alarmed shouts were shrill, and Miki precariously bent over to lift the dog off the ground. His knee joint protested being twisted around but held as he stood back up.

"Dude, cut your shit," he scolded, hefting the dog under his arm.

"Miki! Over here! Is this man your new lover? Have you finally gotten over Damien's death?"

"There's a rumor the Mitchells are suing you over the rights to Sinner Gin's songs. How do you feel about that, Miki?"

"Is this the detective investigating your prostitution charges? Do you have any comment about that?"

That caught Miki's attention, and he narrowed his eyes at the reporter as he limped past the swarm to where Kane was shouting at the man he'd pushed. Dude squirmed in Miki's arms, barking his head off at the people trailing after Miki like lost ducklings. The noise level rose and overwhelmed him, a buzzing cacophony he'd not missed since he was released from the hospital. The badgering stalked him with every step Miki took. Questions followed him, voices shouting after him about his injuries, his damaged relationship with Damien's parents, and the dead man found in his garage.

"Let's go back inside," Miki shouted at Kane so the man would hear him above the fray. "I'll call the cops."

"I *am* the fucking cops!" Kane growled back. "God, I'm going to shoot one of these assholes."

"You don't even have your shoes on, and I think you left your gun in the house." He laughed, then nearly toppled over when someone pushed him from behind. "I own this end of the street. It's private property. There's a sign and everything. I'll call them in for trespassing."

"I'd rather fucking shoot them," Kane grumbled. "Give me the dog. I'll hold him."

"How about if I hold him and you shove us back to the house?" Miki nodded to the front door. Dude snapped at a cheek that got too close to Miki, taking a nip of skin with his bite. The man howled and clutched at his face, a small pinch of pink skin peeking out between his fingers. "Or I could just hold him in front of me like the Cleaners from *Labyrinth*."

"I'm going to sue! Your damned dog bit me!" The scream was lost in the blizzard of shouts and cameras whirring for the perfect shot.

"Talk to that asshole." Miki jerked his chin toward the photographer who lost his camera to Kane's temper. "You guys can go in on a lawyer. Now get the fuck off my property. All of you."

It was hard going, much more difficult than most of the paparazzi crowds he'd dealt with before. Not for the first time in his life, Miki wished Damien was around. The guitarist seemed to have snake-charming ability to fend off the packs of photographers who stalked them. With Kane's arm around his shoulders, Miki held the terrier as firmly as he could while the cop led him back into the house.

The crowd was reluctant to let them escape, blocking the front door. The press of bodies grew too hot for Miki to stand, and he gulped in large pulls of air, hoping to escape the claustrophobic walls of people. Kane shoved hard, pushing through the mass to give Miki room to walk.

It took Miki some time. The dog squirmed, eager to catch another bite of someone's face or arm. Dude's teeth came dangerously close to a woman's nose, and she jerked back, toppling a cameraman behind her. They scattered and fell, human dominoes stacked too tightly together for comfort, taking Miki down with them.

He felt himself falling forward, his foot catching on someone's leg or ankle. Miki twisted, holding Dude close to his belly when he went down. He hit the pavement and choked on the air rushing out of his chest. Something gave in his leg, a tearing heat spreading out from his knee to hook into his balls before twisting a snarling pain through his body.

Gasping, he let go of the dog and rolled over, covering his head to protect himself from the stampede of people around him. Dude jumped free, landing gracefully on the grass. Waves of pain hit Miki's spine, and he let his stomach have its way, puking out what little he had left in him. Miki heard Dude barking and snapping at the people around him, but he couldn't focus on the furry blond blur long enough to yell at the terrier to stop.

Strong hands grabbed Miki's upper arms, hoisting him up. The world tilted, brightening when he was lifted up over the bodies around him. Slung across Kane's shoulders, Miki hissed when another wave of pain hit him, and he horked, dry heaving over Kane's chest.

"Shit, you sound like my mom's cat. Hold on." Kane turned, shoving people aside with his bulk. Miki was precariously balanced across his back in a half-assed piggy back. Hands were grabbing at his sweats, threatening to pull them down off his slender hips.

Bodies jostled them, and Kane pushed back as much as he could. "Dude! Get in the house! Now!"

The dog took one last look at the throng, gave a final defiant bark, and trotted back into the house, tail up high in insult.

"Put me down," Miki growled. "I can walk."

For a second, Miki thought Kane was ready to dump him onto his feet on the sidewalk, but the cop was only shifting his hold on Miki's arms. Draped down Kane's spine, he had to duck his head when the man plowed through the last of the crowd. A brush of cold air kissed Miki's bare hip, and he made a grab for his sweats, tugging them back up over his leg.

The press of warm bodies followed them to the threshold. Kane gently put Miki down, his eyes narrowing when Miki yelped in agony. His knee buckled, and he grabbed at Kane to keep his balance. Clutching the man's arms, he bent his head down and panted, forcing himself to work past the crippling pain. He let go of Kane suddenly and pushed against the man's broad chest.

"Close the door," Miki spat out. "If they stick their fingers in, just slam it harder."

Someone snagged Miki's arm through the opening of the door, and Kane pushed back. Shoving at the man holding Miki, Kane balled his hand into a fist and let fly. His knuckles connected with the reporter's nose, crunching it to the side. Wedging himself into the doorframe, Kane stood his ground, keeping his body between the horde and Miki.

"Get inside, Miki," Kane growled. "We need to get somebody down here to get these assholes off your property."

A camera stuck through the opening clattered to the floor as its owner's wrist was caught against the door. From the resistance against Kane's shove, Miki guessed the man caught more than one person's fingers. The door bounced slightly as Kane gave the reporters space to pull out their various body parts. Then he shoved it closed again, snapping the door tightly against the jamb.

Miki hobbled over to the couch and grabbed at the back for support. His left leg hurt from taking all of his weight, and the twinge in his right ankle was a warning he'd injured more than his knee. Sitting on the far end of the couch, Dude lolled a smile at him, clearly pleased at the battle he waged against the people outside.

Kane stood by the door and stared at Miki, stiff, furious, and brimming with energy. The man's deep blue eyes were snapping with anger, and Miki almost winced under the intensity of Kane's stare. As calmly as he could, he edged around the arm of the couch and tried to ease into the cushions without making too much noise.

He failed miserably.

The pain was intolerable, jerking his nerves up his spine and tingling shockwaves into his teeth. His mouth thickened with viscous spit, and Miki gulped, choking on the sudden mouthful of liquid moving across his tongue. Grabbing at the sofa with both hands, Miki tilted forward and panted, riding out the scorching heat traveling up his leg.

"Come here," Kane murmured, stepping up behind Miki.

He tried shoving the cop away, but Kane's arms were already around his waist, lifting him up to ease the pressure against his joints. Kane ducked his head, nudging Miki's arm up over his shoulder.

"Hold on to me. Let's get you into the bathroom." Kane hitched his stride short, gently easing Miki to the bathroom. "I'll grab some ice for your knee, and you can sit in there with your leg up while I hunt you down some drugs."

"I've got some Jack on the fridge," Miki grumbled. "God, this fucking hurts."

"Whiskey isn't the answer," Kane sighed. "As much as I'd like to get stinking drunk with you, I think it's time to give some of the crap the doctors pushed on you a try."

"Don't want to get addicted to that shit," Miki said, shaking his head. "I've got to watch for that. They think I had some shit in my system when they found me."

"You were like, what? Two? Three?" Kane stopped walking and peered down at Miki. "Jesus Christ."

He shrugged. It wasn't anything he thought much about, not after so many years of not knowing where he came from or even really giving a shit about the people who let him wander out into the street covered only in a dirty diaper.

"Doesn't matter." Miki sucked in a mouthful of air, and Kane lifted him up again. "Old news. No one gives a shit about it now, especially me. Don't get your panties up in a twist."

"It's still not fair." Kane grimaced. "Yeah, I know. I'm a cop. Life isn't fucking fair, but shit, sometimes I hate people."

"Yeah, me too," Miki admitted. "Especially the ones banging down my door right now."

"Bathroom first." Kane's voice dropped an octave, a grumbling roar that tantalized Miki's cock more than he'd like. "I'll call the station and get someone out there to chase them away. Hell, I might not even wait for someone to show up 'cause I'm serious about going out there and shooting them for doing this to you."

"Yeah, just don't go do that before you get me the ice." He grunted when Kane eased him onto the long bench next to the whirlpool. "And if you really fucking loved me, you'd make sure that ice has some whiskey around it."

CHAPTER TWELVE

I promised to take you, take you to the stars.
Way past Pluto, once we clear Mars.
We'll dance in the black, and I will right all my wrongs,
And before our fall from Heaven, we'll sing our old songs.
So long that we've danced, we'll forget how they go,
Mumble a few words, then bask in our glow.
I'll teach you to fly, And you'll teach me to win.
Made me survive, and taught me to sin.

—Letters D and S

HE LEFT Miki asleep in his bed. The afternoon had been filled with cops, questions, and curious looks that made Miki shuffle his feet and retreat behind an icy mask of cynicism and aloofness. It'd gotten to the point where Miki couldn't even put together the timeline of events, and he stumbled when trying to get his thoughts together. His body grew tense, tightening with stress as each minute passed, and Kane finally broke off the questioning, secreting Miki back in the warehouse where he could collapse on the bed.

A call to the station ensured the presence of a patrol car in front of Miki's warehouse, but Kane still scanned the main street as he drove away, memorizing the cars clustered near Miki's driveway in case they needed to be rousted when he came back.

In a city whose lifeblood was tourism, finding a quiet spot was still relatively easy. Driving from Miki's place, he slid into Chinatown's busy traffic, heading toward Mission street. The spiced aroma of sizzling meats wafted through the district, and locals fought for space on the sidewalks alongside visitors, heading to favorite hole-in-the-wall places for a late lunch.

He pulled into a space near St. Patrick's and strolled to the tall brick building, stopping on the sidewalk to let a pair of wind-burnt women in floppy hats finish taking pictures of the church. Kane mounted the short flight of cement steps, entered the church where he'd spent his childhood Sunday mornings, and took a deep breath, inhaling the sweet scent of ancient wood, candle wax, and old paper. After dipping his fingers into the font, Kane crossed himself, dabbing the water on his body. Dipping his head toward the central altar, he continued to walk along the back aisle, then slid into a pew at the rear of the left conclave.

It was an old church with a history that stretched back decades before the Great Quake. Originally built to serve the area's Irish community, the congregation grew to embrace the Latino and Filipino families that moved into the area. The ornate altar and stained glass windows were framed by arched ceilings and slender marble columns, the cream interior softened by years of burning candles and seasoned stone. The building continued on through the worst of the city's times, opening its door for those who needed its gentle grace, especially to a growing Morgan family.

It'd become Kane's sanctuary, one he'd come to when he needed to find peace, whether it was inside or out.

Leaning into the hard wood, Kane closed his eyes and took another breath, letting the cool quiet of the church seep into him. He had a couple of hours before the five o'clock mass, and St. Patrick's was empty, giving him some solitude. He'd only steeped in the calming silence for a few minutes when a heavy hand clasped his shoulder. Jerking up from his slouch, Kane hissed in slight annoyance when his brother Connor slid into the pew next to him, jostling him with an elbow jab to his left side.

"Stalking me?" Kane muttered.

"Nah, I could smell you from across the city, so I stopped by to tell you to bathe," Connor murmured back under his breath.

They kept their voices down, more from habit than fear of disturbing anyone else in the empty church, but it was a long-ingrained behavior neither one of them could break. Sitting in the pew next to Connor, Kane felt like he was a little kid again, edging his brother with a few well placed kicks to get Connor to move down to give him more room. The Morgans once took up an entire pew, slowly filling out to two and then three when the boys reached their full breadth. Now their schedules made it hard to attend, but their parents still had a few offspring sitting beside them in the back of the church, as if they still ran the risk of their father taking them outside for misbehaving.

"I saw your car parked across the street," Connor said, leaning forward to rest his forearms on the pew in front of them. "I was heading up to the house, and thought I'd stop in to see what you were up to."

Kane grumbled and shoved Connor's shoulder with his fist. "Nice of you to stop by, now go on to Mom and Dad's."

"Did you call Mom to tell her you weren't coming to dinner?"

"She wasn't home. I left a message," Kane replied. "Things got... fucked up. I don't want to leave Miki alone for too long. I've got a couple of uniforms in front of the house right now, but I've got to head back."

"So you came here?" Connor swept his hand in front of him, waving at the church's Irish-influenced interior. "Thought you and God weren't on speaking terms."

"God and I are good." He snorted. "It's me and the Church that's got some problems. Doesn't mean I'm not Catholic. Just means they've got to get their shit together a bit. Not like I came here for the cookies and juice."

"True, they suck," his older brother murmured. "Yeah, I guess if Mom and Dad still love you, I'm pretty sure God's okay with you too."

Resigned to his brother's company, Kane shoved his hands in his pockets and gave Connor a sidelong look. "Okay, tell me the real reason you're here. Mom sent you to hunt me down, didn't she?"

"Nope." Connor winked at his younger brother. "I really stopped because I was worried about you. Last time I saw you, you were wrapped up tight around that kid I left you with. Now, I find you here looking for God. You don't think I'd be worried?"

"I'm okay, dude," Kane reassured him. "I just needed some thinking time. And Miki's not a kid. He's only a few years younger than me."

"Looks like he just rolled out of high school. You sure he's old enough to buy booze?" The man rumbled as he spoke, and Kane smirked, recalling when his brother's voice squeaked and jerked down as he shot up in height. Kane soon followed, their gawky bodies stumbling over their growing feet and slamming into walls that suddenly seemed to narrow in on them. He'd been a bit jealous that Connor outstripped him in bulk, always the older and bigger brother, but with his brother sitting next to him, Kane found an odd comfort in his brother's mass.

"Yeah, he's old enough," Kane replied. "Old enough for a lot of things, but that's… kind of the problem."

"Talk to me, K." Connor turned his head to look at his younger brother. "You can tell me what's bugging you."

Kane knew he could. While he'd been close to Quinn, it'd been Connor he turned to when things went to shit. His big brother was the rock in his life, the person he bounced his insanity off of before he had to trot out his problems to his parents. Even from a young age, Connor had been serious, a stalwart and calming influence on everyone around him. He'd been the one to lead the charge when the Morgan boys finally had enough of the Delany clan's bullying.

Connor also took the blame when Kane knocked out five of Mike Delany's teeth and broke his jaw enough that it had to be wired shut. He'd been set to cleaning out the garage and basement for punishment, only nodding in silent thanks when Kane and Quinn joined in to help.

"It's your Miki, huh?" Connor grunted and settled back besides his brother. "He seemed nice. Stubborn. Kind of fragile but okay."

"He's… strong and… yeah, stubborn." Kane couldn't stop his smile and bashfully ducked his head when Connor teasingly poked him in the ribs. "There's just so much crap he's lived through. It's fucking hell to deal with, and I feel like shit saying that."

"Why?" his brother asked. "Just you and me here, dude. You can say anything you want."

Kane lifted his chin up and stared down at the rows of pews. Sifting through the tangle of thoughts clouding his mind, he settled on the first thing surfacing amid the noise.

"I'm scared to love him. He… fucking scares me so much." He shook his head, unable to find the ends to the shattered emotions inside of him. "He's really screwed up, Con. There's nothing inside of him to build on. He's got a fucking dead best friend who's the closest thing to family he's ever had, and now there's these two assholes who raped him when he was a kid standing in front of him like vengeful ghosts. He left those guys behind, and here they are again… one's dead and the other's probably a stiff too, but it's like they're alive and walking around him. I'm scared to touch him. I'm fucking scared to want him because all I can think about is if he'll feel them on him when I touch him."

Kane's voice broke, and he gritted his teeth, refusing to give in to the confusion overwhelming him. Connor's hand formed a solid warmth in the middle of his back, and Kane took a breath, trying to steady himself before he spoke again.

"Did you tell him that?" Connor asked. "Did you tell him you want him?"

"Yeah." Kane nodded and ran his hands through his hair, frustrated at the man he'd left behind in a bed he wanted to share. "We've known each other for what? A couple of weeks? It's not some damned fairy tale where I kiss him and everything's okay. He's fucked up, Con. Really fucked up, and it kills me. I hate that this crap happened to him. I hate that no one gave a shit about him, and I don't know what the hell to do about it."

"Do you love him?" Connor pressed. "You know what that feels like, K. Do you love him? Or just pity him? You've got enough scars on you from pitying things."

"I don't know," Kane admitted. "Honestly? It's not pity. It isn't. Could I love him? Shit, Con, I *like* him. It's good with us. He makes me feel... electric... inside. I think about him. I wonder what he's doing and if he's eaten something for lunch. I like that he sings when he's not thinking about it. It's like he has a constant soundtrack going. He makes me... *feel*, Con. He makes me feel like I'm more than I am when I'm with him. Even when he's giving me shit about something, it feels good."

"Then love him." His brother rubbed the middle of Kane's back, tapping along his spine with his fingers. "If he makes you feel good, then he's good for you. It's not rocket science, K."

When he was a kid, he trailed after Connor, wanting more than anything to be just like his older brother. Sitting next to him on the pew they'd waged their Sunday battles on, Kane realized not much had changed. He still wanted to be just like his slightly older but much wiser brother.

"What about the other... shit?" Kane turned his head to look at Connor. "What do I do about the crap that he's gone through. Suppose he can't deal with me touching him?"

"Has he had sex before? With other guys?"

"Yeah," Kane said, frowning. "Sort of. Kind of back room shit. Nothing serious. Not a relationship."

"Then don't you think he'll be okay with someone who actually likes him?" Connor asked. "Sometimes, little brother, you complicate shit you don't need to. Talk to him. Kiss the fuck out of him and go from there. If you're going to give him anything, make him feel safe. Make sure he knows he can say no if things get too much for him."

"You think it's that easy?" Kane eyed his brother.

"Nope," Connor said, shaking his head. "I think you're going to have a fucking hard time of it, but let me ask you; is he worth it?"

Kane didn't have to think hard. He remembered Miki sitting up on the counter as he cooked, singing an old tune by Aerosmith while Kane grilled their steaks. He loved the flash of gold in the man's hazel eyes when Sanchez pushed him too hard and the jut of Miki's chin as he defied Kane's temper to defend a dog he loved but was afraid would move on. He wanted to kiss away the pain on Miki's mouth when his knee was bothering him and lick at the man's dark plum nipples until Miki's hands were digging into Kane's shoulders.

Most of all, Kane wanted to hear Miki's husky voice rasp his name as he stretched him open with a thrust of his cock and moan with need when Kane's arms cradled him close.

"Yeah, he's worth it," Kane whispered.

"Then quit being a selfish dick. Stop thinking about how *you're* going to deal with this and concentrate on how he's going to get through it," Connor scolded in his soft, deep voice. "The shit that's happened to him is his shit. So you get a little bit on you. So fucking what? You should be wading in it to reach him… to pull him out of it. You're a Morgan. Act like one. Act like the baby brother I know I have."

Kane smirked, turning his head to the side so his brother couldn't see his face. Connor slapped him on the shoulder anyway, the sound echoing in the vastness of the church's interior.

"Thanks, Con," he said, rubbing at the sting Connor left behind. "For stopping."

"No worries," Connor said. He stood, nudging his brother with his fist. "Come on. You've got to go deal with falling in love. I'll go make your excuses to Mom for you. Call me if there's any more shit that happens."

"Yeah, no problem." Kane followed his brother out, shuffling sideways to get out of the pew. "Tell Mom I said I love her and I'll give her a call."

"Oh no," his older brother replied caustically. "I'll tell her you're skipping dinner. Sucking up to her? You're going to have to do that all on your own, little brother."

HE WAS woken up by a kiss.

Miki felt the skim of lips over his jaw and then Kane's soft breath on his lobe. The Irish-tinted words Kane murmured into his ear were promises, wicked things he wanted to do with Miki until they both were covered in sweat and too tired to move. Kane's teeth nipped at the tender skin beneath Miki's ear, sending shivers down Miki's spine.

He kept his eyes closed, letting Kane's hands roam over his arms, then up over his shoulders. Tilting his head up, Miki gave the man his throat, and he moaned helplessly, driven to distraction when Kane's teeth raked over his neck, then down over the jut of his collarbone. Suddenly, his T-shirt felt too hot, too constricting, and Miki writhed under the fabric, needing to tear it loose from his body. Kane nibbled on his throat again, drawing Miki's shirt up until the fabric pooled near his armpits. His fingers found Miki's nipples, and he pulled at them until they ruched under his touch.

"Let me see those beautiful eyes of yours, Miki love," Kane whispered, lightly pulling on Miki's lip with a gentle bite. "Let me see that gold you hide behind those pretty lashes."

"God, that's… cheesy," Miki accused, but he opened his eyes and found himself staring up into Kane's handsome face. "Hey, where's Dude?"

"Really? That's what's crossed your mind when I'm doing this?" Kane laughed at Miki's snort. "I gave him a bone with lots of meat on it. Thought it would be a good idea to keep him busy."

The late afternoon sun crept past the openings between the heavy draperies slung across the room's windows. A sliver of buttery light fell on Kane's face and bare chest, throwing long shadows behind the ridges of his muscles and bones. Kane watched Miki study him, his cop's eyes taking in everything around him.

A tiny shift of the bridge and a thin white crease marred the strong line of his nose, and from the speck of scarring on his upper lip, it looked like he'd taken a fist to his mouth. Miki leaned forward and blew a puff of air into Kane's face, rolling onto his back when the man jerked up and flailed a hand at him.

"Brat." Kane snorted, trying to clear the tickle from his nose. Glaring at Miki, he grumbled, "A kiss would have been nicer."

"This was funnier," Miki laughed. It was odd having a warm body near him, a sensual length of skin and muscle wrapped around his stomach and lying along the curve of his back.

It felt good.

It felt weird. Weird but good, especially since that body was Kane's.

Miki stretched out, tensing his leg in case his knee rebelled. It ran a little hot, spiking flares up and down his calf, but when he twisted his ankle, his knee didn't do much more than mutter a mild complaint.

His cock, however, had plenty of suggestions for what to do with the man lying beside him.

"Your knee up for this?" Kane's breath whispered over Miki's face, and he inhaled, pulling the man's scent into his chest. "Are you up for this?"

"No, no. I'm good." Miki shifted on the mattress, sliding his free leg up between Kane's thighs. "It doesn't hurt. Okay, it doesn't hurt more than it usually does. I'm okay."

"Yeah?" Kane's mouth turned wicked. "'Cause I can think of a lot of things to do with you like this."

Their kiss was hard, packed with a sweetness Kane could taste down his spine. Kane cupped Miki's face, stroking at the man's cheekbone briefly, then sliding his thumb into the crease of Miki's lips. Gently urging with a press of his hand, Kane plundered Miki's mouth, driving his tongue deep into the man's hot moistness. Moaning, Miki arched, working his hips up until he fit into the curve of Kane's belly. Twisting the rest of the way, he partially lay on his side, sliding his left leg carefully between Kane's thighs.

Kane's cock thickened when Miki's cotton-covered thigh brushed against it. Even through the layers of clothing, Miki's heat engorged Kane's shaft, and the cop moved into the touch, ignoring everything beyond stoking the fire raging between them.

He bit Miki's lower lip, a light brush of his teeth on the plumpness he'd wanted to gorge on for the past couple of weeks. The moans coming from Miki's mouth made Kane's cock harden, and he mindlessly ground his hips against Miki's thigh. Grasping Miki's wrist, he guided the man's hand down until Kane could feel the press of Miki's fingers against the denim barrier between them.

"God, I want in you so bad," Kane murmured into the recesses of Miki's mouth.

Teasingly, the man's tongue darted out and played along the width of Kane's chin, scraping the flat over the stubble growing on Kane's jaw. Growling, Kane bent his head and nipped at the tender skin on Miki's neck until the man arched his spine and threw his head back, exposing his long throat to Kane's teeth.

It was an invitation Kane could not ignore.

There were so many things Miki wanted to say... to scrape loose from his brain and rip his heart free. Kane's murmuring kisses felt so damned good... a deep good that touched places inside of him he'd always thought would remain dark. He couldn't trust that feeling. It was too frightening... too new... too sweet of a taste for his soul to handle.

And he wanted more of it.

Miki didn't want it to fucking end. And he was scared to death he'd see Kane walk away before he could get his fill.

"You make me want weird things, you know? Like, normal things." He eyed the man lying over him. "It's stupid and sick. Like one of those cards you open up and it sings Carly Simon at you."

"Is that a bad thing?" Kane's expression sobered, and he stared down into Miki's face, searching for something, but Miki couldn't imagine what. The man's fingertips were a soft, feathery touch on his cheek, and Miki leaned into Kane's palm, enjoying the roughness of the man's hand on his skin. "The normal things you want, not the singing card. The only thing I want singing is you."

"Okay, *that* was cheesy." Miki wrinkled his nose at Kane. "Worse than that other thing."

"I mean it, you know." He bent his head down and ghosted a kiss over Miki's mouth. "You make me *want*. And crazy. You make me nuts, Miki boy. I like the crazy you make me."

Miki's shy smile earned him a kiss. Then another until Miki couldn't breathe. They broke, separating long enough for him to get a gasp of air in, and his lips burned with the memory of Kane's mouth. The man's hands moved up under Miki's shirt, peeling it up over his shoulders. They fought with the shirt as it clung to Miki's skin and arms until Kane tugged it free and threw it to the side.

"You're wearing too much clothes," Miki grumbled. He tried to reach Kane's waistband, but the man grabbed his wrist before he could undo the metal button.

"I need to talk to you first," Kane murmured, leaving a searing kiss on the corner of Miki's mouth. "I need to talk to you about Carl… and Shing."

Kane was serious. Miki could see the worry and concern in every line of Kane's body. Even the skim of his fingers over Miki's throat was a stuttering, feathery touch, as if the man was afraid he'd break.

"I don't want them in this room with us," Miki growled and captured Kane's face in his hands, forcing the man to look straight at him. "I didn't bring them in here. I don't want you to either. For once in my fucking life, Kane, can't I just be with you? Without having anyone else inside of me? 'Cause you're the only one I want inside of me. Not them. You."

CHAPTER
THIRTEEN

He found me on a staircase of steel.
Nowhere near Heaven, a Devil making a deal.
Come on down, son, my Satan said with a grin.
Come with me and we'll make Sinner's Gin.

—Gin and Demonic

"NO, THERE'S just me," Kane whispered finally. "Just you and me, baby."

"Good," Miki whispered. "Because I don't want to think about anyone else. I want this. I want you, Kane."

Kane felt good against him. Too right on his skin. A part of him wanted to shove the man away… to shove Kane as far out of his life as he could, but the selfish child inside of him whimpered at the thought. It'd been too long since he'd been held. Too long since a man whispered how much he was wanted. Too long since he heard all of the lies men told him when they wanted him to spread his legs so they could fill him with their release, only to walk away leaving him empty and wanting something more.

It was wrong to believe Kane when the man said he would give Miki more, but Miki wanted to believe him.

Even if it was too much of a lie to believe.

Kane's palms were rough on his skin. Small imperfections and calluses caught against the smooth landscape of Miki's stomach, and then Kane smoothed over the roughness with a gentle feathering of his fingers over the reddened spot. The man's stubble-burred jaw scraped Miki's neck, and then the sting of Kane's teeth in the hollow of his throat made him gasp. Digging his fingers into Kane's shoulders, he shifted under the man's heavy body, easing his right leg out.

Then Kane moved away, leaving Miki's heated skin to cool.

He didn't want to beg. He'd be damned if he begged, but Miki's throat widened with the barbed words anyway. Swallowing at the lump forming at the back of his mouth, he tried not to spit out his anger at the man drawing off of him, but it was hard.

"Where the fuck are you going?"

"I want to taste you first," Kane whispered.

"We can...." Miki was silenced with a punishing, hard kiss, and he gasped, trying to regain his breath.

"Let me do this for you," Kane said. "Let me take care of you. For right now, lay back and let me make this all about you. When was the last time someone did that for you, huh?"

He didn't want to say never, but it hovered on his lips. His past sexual encounters were mostly fumbling dark-alley blowjobs given to guys who wanted Miki's mouth on their dicks, not the other way around, and when Sinner Gin had finally broken out on stage, he was working too hard and drove himself too fast to do more than quick hand jerks given to him by faceless, sexless fans in backstage corners or in the shadow of Sinner's Gin's tour bus.

Miki wanted more than what he'd had in the past. He needed Kane to be with him, to take his time with Miki's torn body. Falling back onto the bed, he reached out and hooked his hand around his lover's neck, pulling Kane in for a kiss. When Miki gasped for air, Kane broke free and began to run his tongue over Miki's bare skin.

Kane spending time licking at his body was far more than Miki ever dreamed about, much less hoped for.

His nipples were as hard as his cock, maybe even harder once Kane's mouth closed over his left nub. The man's tongue flicked over the dense bit. Pinched lightly between Kane's front teeth, his nipple throbbed, and his body responded to the wet, sweet pain of the man's bite. Kane's fingers stroked first at his other nipple. Then, when he moved over to lave at Miki's unattended nub, that same hand traveled downward, snagging the drawstring loop of Miki's pants. Kane's nimble fingertips made quick work of Miki's waistband bow. Plucking the ends loose, he dove in slowly, the back of his hand scraping across the slender down trail below Miki's navel until he reached what he was searching for.

"Kane….," Miki growled, torn between wanting the man's touch and the crawl of tingling nerves as his dick responded to the whisper of fingertips at its root.

"Just hold it in, babe." The tantalizing hand withdrew, and Kane rose up onto his knees, straddling Miki's thighs. Hooking his fingers into Miki's waistband, he slowly drew the cotton fabric down, taking extra care not to jostle his right knee. Kissing the trail of barbed-wire scar around the joint, Kane traced it up until its end, a faint starburst on the inside of Miki's thigh.

Sprung free from its prison, Miki's cock jostled for attention, a glistening curve of ivory tipped with pink. Kane leaned forward to kiss its tip, and Miki gasped, jerking his hips back. Grinning at the sensitive response, Kane clasped Miki's hips and held him steady, adjusting his stance until he was kneeling between Miki's legs. The man parted his thighs and panted out a guttural moan when Kane moved his right knee over a pillow.

"You okay?" Kane reached up with one hand and cupped Miki's cheek. "Do you want me to stop?"

"No….," Miki groaned, digging his shoulders back into the mattress. "I just needed it up on a pillow. It's okay. God, don't stop. I'll kill you in your sleep if you stop right now."

"Now, if that isn't incentive," Kane murmured. "Hold on to me, babe. Hold and just… let go."

Miki didn't know how long he could last. Certainly not longer than they'd already been kissing, and when Kane's hot mouth closed over the tip of his cock, he almost exploded into Kane's throat. The man pulled back, coaxing a low, groaning keen out of Miki's throat when he laid a skim of butterfly kisses down Miki's hard shaft.

Gripping the base of Miki's sex, Kane gently stroked the slick skin and sparse hair with his thumb.

"Kane," Miki gasped and pushed at the man's shoulders lightly.

"What, Mick?" He didn't stop long enough to do more than whisper those words before he dropped back down to lick at Miki's cock tip, parting the slit with his tongue.

"Can you...." Miki shut his eyes. Something inside of him lingered dark and heavy in his chest, and he reached for Kane's hard arms, anchoring himself in the moment with the feel of the man straddling him. "Can you take off your clothes? Please? I... I've never had anyone with me long enough to.... It would be like you're staying, you know?"

Kane stopped and drew himself up, staring down at the man he'd brought to a frenzied need. For a moment, Miki wondered if he'd go insane waiting for Kane's answer, but then the cop slid off of the bed and began pulling his clothes off. As he stepped out of his jeans, Kane's erection drew Miki's attention first. He stood at the end of the bed, letting Miki get a good look at the man who battered down the walls he'd put up around himself.

"Take a good look, Miki love." Kane's voice was a rough pour of Irish over sex. "Because I'm staying."

Years of working with wood and training for the force sculpted Kane's body. His arms bulged as he tossed his shirt aside, and as he twisted, his ass muscles tightened into dips before relaxing into firm rounds. The cut of his abdominal muscles was framed by his hips, and a thick black pelt surrounded the heavy weight of his stiff, long sex. He held his arms out, giving Miki a cocky smile, and turned around, laughing when the singer blew an off-key wolf whistle at him.

Kane's smile was silly enough to ease the razor-fanged butterflies feasting on Miki's stomach.

It wasn't a perfect body. Instead, it was the body of a hard-muscled man who grew up with a band of rowdy brothers and lived a life as fully as he could. There were scars. The largest, a thin line of white through tanned skin, ran from Kane's left hip up his ribcage. Another, a lighter swatch of brown, marked the space under his left knee. Miki didn't mind them. He had his own scars, both inside and out.

Kane's stomach rippled when he moved toward the bed, his muscled chest and arms flexing as Kane put his hands on the mattress to balance himself while he kissed the jut of bone on Miki's right ankle. A light constellation of freckles spanned the top of Kane's shoulders, and Miki made a silent promise to himself to kiss every single coffee-splash dot before Kane slipped away from him.

Taken as a whole, Kane was the most beautiful man Miki ever had the pleasure of seeing.

Then Kane's hands roamed up his calves and over his hips, and Miki forgot everything other than the touch of the man's mouth and tongue.

He knew he wouldn't last. Not after so many years of being unable to do anything more than cry, but Kane took his time, suckling on his cock and pulling back up its length when it seemed like Miki was about to lose himself. Clutching at the root, Kane held Miki's release tight, slowing down his strokes until they became whisper-soft touches. When Miki was finally able to see again, Kane began anew, wrapping his lips around Miki's flange and scoring the velvety skin lightly with a brush of his teeth.

His cock grew wet with Kane's spit, and Miki parted his legs, needing to thrust himself deeper into Kane's hot mouth, but the man's broad hand on his hip held him down. Frustrated, Miki threaded his fingers into the soft ruff of Kane's hair and gripped the man's nape.

"Kane, I've got to come," Miki begged. "God, just let me go."

"No, baby," Kane whispered, running his tongue around Miki's head. "I don't want to let you go. Not now. Not ever."

The promise in Kane's voice drew Miki's balls tight, and he lurched up, curling his body around Kane's shoulders. The tears hit, riding fast on the heels of his release, and when the lightning from his cock struck, Miki held on tight to the man stroking him. The heat unspooled quickly, spreading through his body in a wave of overwhelming sensations Miki had no name for.

His throat tightened, and he struggled to breathe, jerking with the intensity of his orgasm. It built up from his balls, choking past the tangle of nerves at his cock's base, then spilled out in a stream of hot liquid. His climax hit again, the second wave drawing itself out longer, and he held on tighter, feeling Kane's skin give beneath the press of his nails.

Miki tasted blood, and he licked at his lips, not surprised to find he'd bitten through the tender flesh. His insides begged for Kane's touch, and when he thought he couldn't stand much more, the tip of Kane's spit-damp finger edged into his opening and slid in, spreading him enough for Miki to have a taste of what it would feel like to have Kane's cock delving into him.

His orgasm ripped through him, and Miki screamed Kane's name. The man wrapped his arms around Miki's waist and rocked him, hissing when Miki's teeth sank into the meat of his shoulder. Miki held on, his cock reveling in its awakening. The skin on his shaft tightened and gave when his balls emptied again, the head growing too tender to be touched. Miki ached along the length of his sex, and still, his body continued to release, spilling out every drop of want and desire he'd held in for too long.

Miki's jaw ached, and he finally let go of Kane's shoulder, horrified at the deep purpling beginning to spread over the spot he'd bitten. Weakened, he murmured an apology, but it came out a whisper of nonsense and pleasure. Grinning at Miki's insensibility, Kane leaned them both back into the pile of pillows scattered at the head of the bed and shifted Miki's boneless body into a more knee-friendly position.

"I'll give you a few minutes to rest." Kane kissed Miki's bitten lips. "You strong enough for me to take you bent over the bed?"

"I don't know. That's a lot of standing I'd have to do," He blinked and snorted, cradling Kane's arm when he draped it over Miki's chest. "And maybe I want to have *you* bent over the bed."

"I'm the one who got the condoms and lube," Kane whispered, stealing another kiss from Miki's open mouth. "I get first dibs on your ass. You can have me later."

A RUMPLED, naked Miki was possibly the sexiest thing Kane ever saw in his life. The man's legs seemed to go on for miles, and as the singer bent forward to grab at the bottle of lube Kane tossed onto the bed, Kane was tempted to bite down on the ripples of bone along the man's rib cage.

Miki's shocked yelp was well worth the slap Kane got when he sank his teeth into the man's side.

"Shit, we didn't eat. I might be a little hungry...." Miki began to crawl off the bed, but Kane grabbed him by the hips and pulled him back.

Kane sent a mental thank you to the designer who stocked Miki's home. The bed linens were luxurious, a satiny cotton that made it easy to slide his lover over. He swallowed Miki's laughing protest in a fierce kiss and worked the man's fingers off of the bottle of lube, letting it drop onto the mattress.

"We'll eat later," Kane promised. "Right now, I've got other things for you to do."

It took delicate maneuvering, but Kane's hands were insistent, and he edged Miki over onto his lap. The singer's long legs wrapped around Kane's hips, and he caressed the man's injured leg, working a gentle massage over the scars running a hopscotch around his knee.

"You okay?" Kane asked softly, returning his mouth to the column of Miki's throat.

"Yeah, it feels more stretchy than hurting," Miki murmured. "It's... not bad."

He was learning to love the blushing pink marks his teeth made on the man's pale skin. The tender area on his throat was an erotic zone for Miki, and with every bite and rake, the man squirmed and moaned. Suckling at the crease between Miki's throat and shoulder, Kane drew up a welt, scoring the spot with his bite as he rolled the skin with his teeth.

Miki's cock was hard again, leaking a clear dribble of need when Kane's fingers danced over its head. Smoothing the liquid into the velvety skin, Kane slid his hand slowly down the man's shaft, tightening his grip when he reached Miki's balls. Cupping the delicate sac, Kane played with their weight, tugging gently until he felt the bite of Miki's fingernails digging into his arms. He dropped his hand further down, teasing the opening hidden between Miki's cheeks. The furl gave slightly under the pressure of his fingers, and he lightly circled the man's entrance.

"You like that?" Kane whispered against Miki's parted lips. "Want more?"

"Yeah," Miki rasped. "God, yeah."

The lube was scented, a sweet almond aroma that spread to fill the room when it hit Miki's hot skin. Kane's fingers were coated with the slick, and it ran down into his palm as he parted Miki's opening with a delicate pressure. Miki took the foil packet from and bit into its corner to open it. Then spat out the dribble of lubricant he got on his tongue from tearing open the wrapper. Scraping at his tongue with his front teeth, he made a face at its taste.

"Don't laugh at me," Miki grumbled at his smirking lover. "That shit's nasty."

His cock eagerly stood for the condom, and Kane fitted the tip over his head quickly, shoving it down until it caught on his root. A stroke down seated the latex tightly on his shaft. Then Miki gasped when Kane's fingers dipped into him, spreading him apart.

"Shit, warn a guy," Miki growled into Kane's shoulder.

"Okay, hold on," Kane warned. "I'm going to be fucking you. Hard."

Miki shuddered in anticipation from the heavy promise in Kane's words. He wiggled against Kane's hips, his shins taking most of his weight as he balanced on the mattress. Angling his ass up, he fell slightly forward, rubbing his chest against Kane's with a slow, erotic burn of sweaty skin on skin.

Kane pushed deeper into his lover's heat, pulling out a rumbling groan from Miki's open mouth. With the singer pressed against him, Kane had a good view of the man's pretty face, softened with arousal. His full lips were dappled from being bitten, and a long trail of slightly raised welts danced down Miki's throat and across his collarbone. The man's rich brown hair cascaded across his cheekbones, dusting over Kane's chest, and Miki's hands were clenched into fists, resting on Kane's shoulders.

Kneading his hands against Kane's body, Miki held as still as he could while Kane worked his fingers in until his palm lay flush against the underside of Miki's ass. Once entrenched, Kane let Miki rest before he parted his fingers to work his lover's tension free. The muscles in Miki's body responded to Kane's touch, and the singer relaxed, taking in more of Kane's fingers with a sighing murmur.

"Not enough," Miki pleaded. His head was down, so Kane couldn't see the spark of emerald he wanted to flash in Miki's eyes before he seated himself into Miki's body. Cupping the man's chin, Kane guided Miki's head until he could see his face.

He was in love with Miki's face. Kane could admit that easily without letting the rest of his heart murmur its pleasure at Miki's presence in his life. The man's thick black lashes and exotic features were dominated by his enormous green-gold eyes and sweet mouth. Framed by his rich mahogany-shot hair, Miki's face could make angels weep and haunt a cop's dreams. Somewhere, someone made the perfect beautiful male and tossed him away, letting Miki drift like flotsam until Kane found him. It broke a part of Kane's heart open, and he wanted to kiss away the sadness lingering in the shadows of Miki's gaze.

"There you are," Kane whispered. Slanting his mouth over Miki's open lips, Kane drew his hand away from Miki's ass and licked the roof of his lover's mouth when he began to protest. Murmuring softly about how good Miki felt straddling him, Kane shifted his legs and guided his cock to the slick, gaping pout waiting for him.

Slathered with lube, Kane slid into Miki as if he'd been created to fill the singer's body. Parting Miki's opening, Kane took a deep breath when Miki canted his body and took him in. As Kane inched further into Miki's passage, Kane rubbed at his lover's spine, stroking him gently while Miki struggled to find air. Gasping, Miki dropped his head down until his forehead rested on Kane's muscular shoulder. He lifted his arms, wrapping them around Kane's torso, and quivered, panting with the pleasure of being filled.

"I've got you, Miki love," Kane's fingers tangled into Miki's hair, and he caressed the man's nape, feeling Miki slowly relax around his erection. "We'll take our time."

Pulling himself up, Miki kept his head down as he pushed against Kane's thighs. A change in the angle of his hips, and Kane's cock nearly slipped free of his ass, but Miki ground his hips back, moving in a small circle to recapture Kane in his tight grip. Kane shivered from the sudden plunge of his cock into the cold air of the room, only to be engulfed by the simmering warmth of Miki's slick hole. Another tilt, and Miki gave a whispering moan, filling himself again with Kane's heft. Reaching forward, he palmed his own cock, only to have his hand pushed away.

"Let me," Kane insisted. "I want to do that for you, baby. I want to make you explode."

Kane's fingers found him, stroking at his length until Miki's hard cock jerked and twisted in his hand. Murmuring encouragement, Kane began to thrust up, piercing Miki's core with a solid push of flesh. They began to move, finding the pulse between their bodies. In a few heartbeats, Kane found the right hook to follow, and he gripped Miki's hip with his free hand, guiding the man into a steady rhythm.

Miki's tight, velvet grip around his cock drove Kane wild as he plunged in and out of his lover's body. Buried inside the man for the first time, he pushed himself deep to stroke against Miki's pleasure. He struck the spot, and Miki's body untangled around him in a sudden, frenetic squirm. Miki grunted for more, and Kane tried to time his strokes with the roll of his fingers. The lube on his hand turned Miki's cock to a satiny-hard shaft, and he worked down its length, burnishing the head with his palm before fondling his way back down to the base.

Unable to hold himself back, Miki covered Kane's fingers with his own hand. They slid up and down Miki's sex with their tangled fingers, its lube-slick skin rolling over the shaft in time with the thrusts of Kane's hips. Encouraged by Kane's whispers, Miki drove down to meet his lover with each stroke.

"I can't last, Miki. Gonna lose it." Kane shuddered, trying to slow his own release.

The spiraled clench of Miki's passage on him was nearly too much to handle, and he felt the rush of his seed beginning to boil up from his sac. Quickening, he flicked his thumb over Miki's entrance, running the spread of lube around the rosette so he could pound Miki harder. The rough feel of his finger against Miki's crinkled entrance drove Kane to lose himself in the feel of his lover's skin sliding against him.

"Too much, Kane," Miki gasped. "Going to come."

Grasping himself firmly, Miki pulled his sex hard, jerking his palm over the head as he tried to match the thrusts pounding up inside of him. His shoulders and stomach trembled with the release building along his erection, and Kane began to rock faster, determined to drive Miki over the edge.

Nearly painfully hard, Miki's cock throbbed once, then spurted a thin trail of white. It spread over his fingers, seeping down between the cracks of his knuckles. A moment later, another climax hit him, and he shot wide, splattering Kane's chest with a blast of hot seed. Continuing to rock on Kane's sex, Miki lunged forward, dropping his shoulders and pushing back onto the other man, driving Kane as far in as he could take him.

Kane picked up his pace, moving in time to the man's encouraging grunts. Digging his fingers into the small of Miki's back, he regained his control long enough to hold on, slapping their bodies together in a wet slide of skin on skin.

A spark of release hit Kane hard, and he leaned back, nearly losing his balance as his cock erupted. Miki crested again, and Kane cried out, driven to his orgasm by the clench of Miki's muscles around his shaft. Pulled in by the man's contractions, Kane gritted his teeth and came hard. Sweat dotted his chest and ran down his torso as he gripped Miki's shoulders and drove his lover down onto his throbbing shaft.

Engulfed fully, Kane thrust one last time into Miki, the tight sac under his erection giving to his release and curling up into the hollow of his thighs. The hot spill bloomed into Miki's passage, working a flood of sexual desire through the tight space between them. The latex swelled, filling to the brim with Kane's seed, and Miki gasped at the volcanic rush coursing from Kane's shaft, his own cock seeking its final, fluttering release.

Kane eased Miki down, reluctantly laying the panting man onto the mattress. The singer complained softly when Kane's softening erection slid free of Miki's rippling entrance. Bound by sweat and drying lube, they kissed what parts of each other they could reach, wet skin slick under their palms, and the smell of musky sex blended with almond oil.

"Fuck, that was nice," Miki finally gasped. Panting slightly, he stretched out over the bed, sucking in as much air as he could. "I'm going to hurt like hell tomorrow but it was worth it."

"Nice?" Kane muttered. The muscles in his legs were rubbery, and there was a creaking ache beginning to form in his spine. Next to him, Miki looked well-fucked, his skin glowing gold and his mouth slightly swollen from Kane's tongue and teeth. "Fucking hell, it was more than nice. You wore me out, and I get *nice*?"

"Yeah, nice." Miki turned his head, sleepily winking at the man lying next to him. "Maybe next time, we can aim for pretty good."

"What do I have to do to get a fucking fantastic?" Kane eyed his lover suspiciously.

"Make me forget my name," he murmured, his green eyes gleaming with satiation.

"Deal." He chuckled, rolling over to give Miki a slow, simmering kiss. "Just so long as you don't forget mine, Miki love, because you're going to be screaming it for a very long time."

CHAPTER
FOURTEEN

We are lost somewhere in Boon Fuck E.
The van's all broke and we don't have tea.
Damie's driving us to hell and gone...
Sinjun, if you don't shut the fuck up, I'm going to take that guitar
and shove it down your throat.
Hey, what rhymes with gone? Maybe I should change it to back.
That way I can use black.

—First Tour of the Americas, location unknown.

KANE jerked awake at the sound of a deep, lolling chime echoing through the warehouse. He debated ignoring the doorbell, then thought better of it when Miki shifted in his sleep and grumbled into the pillow he'd curled up around. After sliding out from the tangled sprawl of the man's limbs, Kane grabbed a pair of sweats from the floor and tugged them up over his hips. The chime sounded again, a low, mournful sound and Kane shook his head.

"Sounds like you should have Lurch answering your door there, Miki boy," he mumbled to the sleeping man. Dude opened one eye from his post at the end of the bed and rolled over, showing Kane his extreme disinterest in getting up in the form of his blond-furred belly.

According to the green light displays on Miki's living room electronics, they'd slept the afternoon away and were quickly heading toward early evening without either of them having much in their stomachs. Somewhere close, someone had cooked a dinner rich with garlic and cabbage, and his insides protested the emptiness sticking to his ribs. Shuffling to the front door, Kane peered through the fish-eye peep hole and stared in shock at the person standing on Miki's stoop.

"Oh, fucking hell," he whispered under his breath.

He would rather have taken on another pack of reporters. Hell, he'd even be willing to tackle Connor's team of glorified thugs who thought they were *real* cops. No, instead God chose to deliver onto Miki's doorstep the source of all Morgans' nightmares following a missed Sunday family dinner—a short, red-haired Brigid Finnegan Morgan carrying casserole dishes in the bright pink paisley fabric tote Riley got her last Christmas.

"Fucking Connor. You were supposed to tell her I was missing dinner, not send her here!" His brother had to have told her where Miki lived, and it was no use pretending he wasn't there. His SUV was parked only a few feet from Miki's front door, and he'd turned on the living room lights so he could see his way to the door without tripping on one of Dude's tennis balls. "Okay, come on. You're an adult. Take the food and turn her back around."

Kane knew he was lying to himself before he even turned the knob, especially when the garlic and cabbage aroma bloomed in his face when he opened the door and his mother shoved her shoulder through. A second later she was inside, tottering in on a pair of flame-red leather pumps she usually wore only to church or to visit people she wanted to impress.

Obviously, Brigid Morgan had also decided they were appropriate footwear for kicking her son's ass to the lower circles of Hell where she thought he belonged.

"Since you couldn't seem to find yer way home, I had Connor tell me where you've been hiding. Where's the kitchen, Kane Aodh Morgan? Never mind, I can see it plain as day from here."

A heavy dram of Ireland lived in his mother's words, a strong reminder of the home she'd left behind to chase Donal Morgan's dreams. When she spoke, her rolling words shouted green hills and a douse of Emerald Isle rain, but Kane could hear the promise of a peat bog in his future if she didn't get an answer to why he'd not shown up at the family gathering for over a month.

His mother stalked past him, her heels clomping on the wood floor, leaving Kane by the front door. She came to a screeching halt at the open archway and stood there, gaping.

Kane knew what she was staring at. He'd just left a naked Miki still asleep on his stomach and lying on a web of tangled sheets, bared to God and kissed to submission. The memory of the man's green-tea-and-sex-scented skin was burned into his brain so deep he was surprised he could smell his mother's cooking through it.

In that moment, he was fourteen again, and his mother had walked in on him jerking off in the bathroom. It'd been the perfect vantage point, overlooking their backyard where his brother Connor and his friends were playing chicken fight in the pool. Their toned, wet bodies had been too much for him to take, and he fled to the relative safety of the old-fashioned bathtub's wide rim to satisfy himself.

If only he'd locked the door.

If only Miki *had* a door.

"Yer telling me that in this big, expensive place, you couldn't be finding that poor boy a door for his bedroom?" Brigid gave her second son a withering glance. "And you call yerself a woodworker. I'll be heating things up in the kitchen. Yer going to wake up that young man so he can get some food in him. Yer a sorry excuse for a son if yer letting him starve himself to bones."

Kane wondered if he could get Miki dressed and bundled up in his car before his mother noticed they'd fled, but Dude was a complication. The dog would probably sniff out the food and go investigating. He'd notice Kane squirreling Miki away, especially if it included a car ride.

The skitter of nails on the wood floor confirmed Kane's thoughts on the terrier, and Dude barely spared him a glance as he trotted quickly by him, his twitching nose leading him to the kitchen.

"Fucking mutt." Kane padded into Miki's bedroom and stood at the end of the mattress. He was reluctant to wake the man. The shadows under Miki's eyes were only just starting to fade, but arguing with his mother was useless. As far as she was concerned, if there was food on the table, everyone in the house showed up to eat. Even if it wasn't her house and there wasn't technically a table.

Miki's foot twitched, and Kane grabbed his big toe, tugging lightly. The singer mumbled and kicked Kane's hand away, burying his face into the pillows. Kane was tempted to let him sleep, but when Miki squirmed on his belly into the rumpled sheets, Kane got a good view of the man's naked, firm ass.

"Damn. You hate me, don't you?" Kane threw a glance up at the heavens. Unless he wanted his mother to learn firsthand about how two men had sex, he didn't dare touch Miki's bare skin, but short of tossing a bucket of ice water on him, Kane didn't have much choice. "Aw, screw it."

Stretching out across the enormous mattress, Kane lay perpendicular to Miki's lean body. Tucking his elbows under him, Kane supported himself on his forearms and blew a fierce puff of air into Miki's left nostril.

"What the fucking hell?" Miki shot up, scrambling to rub at his face. Rubbing hard at his nose, he slapped frantically at the sheets for a moment with his other hand. His hazel eyes focused on Kane, and he glared. "Fucking asshole. Face is okay, but never the nose."

"It was either that or kiss you." He gave Miki a cocky smile. "It was safer for my dick's sanity not to kiss you."

"Never ever fucking do that to someone who's lived around roaches," the singer grumbled, taking a final swipe at his nose. "I have nightmares about those bastards climbing into places I can't get them out."

Kane winced. He'd stupidly complained about the Irishwoman who, at that very moment, was clanging around Miki's kitchen because she missed him, and Miki's first thought at being tickled was roaches. He leaned in and kissed the corner of Miki's frown, murmuring, "I'm sorry. I didn't know."

Miki snorted and shrugged it off, rolling his shoulders. The crack of his spine was loud enough to make Kane wince, and the popping from his neck almost echoed in the cavernous room. Stretching his arms up over his head, Miki shifted his legs out and sniffed. "You ordered dinner?"

"Worse, dinner came to us." Kane grimaced playfully. "My mother's here. She brought food. Smells like roast beast a la Morgan and cabbage rolls."

Miki raised his eyebrows. Then his eyes widened, his pupils nearly pinpricks amid the green and gold. "What the fuck? Your mom? How the... oh fucking hell... fuck me."

"Yeah," Kane agreed. "I'll do that later. Hopefully, I can wait until your knee's better, but I'm not promising anything."

"Dude, I don't do parents," Miki mumbled in a panic. "Fuck, they hate my guts. You've got to get rid of her. Why the hell did she come here?"

"You're cute when you're nervous." He laughed and slid off the bed. "Go pull your pants all the way up and go wash up a bit. You'll be fine. She's nice. It's me she's pissed off at. You, she'll love. Just be yourself."

"Are you fucking kidding me? You've met me!" he grumbled and searched for his shirt, finding it balled up under the sheets. "God, this is the worst fucking idea."

"I've had worse," Kane promised. "Remind me to tell you about my baby brother Ian's adventures of seeing what his dick would fit into when he was sixteen. Having my mother here will seem like a walk in the park."

"Who the hell walks in the park?" Miki sighed and flung himself back on the bed. Kane nudged him with a poke in the ribs, and he yelped, rubbing at the ticklish spot. "Fine, go keep her company so I can sneak into the bathroom, but I swear to God, if she hates me, it's all your fault."

KANE'S mother loved Miki.

She'd been thrown by the Spartan warehouse and the seemingly overwhelming supply of packaged ramen in the pantry, but when the gun-shy, wide-eyed, disheveled Miki emerged from the bathroom, Brigid fell in love.

Kane almost bit through his upper lip to stop from laughing when Brigid clasped Miki's fine-boned cheeks. His deep hazel eyes flew open in surprise, and he stumbled back, caught short by his injured knee. He was nothing like her own sons, with his haunted, startling eyes and pretty face, but that didn't stop Brigid from clasping him to her not inconsiderable bosom and tsking over his lean body.

"Mom, leave him be." Kane pulled a shell-shocked Miki out his mother's grasp. "Mick, grab the plates. We'll go set up in the living room."

Miki snatched the plates, forks, and napkins from the counter and limped out faster than Kane thought humanly possible. Dude glanced up at Brigid once, obviously contemplating his options. It was decidedly easy once Brigid began trimming the fat off the roast beef she'd set into the oven to warm and slid the finely slivered trim into Dude's dish.

The lack of dining room table perplexed Brigid for a moment, but she rallied admirably, ordering Kane to set the pseudo-coffee table once it was cleared of game controllers and a stack of notebooks with worn edges. Miki grabbed them before Kane could get ahold of them, and stashed them in a milk crate set on its side by the couch. A swipe of a damp sponge took off most of the dust, and Kane grinned when Miki hurriedly shoved a couple of DVDs under the couch before Brigid could see them.

Kane left Miki to figure out how he was going to set up the coffee table and ambled back into the kitchen to see if his mother needed help.

"He doesn't eat healthy," Brigid said accusingly when Kane joined her. "You call yourself a boyfriend? Look at what he has in his fridge!"

"Mom, he's not...." Kane stopped himself. "I know what he's got in the fridge. I put some of it there. I'm not going to tell Miki what to do. He's a grown man."

"Where's his mother? Doesn't she care about him?" Kane shook his head at her warningly, and she sniffed haughtily, a strong condemnation against Miki's absent parents. "It looks like I sent a five-year-old to the store. I worry about him."

"You just met him." He knew it was useless to point out the obvious, but he tried anyway, reaching over his mother's head to grab the long platter he'd found above the fridge. "You can't worry about him yet."

"I'll worry if I want to. Yer not one to tell me I can't." She waved the business end of her wooden spoon at his nose. "Put that there. I'll use it for the cabbage rolls. Does he like cabbage?"

"I'm guessing he's never ever had those before," Kane admitted. "But you never know. He might love cabbage."

He was saved by his cell phone skittering across the kitchen counter as it sang about a private dick who was a sex machine to all the chicks. Smiling a fake apology at his mother, he grabbed the phone to answer it just as Brigid headed out into the living room to interrogate Miki about green, leafy vegetables and his fondness of them.

Stepping over a food-engrossed Dude, Kane ducked out of the kitchen. "Hey, Lieutenant. What's up?"

"That rock star of yours got a television?" Casey barked into the phone.

"Yeah," Kane said, peeking down the hall to watch Miki being quizzed by his mother about cabbages. "Uh, I don't know if he actually watches anything on it. I think it's just for video games."

"Well, if you were so inclined as to turn on the damned thing, you'd see you're plastered all over the fricking news for punching out some camera guy in front of Miki St. John's place." The phone buzzed as Casey's voice got louder. "Is that what you think it means when I say keep a low profile?"

"Fucking hell." He leaned against the wall. "Guy stuck his camera into my face. What was I supposed to do? Kiss him?"

"If you'd kissed him, I wouldn't have gotten a phone call from the damned Chief's office asking me to explain what you're up to!"

"Sorry. Next time, I'll drop to my knees and blow him, sir," Kane quipped, teasing the man who took him out for his first beer when he graduated from the academy.

"Good thing you remembered that *sir* part, boy, or I would have had your ass for breakfast," Casey growled.

"Too late, sir," he replied. "Mom's here. She's first in line for breakfasting off of my ass. You can have lunch if there's any left over."

"I'll order a salad, just in case. I don't think she's going to leave me much." The man sighed heavily into the phone. "Do you know what they wanted me to do with you, Kane?"

"Park me behind a desk?"

"Actually, they wanted you parking your ass someplace on a corner wearing a safety vest, waving a flag so the kiddies know when to cross the street." There was more than a tincture of menace in the man's voice, and Kane's stomach dropped down to his knees.

Kane whistled under his breath. "Fuck that. I don't look good in orange."

"I don't like it when people tell me what to do with my cops, especially when he's been assaulted on private property by some asshole looking for something juicy to report. Then, right after I pulled the Chief's butt monkey's head out of his ass, it sounds like St. John's lawyers went to work on him." Casey grumbled. "So, Morgan, consider your ass… and badge… saved."

Kane's belly unclenched, and he exhaled hard. "Thanks, sir."

"Don't thank me yet. I'm going to work you until you bleed," Casey barked. "Did Sanchez call you about the photos?"

"Yeah. Kel's pissed off about them getting out. He thinks someone on the inside leaked them."

"He was right. It looks like an admin clerk found a way to make a quick buck. I'll be talking to that little asshole tomorrow morning."

"I'd offer to help you do that, sir," Kane interjected. "But I don't think there'll be much more of him left. I told Miki about them. He's pretty *whatevers* about the whole thing. Says it's part of the gig of being in the public eye."

"Tell St. John to get a gate put up across that street and to have us on speed dial if he even sees a reporter's nose hair. I want you and Sanchez to put this thing to rest. So, tomorrow morning, you polish that damned inspector badge, show up for work, and do your damned job."

"Yes, sir." Kane chuckled. "Thanks."

"And Morgan," Casey snapped. "If I see one photo of you outside of a frame on one of your siblings' desk, I'm going to cut line in front of your mother and wipe that breakfast buffet clean. Do you understand me, Morgan? And tell your rock star to keep his nose clean and his head down. I don't want the next call I get from the morgue telling me they've got him there waiting for you."

THE woman was a tsunami of chittering stiletto heels and corkscrew red curls.

She also scared the shit out of Miki.

Taking one last look around the room for porn or used tissues, Miki nearly jumped out of his skin when Brigid came out of the kitchen and looked up at him. Nervously peering around her, he spotted Kane talking on his cell phone. The man's broad back was facing the living room, and Miki tried clearing his throat to catch Kane's attention, but the cop was too engrossed in his call.

"Hi!" Miki tried for a welcoming grin, but it felt more like a terrified grimace creeping his cheeks up into his earlobes. "Um, I set the... table. Sorta."

He'd never planned for guests. Hell, he'd never imagined anyone but Dude ever crossing the threshold. Now Kane was practically living in his armpit, and a scarlet-haired dervish appeared on his doorstep. If he had a dining room table, it was packed up tight under cellophane wrap and plastic ties along with the rest of the furniture the interior designer had picked out for him. He had no idea where to go looking for the table, even if he knew for sure he had something to eat off of at all.

From the looks of her, she'd also want the matching chairs. The best Miki could offer her were that his plates were all the same size. Mostly.

"It looks lovely, Mick love." The smile she gave him was worthy of a Pulitzer instead of just for folding a few paper napkins and arranging the utensils together. Touching his arm, Brigid moved around Miki and sat down on the couch, then patted the seat next to her. "Come. Sit down. It's a bit of time before dinner. The cabbage rolls got too cold on the way over here. Spend some time with me. Yer liking cabbage, aren't ye?"

"Uh, yeah. Sure," he mumbled. After staring at the cushion for a moment, he shuffled over and sat down at the end of the couch, sucking at his teeth. Searching for something to say, he nodded. "Cabbage is great."

Brigid shifted closer, and Miki eyed her suspiciously. On the surface, she looked like the type of woman they'd cast as the warm-voiced mother on some drama where one of her kids caught a tragic disease. Then she spent the next couple of hours tracking through the jungles, looking for the one plant in the world that could cure him.

While wearing those heels. And flipping blueberry pancakes. And slinging an Uzi across her shoulder to fight off a horde of pirates.

And smiling in that crazy, happy way she was smiling at Miki because he put a couple of napkins and forks down on the table.

"Get off the fucking phone, Kane," he muttered under his breath, hoping Brigid couldn't hear him. Briefly wondering if he could fall off the couch and knock himself unconscious, Miki returned Brigid's smile, then shifted his gaze back to Kane's broad shoulders. That's when he noticed the crazy left Brigid's smile only to be replaced with something softer he didn't recognize.

"Yer nervous," she said, nodding. "I didn't think you'd be nervous. Connor said yer a music star. My littlest's got ye on her wall. I guess I got too used to seeing ye and yer boys screaming at me when I went in to put away laundry. It's like I almost know ye."

"Oh God, fucking hell," Miki exclaimed, burying his face in his hands. He tried to stand, wobbling when his right knee refused to do more than throb while his left knee worked fine. Miki made a grab at the table to steady himself. "Jesus, I have no fucking clue here. Sorry, I kept telling Kane... I'm no good with the whole... family thing. I mean, thanks for coming over but...."

"Yer younger than I thought ye'd be," Brigid replied softly. Her hands lifted up and eased Miki back down onto the couch. "Not much more than a boy, aren't ye? It's okay to be nervous. From what Kane's said, it doesn't seem like ye've had much of a good run with family."

Sitting next to him, she seemed smaller, more like a hummingbird, with her generous cleavage and delicate features. He could see a hint of Kane in her face. It was there in her mouth and the slant of her eyes. He laughed like she smiled, throwing his full heart into it, and Miki wondered how the hell the world was big enough to hold an entire clan of Morgans' passion and mirth.

She studied him with those large, too-green eyes, and Miki felt peeled open for her to pick through his bones and thoughts. He wanted to call out to Kane, but the man's damned phone rang again, a brisk, sex-inspired tune Miki half remembered. Sighing, Miki consigned himself to Brigid's interrogation

"How old are ye, Miki?" she asked softly. "Ye don't look much older than my Riley, but ye've got a sweet face so it is hard to tell."

"Um, maybe twenty-five? Twenty-six? Don't really know." Struggling to find his footing, he studied his nails for a moment. "Which one's Riley? Shit... you've got a lot of kids. How the hell do you keep them straight?"

"Well, there's enough so I'd be fine killing off a few of them when they make me mad," she teased.

"So it's not just me." Miki breathed a sigh of relief. "'Cause I want to kill Kane all the fucking time."

He was right about Kane having his mother's laugh. She threw herself into it, an audible confetti of glee. Wiping a tear from the corner of her eye, Brigid leaned forward and wrapped her arms around Miki's shoulders, pulling him, stiff and reluctant, into a tight embrace. His breath shortened, and then he finally simply held it, waiting for the woman to let him go.

A second passed, then three, but Kane's mother showed no sign of giving him his freedom. Her fingers stroked the back of his head, tangling through the soft strands of hair at his nape. As he blinked furiously, the world swam behind his wet lashes, and he shifted in her arms.

Brigid's hair tickled his nose, and he turned his face, catching a whiff of tangerine and lemon on her soft curls. Like her son's, the pale skin at her collar was dappled with a dusting of golden freckles, and a faceted purple stone twinkled in the ear she'd been pressing into Miki's cheek. Short of clawing free, he was trapped, cocooned in a baby powder, citrus motherly prison as Kane's Irish-born mother slowly wrapped strand upon strand of affection around him.

"Someone should have loved ye, sweet boy," Brigid crooned, a husky murmur laden with honey and cracked sorrow. "But ye've got the Morgans now. Kane'll take care of you. All of us will."

"Oh, God fucking help me," Miki swore and tore himself free before he drowned in Brigid's concern. He couldn't meet her eyes. She saw through him, through everything. From every steak he'd shoved down the back of his pants while shoplifting for food when he ran out of money to the times he helped Damien siphon off gas from cars in a club's parking lot so they had enough to get their equipment home… she saw it and knew he'd done wrong.

He slid as far away from the woman as he could without falling off of the couch. Brigid looked startled and reached for him. Miki recoiled, and he scrambled back, losing his tenuous balance on the soft cushions. Landing hard on the floor rattled Miki's teeth in his head, and his leg went sideways, banging the edge of his kneecap against the couch's hard frame.

"Mom, feed him. Don't smother him." Kane strode into the room. He reached down between the couch and the table to pull Miki up off the floor. His thick eyebrows met above the bridge of his nose, and he ran his hand over Miki's injured knee, scrutinizing the man's expression. "Are you okay?"

"Yeah." He swallowed. Leaning forward, Miki whispered into his ear. "She's fucking killing me, dude. I don't know what to do with her."

"Just eat the food and smile. Nod if you have to," Kane advised, kissing the tip of Miki's nose. "And don't agree to have dinner with the family. Mom, don't touch him until I come back. Or better yet, head home. I'll call you in the morning."

"Yer leaving?" Brigid stood up, her heels clicking when they struck the floor. "Do ye want me to make up something to take with ye?"

"No, I'll grab something when I come back." He was talking to the air. Brigid was halfway to the kitchen before he could protest. Easing Miki back onto the couch cushions, he slanted his mouth over the other man's lips, savoring a kiss before resting his forehead on Miki's temple. "Mind if I come back?"

"No, so long as you're taking her with you." Miki eyed him. "She's... fucking scary, man. No wonder all of you are cops. Nothing can scare the shit out of you. Look at what raised you."

"No, babe," he whispered, stroking the hair from Miki's face. "She's just a mom. I'll talk to her. Tell her to take baby steps."

"Dude, I know she's your mom but...," he whispered hotly. "Man, she's always touching, and she hugs a lot. And she doesn't let go. It's weird."

"Baby steps," Kane promised. "Now, I'm going to grab her and see if I can't shove her into her car when I head out. Sanchez just called. We pulled a body that might be Carl. There's a patrol car heading over here to keep watch while I'm on the scene. I've got to go check it out, but I'll be back in a couple of hours. If you want me back."

"Yeah," Miki growled. Hooking his fingers into Kane's shirt, he shook the man lightly. "Just don't leave me here alone with her. She'll be having me make gingerbread houses or something before you come back. I just fucking know it."

CHAPTER
FIFTEEN

They say I'm nobody to fear
And no one to love,
Soul blacker than ink.
Sin fits like a glove.
And the soft damning whispers,
Follow me where ever I go.
They can't hear me crying.
Even as they kill me real slow.

—Forgotten Son

DISPATCH gave Kane an address that led to a worn-out strip mall straddling the line between decrepit and seedy. Several police cars blocked off the two driveways leading into the cracked asphalt parking lot. A small group of Hispanic women clustered at the doorway of a small Laundromat at one end of the strip mall's L, watching the steady stream of people going in and out of a boarded-up Mexican taco shop thinly disguised as an Italian ristorante. From the plywood sheets and cut chains dangling from the steel mesh doors, the neighborhood didn't care much for spaghetti and antipasto.

From the looks of the people gathering near the sidewalk, the area needed more in the line of entertainment. A Mexican fruit salad vendor dealt a swift business on the corner, loading up plastic cups of tropical fruit before sprinkling the mixture with lime juice, salt, and chili peppers. Kane's mouth watered at the sight, and his stomach grumbled, reminding him it was empty.

"Trust me, belly, you don't want anything in you when we walk into this shit." Kane flashed his badge to get past the uniforms and parked his SUV next to Sanchez's Porsche. Climbing out of his car, he nodded to the pair of older women gossiping at the front of the check-cashing place kitty-corner of the restaurant.

Passing them, he gave them a winning smile and a nod. "Ladies."

He jostled the chains as he edged past the steel door, and the foul smell of rotten meat hit him hard. Enormous spotlight tripods were set up to illuminate the scene, chasing away any shadow that might hide a sliver of evidence. Standing in the middle of the room, Sanchez looked like death warmed over, lack of sleep hanging creases beneath his dark eyes. Still, he was a damned sight prettier than the man strewn all over the cement floor of the abandoned restaurant. Handing his partner one of the coffees he'd grabbed from a drive-thru, Kane stepped around the circle of carnage in the middle of what was once a dining room.

"This guy is a butcher," Kel muttered. Sipping the hot coffee, he sighed in gratitude. "Thanks for the hit. This case is killing me."

"Yeah, tell me about it." He looked around the place. "Who called this in?"

"Lady across the street. Her cat brought home a nose. She figured she should tell someone about it." Sanchez handed Kane a pair of plastic booties and gloves. "Suit up and I'll show you what's left of our pedophile."

The restaurant wore its history on its walls. Dust and cobwebs covered nearly every flat surface, and the industrial gray rug was mostly ripped up off the floor. Only wide swaths of the gummy patterned carpet remained near a broken podium that had probably served as a hostess station. Plastic grapes and fabric ivy vines looped over nails to frame the Spanish-style arches at the entrance. More baskets of grapes and straw were fastened to the walls, a few sagging from the molly bolts giving way under their weight.

A faded mural of a salsa dancer took up most of a long wall, its background altered by a less-skilled artist to depict what Kane guessed was supposed to be an Italian vineyard. Even in the gloom, the splotches of bright purple and yellow squiggles looked more like disease cells than something he'd want a wine squeezed out of.

In the middle of the grime and filth lay a man Kane would say was the dirtiest thing in the room.

Lack of circulation hung the stink of Carl Vega's body in the air, covering everything in a greasy feel from the gaseous expulsions of his intestines giving way. It was hard to tell what was left of Carl. Too much of him was scattered about the area, and Kane thought he spotted an ear beneath one of the banquette tables sitting askew against the wall. A circle of black dried blood pooled around the remains, its edges marred by a series of boot prints leading in and out of the mess.

One of the technicians stood near the blood mass, snapping pictures of the clearest prints. He lifted up his foot to reposition himself into a different angle and to avoid the flap of scalp and hair that had been tossed away from the body. From what Kane could see, most of the skeleton was present, although broken apart as if a wild animal had ravaged the corpse. Long shreds of skin were spread out from Carl's kinked spine, giving the remains curling, dried fragments of wings.

"Jesus, what a fucking mess," Kel muttered, snapping on his gloves. He snagged a tech standing nearby with a clipboard. "Did we get positive ID that it's Vega?"

"Yes." The man began to rattle off particulars of fingerprints and blood type, but Kel wandered off to inspect the evidence the techs had already gathered, leaving Kane to take down the details. "I've got ID on Vega but nothing on the perp other than boot prints. He smeared the hell out of anything he touched, so we're assuming he was wearing gloves."

"Still, it was a fast ID," Kane murmured. "Thanks. We owe you one."

"We were processing the other fingers from the St. John crime scene. Since the remains are missing quite a few digits, it made sense they were connected." The tech nodded. "We've been here a couple of hours already. Once we got positive identification, the call was made to you guys. Until then, Browne over there caught the case. He can tell you about the call."

"Thanks." Kane took a few steps over to where Browne, a grizzled salt-and-pepper haired inspector, stood near the hostess podium. He'd come in after Kane, obviously returning from a hunt for a hot cup of coffee, and lifted his hand to wave Kane over.

Mark Browne was a stereotype of a cop. He wore ill-fitting polyester pants and cotton button-up white shirts that invariably had a coffee or food stain down the front. Often, he wore ties that were obviously gifts from his children, silkscreened cartoon characters or oddly colored plaids bright enough to hurt the eyes, but hidden behind the stomach paunch, thinning ginger hair, and walrus mustache lay a bloodhound of a cop most of the district admired.

"How are you doing, Morgan?" Browne slurped at his lidless cup, dunking most of his mustache into the creamy liquid. He licked at the coffee, careful not to drip on the floor. "Just sent your baby brother outside. Might as well make him good for something."

"Riley?" Kane snorted. "He's doing walkarounds in the neighborhood?"

"Yeah, I figured a pretty face will get people talking if they know anything." The inspector grunted. "Might as well put that Morgan charm of his to use. Don't know if he'll get anything. Spoke to one Charlene Martes. She's the one with the cat. Nice lady, used to be a schoolteacher, so she wasn't all that panicky when Frisky dropped a piece of Vega down in front of her. She thought it was a lizard but then got a small shock when she grabbed it with a paper towel. Dialed us up right after that."

"How long did it take you guys to find him?" Kane rocked back on his heels, watching the forensics techs scrape and gather up what they needed. A body bag lay on a gurney, waiting to transport the remains, but there was some discussion going on about the whereabouts of Carl's facial bits.

"Not long. Let's go outside for a bit. The air in here's thick, if you know what I mean," Browne nodded toward the expanding sacks of organs on the floor. "He couldn't have been here too long. The heat in here's going to make those bits pop, and I don't want to be in here when they go."

The check-cashing storefront gave up on its evening business and was closed up tight when Kane and Browne emerged from the restaurant, but the Laundromat looked like it was doing a bang-up business, even though it appeared no one was actually washing or drying clothes. Outside, the chilled air was steeped with the smell of car exhaust and a whiff of garbage from a pair of dumpsters set up against a wall the stores shared with an apartment building next door.

Even as sour as the air was, it was still a cleaner smell than what lay stagnant inside the restaurant. Browne fumbled at the inside of his jacket, then sighed heavily, giving Kane a remorseful look. "Gave up smoking a few years ago when my wife got pregnant. I love my daughter to death, but, fuck it, I miss having a cigarette sometimes. I'd been smoking since I was sixteen. What the hell do I do with my hands?"

"Never smoked," Kane admitted. "Have you met my mother? She'd have skinned us alive if she found one of us smoking."

"You think that's what happened to Vega?" Browne jerked his chin toward the restaurant. "Your mom caught him smoking?"

"Nah, but who ever did that to him really was pissed off." He shuffled his feet and glanced around at the faces of people gathered around the corner strip.

Someone, a person probably still in the crowd, had taken a few sharp knives to Vega's still-quivering body and carved the life out of him. It was a brutal act and a selfish one. Someone wanted to take credit for it, even if it was merely watching the cops taking Vega's body out in a bag. Kane scanned the crowd, looking for someone alone trying to look nonchalant, but everyone clustered about seemed to be in packs and talking, more curious than disinterested.

Until he spotted a tall young man smoking a cigarette directly across the one-way, single-lane street where Kane and Browne stood. From a distance, he looked like he was waiting for someone, leaning against a bus-stop post and glancing down the street, but Kane saw the catch in his gaze when he let his eyes roam over the police cars and the soft tug of something smug on his thin lips before he brought his cigarette up for another drag.

That was when Kane noticed the dark marks over the man's knuckles, deep gouges barely scabbed over and cracking when he flexed. His attention was keenly on the uniforms when Kane stepped forward, but he swept his eyes up the street and caught Kane staring at him.

The man was about Miki's age, and his look of shock would have been comical if it hadn't been quickly replaced by something more sinister. A dirty blue beanie masked most of his hair, but strings of dark strands escaped near his temples. His brows were nearly black, bushy, crawling things that jerked when his eyes skittered away from Kane's face, and his barely grown-in mustache fluttered when he licked at it, spitting out something caught on his lips. His fingers trembled slightly when he brought his cigarette up again, his bare forearm rippling with sinew and muscle as he moved. There was a coiled strength to him, a nervous energy balled up under his skin, and Kane tapped Browne on the shoulder, whispering under his breath.

"See that kid across the street? The one smoking, wearing a cap?"

"Yeah," Browne casually skimmed the crowd, seemingly unengaged in anything other than what Kane was saying. "Seems kind of jumpy."

"Yep, funny, isn't it?" Kane stared out into the parking lot, then dragged his gaze back down the street.

The jittering young man was still staring at him, shifting back and forth between the people passing by. The crowd parted momentarily, and Kane could see him more clearly, taking in the torn jeans, much-laundered shirt, and army jacket he wore. The sight of the young man's worn Sinner's Gin T-shirt peeking out from between the jacket's lapels froze Kane's blood solid, and his heart seemed to stop in midbeat.

They stared at one another for a split second; then the man let his cigarette tumble from his fingers and took off running.

"That's him!" Kane shouted at the other inspector and sprinted across the street. Drawing his badge, he shouted at the people gathered on the uneven sidewalk. "SFPD! Get out of the way!"

There was something sadistic about San Francisco. Either the reputation of thumbing its nose at authority seeded little pockets of anarchy in people, or its residents were more curious than possessing common sense, because instead of parting to let Kane through, the crowd clustered in to watch Kane's lanky prey bolt down the narrow alleyway.

Cursing, Kane shoved past a group of teen girls snapping pictures of themselves in front of the lit-up police cars and took off down the tight causeway. He could hear Browne behind him, his heavy feet slapping at the concrete as he struggled to keep up with Kane's long strides. Despite his bulk, Browne kept up a good pace, and Kane turned the corner between buildings, pausing only long enough to hunt for his suspect.

The blue beanie bobbed up and down behind a dumpster, getting smaller by the second, and Kane took off again, dodging a pile of pallets left on the concrete drive. Cut behind the block of buildings, the alley served as a way station for dumpsters and back-door deliveries. Between the chaotic angles of the garbage bins and that the only lights warding off the dark evening were bare bulbs above stores' rear entrances, it was difficult to see where the man was.

Rotting food set out for slop pickup made running a slippery business, and Kane nearly lost his balance when he hit a slimy piece of bok choy. Careening sideways, he slammed into the brick wall of a restaurant, jolting him down to his teeth.

"Hey!" The shout was heavy with a Cali-Mex accent and followed by a few curse words that would have made Kane's mother blush. A few feet away, a green dumpster blocked much of the alleyway, making it hard to see down the walk, but from the sounds of things, Kane's prey had run into some trouble.

Recovering from his spill, Kane scraped the rotten vegetation off of his foot as Browne pushed aside the pile of stacked, wet cardboard boxes as he ran past him. The sounds of a struggle reached them, and they got around the bin in a hurry. Twenty yards away, Kane's suspect wrestled to get away from a large-bellied Hispanic man dressed in kitchen whites. A crushed, still-smoking cigarette lay on the ground by their feet, and the cook's beefy hands were clamped tight on the man's shoulders. They twisted about, and Kane saw the flash of a knife in the young man's hand as the dim back-door light caught on the crenulated blade.

"Shit, he's got a knife!" Kane shouted, pulling his gun.

It happened too fast, too far away for them to do anything, but even with the cook's back to him, Kane knew the blade slid in and cut deep. The Hispanic man's spine stiffened, and his shoulders suddenly went slack. His hands clawed at the young man's jacket, crumpling the khaki-green material as he hooked his fingers into the fabric. With the bloody knife still clenched tight in his fist, the slender man shoved against the cook's body hard, sending him to his knees.

Gasping, the cook went down on his knees, trying to keep a hold on the man who'd stabbed him, but as the blood poured out of his side, his muscles went slack and he fell, slamming into the concrete slab. His head bounced with a sickening thud, and the sliced apart tie of his apron flew up, exposing his gaping wound. The white T-shirt he wore beneath was soaked through, and the rent in the fabric parted under the gush of an intestinal coil escaping his sliced-open abdominal wall.

By the time Kane reached the cook, his quarry had been swallowed up by the shadows.

There wasn't a question of what he'd do. Despite being so close to catching the man terrorizing Miki, Kane kneeled down and pressed in on the cook's wound. The man's hand trembled as he reached for Kane, and blood dripped from his palm, dribbling down his arm.

"Está bien. Yo soy un policía." Kane struggled with his broken Spanish, trying to say something that made sense from the lessons he'd had drummed into his head. Applying pressure on the gut wound, he murmured, "La ayuda está en camino."

"I've called it in." Browne bent over and clasped his knees, panting to catch his breath. "Medics were on the scene for the body. They're bringing the bus around for him. Hold on."

"I'm holding," Kane muttered. "Hey, stay with me, sir."

The man mumbled something too rapid for Kane to catch, but his grip on Kane's wrist was bruising. What seemed like an eternity later, the tight alleyway lit up with red lights, and a blue-uniformed paramedic squatted next to Kane's legs. Other men came rushing out of the back door of the restaurant, peppering the air with a multilingual confusion. An older man with hang-dog features slammed the door behind him and hurried over to where Kane and the cook were. The paramedic gave the man a nod and made a motion for him to keep back.

"Mi hermano," the older man asserted, motioning to the cook, then to himself. "This is my brother. I won't leave him."

"No, you can stay. Just stay out of the way, please, sir." The blond EMT smiled down at the cook. "Hey, how are you doing? ¿Prefieres que hable en español?"

The cook nodded, and the blond man fired off a rapid string of Spanish Kane couldn't understand, but whatever he said eased the tension in the man's face. Browne moved to the side as the other paramedic, a brawny black man whose arms strained at the seams of his sleeves, wheeled a gurney over and set down a body board next to the cook. The blond placed his hands over Kane's and pressed down, counting to three before instructing Kane to pull away. They swapped places, and the cook groaned loudly, rolling his head to the side.

"Intestine's intact. No sign of perforation or seepage," the blond rattled off to his partner. "Abdominal wall open, but organs appear to be uncompromised. I think we can roll him without too much trouble."

"Good. Let's do a roll and get him on the board," the other paramedic instructed. "We'll get his vitals, then move him up onto the truck. On the count of three."

Kane stepped back, giving the paramedics room to work. The restaurant workers were hustled back inside into the restaurant, but the older man lingered, refusing to leave the cook's side. After a small discussion, he was persuaded to follow the ambulance in his own car. Once on the gurney, the cook patted the man's hand, murmuring reassuring sounds.

A tall, broad-shouldered man wearing a Morgan scowl stepped around the uniforms cordoning off the area. Kane knew from experience that the frown plastered over his friendly features could be wiped away with a well-timed joke or even, if necessary, a few jabs to a ticklish spot under his armpit. While both were highly unprofessional while on the job, as an older brother, Kane still contemplated it. Especially after Inspector Riley Morgan stomped up to Kane and stuck a sharp index finger into Kane's chest.

"What the hell are you doing at my scene?" Riley growled. Although few inches shorter than his brother, Riley still tried to edge his brother back with a push of his palm on Kane's shoulder. "And what the hell are you doing back here? *Trying* to get everyone around you killed? Bad enough I've got Kiki and Dad breathing down my neck. I've got to worry about you too?"

"Easy there, Junior," Browne chuckled. "The case belongs to your brother. It's connected to something he's on. While you're standing there, see if you can't find an evidence bag. Looks like your suspect dropped his sticker over here, Morgan. If I can get your baby brother there moving, we might be able to get something off of it."

"Fuck," Riley swore loudly and threw his hands up. "I should have become a fireman like Brae. He doesn't get a family reunion on every case he gets called on. Last time, it was Connor. Now, I've got to worry about *you* showing up too?"

Kane watched in gentle amusement as his long-legged younger brother stalked off toward one of the cop cars arriving on the scene. Shaking his head, he crouched and inspected the knife lying on the ground. "Blade's been used a lot. God, I'm hoping this is our murder weapon. The jagged cuts on the edge should be easy to match if it was used on Vega."

"Yeah, that's what I was thinking," Browne agreed, standing up with a huff. "Shit, listen to me creak. See? This is why I got a younger partner. So I don't have to do this running shit anymore. Where the hell was he when I needed him? Out knocking on doors and chatting up the ladies."

"No worries. You got an upgrade. A better Morgan to work with for a bit," Kane replied. "Junior, huh?"

"Well, not like I can call him Morgan," The senior inspector scoffed. After laying down a paper ruler strip next to it for scale, he snapped a few pictures of the knife with his phone "Screaming Morgan in a cop house is like yelling for an Oompa Loompa at a chocolate factory. You guys pop up like gophers."

"That's pretty much what dinner's like at our house," Kane acknowledged. "Like a game of whack-a-mole."

Riley returned with an unsealed evidence bag and a magic marker. Handing his partner a plastic-wrap sleeve to grab the knife with, he held the bag open for Browne to drop the knife into. After pressing down on the seal, Riley jotted down the time and place they'd secured the knife and held it out to his partner to sign. The senior inspector grunted a thanks at the younger Morgan and headed over to the lab tech scurrying down the alleyway toward their scene.

Like most of the Morgan boys, Riley ran large, with dark-lashed blue eyes and thick black hair. He kept it closely cropped to his skull, something he'd learned made it difficult for suspects to grab at his head after he ran them down. Newly out of uniform and wearing an inspector's badge, the younger Morgan stood shoulder to shoulder with his older brother, eyeing Kane suspiciously.

"Hey, I didn't know you were paired up with Browne. He's a good cop. You'll learn a lot." Kane slapped his younger brother on the back. Riley stumbled forward a step, then turned to glare back at his older brother.

"You'd know that if you'd shown up for dinner, asshat," Riley muttered. "Mom's about to pop a vein if she doesn't see you soon."

"Trust me, her vein's fine," Kane grumbled. "She showed up at Miki's house with roast beef and cabbage rolls. I tried shoving her into her car before I left, but I don't think it took."

"Good luck with that. There's a reason we never had a terrier growing up. Mom didn't want any competition." He snorted. "Miki's that guy you're seeing? That singer?"

"See? I don't need to show up for dinner," he groused playfully. "Everyone knows what's going on in my life anyway."

"Connor spilled the beans. Says he's prettier in person than in pictures, which had Ryan going. She's going to nail your ass to the wall if you don't bring him around. It's either that or she's going to stalk your front door like some groupie."

"Not going to do her any good. He likes boys," Kane said, jabbing his thumb at his chest. "This one in particular."

Riley jerked his head back toward the street. "So the DB in the restaurant is yours?"

"Yeah, and that asshole with the knife is the guy I think did him." Exhaling, he puffed out his cheeks and watched the ambulance pull away, disappearing around the building. A second later, the sirens hit, and the wailing sounds pulsed through the neighborhood. "This case is getting shittier by the minute. I've got two murders and a stabbing I can put on that guy's head. The DB's wife committed suicide... shit, yesterday? Day before? Dude, I don't know if I'm coming or going at this point. It's been a bit crazy."

"I saw Sanchez," Riley murmured. "He looked like hell. You guys need some sleep."

"Sleep, I've been getting." Kane shrugged, then grinned foolishly. "Mostly. What we need's a break. I'm hoping that knife handle's got a print we can use. I want to find out who this fucker is."

"Wish you luck with that, man," his brother said, patting him on the shoulder.

Sighing, he drew out his cell phone and grinned at Riley. "Betcha this is Sanchez ripping me a new asshole for running off without him."

"Hell, tell him to come over." Riley bared his teeth at his brother in a playful snarl. "I'll help."

Kane ground his teeth when he read Quinn's message. "Son of a bitch, I told her to go home. Damn it to hell. He must be going insane over there. I've got to go find Sanchez."

"What's up?" Riley leaned over and read Quinn's message. "'Get to the house ASAP. Mom's stolen Miki and the dog. Not letting him go until shit going down is done with. Think he's freaking out.' Well, big brother, looks like a murderer's the least of your worries now."

CHAPTER SIXTEEN

I walked onto the Delta, hoping to make myself a man,
Cocky as shit, with my guitar in my hand.
Walked past the Crossroads, paid the Devil no mind.
He didn't reach for me, saying I was already his kind.

—Delta Spawn Blues

ALL in all, it wasn't a bad plan, Miki thought as he looked around the room and calculated what he could move around to block the door to prevent the hordes from descending on him. The studio bungalow attached to the back of the Morgans' two-car garage could be defended fairly easily. He could wedge something into the rails of the sliding glass door leading to the enclosed backyard, and the door connecting the studio to the main house was his only problem. He imagined the Morgans would have a key, so locking the door was out of the question. The armoire possessed great potential. It was heavy and solid wood, a pretty, swirled grain Miki would have admired if he wasn't plotting to use it to prevent the next Morgan siege. Moving it would be a bitch, but he was willing to give it a try.

As soon as Dude was finished romping around in the backyard, where he was occasionally woofing his fool head off.

He wasn't even certain what exactly had happened. One moment he was putting away leftovers, and the next thing he knew, Brigid Morgan descended from whatever mountain mad Irishwomen came from and bullied him into a car, plopping Dude on his lap before screeching off into the night. Another Morgan followed her in, his soulful green gaze an odd change from Kane's brilliant blue eyes. He carried a duffel bag large enough to smuggle a child in, and Brigid shoved most of Miki's clean clothes into it, zipping it up like a woman possessed.

The cops outside were no help. They greeted her by name and waved good-bye, starting up their patrol car despite Miki's protests. The smaller Kane clone with the wrong-colored eyes held the door open for him, giving Miki the illusion that he had a say in the matter, but they both glanced at Brigid climbing into the passenger's seat of the baby monster truck and exchanged a sigh. There was no choice, and Miki got in, grabbing Dude when he gleefully jumped into the backseat.

When they pulled up to the Morgan house, Miki balked at the driveway. The large, rambling Edwardian-style home facing the park was daunting, spreading out from a corner lot with a cheery yellow paint job and window boxes filled with flowers so bright they shone crimson under the soft glow of the street lights lining the walkways. Over the short drive, he'd been introduced to the Kane knock-off, Quinn, who grinned apologetically at Miki when their eyes met in the rearview mirror.

A whirl of people swarmed from the house, and he yelped, actually making a squeaking noise before slamming back into Quinn's immovable body. Kane's younger brother merely put his hands on Miki's upper arms and held him steady as he was shuffled up the drive and into the house, surrounded by a nest of flaming red hair, freckled skin, and the resigned sighs from the men when they saw Miki's stunned face.

He couldn't keep track of names. There were too many of them with nicknames Miki had to remember as well. Quinn introduced him to Kiera, a stunning redhead with a serious demeanor, then called her Kiki when he went in to get some iced tea. Braeden, a brawny Morgan who looked a lot like Quinn, waded in and pulled Miki from the fray, separating him from the youngest, a college freshman named Ryan who was enough like her mother that Miki wondered if Brigid hadn't just cut off a piece of her flesh to grow her in a Petri dish.

More food was shoved at him and enough iced tea to float his kidneys down to his bladder. Dude discovered Brigid's three cats and fawned over them, much to one of the older felines' disgust. A warning shot across the dog's nose left a wide scratch and a spurt of blood on the kitchen floor, but Brigid took it in stride, edging the cat out with her foot while swiping at Dude's nose with a wet paper towel.

Miki was horrified, but Brae shrugged it off with a grin and said, "That's probably the smallest amount of blood that's ever been shed in this house. Don't worry about it."

It seemed like hours before they ended the debate on where to stash Miki, finally settling on the bungalow attachment since it was easier on his knee than climbing up the stairs. All Miki could think about when he saw the apartment was that he could somehow sneak out the door, through the connecting family room, and be out the back door to the garage before anyone was the wiser.

Then Brigid triple-locked the front door after Quinn left, closing the garage behind him, and Miki knew he was doomed, encased in a wooden tomb painted a sunny yellow and filled with a maniacal horde of people who sounded like they'd rip his head off if he tried eating their marshmallow-bit-laden cereal.

At way past midnight, his dog was running around a pool wreathed in chaise lounges and topped off with a waterfall made out of boulders, and Miki still had no idea how he was going to escape.

"Why'd you get in the car?" he scolded himself. "What the hell were you thinking?"

He knew what he was thinking. He'd been caught by the worry trap laid down by Brigid's wide green eyes and trembling mouth when he told her in no uncertain terms he wasn't going to stay at the Morgans' hatching crèche while Kane figured out who was leaving pieces of people at his house.

Brigid's hint of tears broke him, Miki was sure of it, because the next thing he remembered, he was telling Quinn where to find Dude's wet dog food cans and wondering if he needed a pair of boots he hadn't worn since before the accident, just in case they went someplace he couldn't wear sneakers.

"It's like she's a witch," he muttered. "I swear to fucking God, she's a witch. She even *looks* like that witch Dorothy met, but without the squeaky voice. Fuck, she's good."

He was singing to himself when the knock on the door startled him, catching him in the middle of an old Lead Belly tune. Glancing out at the backyard, Miki wondered if there was someplace he could hide in the trees. As he contemplated how long he could survive on pool water, a familiar voice called out to him.

"Miki, I know you're in there," Kane said. "Open up."

"How do I know it's you?" Miki eased himself up onto his feet. His knee gave a twinge, but held. "You could be any one of the clones."

"Because none of the others want to fuck you into a wall," Kane growled. "Now open the damned door."

He stepped aside to let Kane in, but his cop dropped the duffel bag he carried and grabbed Miki by the waist to pull him into a hug. After squirming for a moment, Miki gave in to the embrace, hooking his fingers into the loops of Kane's jeans. Expecting a kiss, Miki frowned when Kane buried his face into the curve of his throat and inhaled the scent of Miki's skin.

"God, you are enough to make a man weep," Kane murmured. "You doing okay?"

"No, your family's fucking crazy." Miki playfully shoved him away with a light push. "Did you eat something? Your mom told me to ask you."

"Trust me, babe, after what I've seen tonight, food's the last thing on my mind." Kane flopped down on the king-sized bed in the middle of the room. He patted the mattress, then raised his eyebrows when Miki shook his head. "What? I showered before I came over. I had to stop at my place to grab some clothes."

"Your mom—" Miki started to say, but Kane cut him off.

"I didn't have anything to do with it." He slid across the bed and grabbed Miki's waistband, pulling him down onto the bed. "But honestly, I like knowing you're here where you're safe."

Kane was careful with him, easing a hand behind Miki's knee when he dragged him over the duvet. It felt good to be taken care of, and Miki's eyes stung a bit as he cuddled into Kane's side, turning over onto his back so he could stare up at the ceiling. The cop waited until Miki got settled, then hooked his arm around Miki's shoulders to let his hand lie on his stomach. Kane tangled their fingers together and kissed the top of Miki's head.

"Dog?" Kane asked softly.

"Outside," he huffed. "Fucker abandoned me to chase squirrels or something. *After* your mom fed him some leftover steak. I hope he pukes in your shoes."

Kane wiggled his bare toes, lifting his feet for Miki to see. "Can't. Left them outside."

"I hope one of your mom's cats fucks your shoes into submission and leaves his spunk in the toes." Miki cursed Kane, nestling into the crook of the man's arm. "And your shoe will like it and cry for more."

"Remind me not to piss you off." Kane laughed, a deep, rolling sound Miki could hear rise up from his belly.

They lay against one another, listening to the occasional bark coming from the backyard and the sounds of the city as San Francisco slumbered. Miki sighed, and he let the locked-in spiral of his muscles ease away. He played with Kane's fingers, remembering the feel of them deep inside of him. His face burned, and the memory woke his cock up, its skin tightening around the shaft.

"Was it Carl?" Miki asked softly. "The call you got? Was it about him?"

He hated that he was curious, but despite shoving Carl as far back into the recesses of his mind as he could, the man loomed large in the shadows, poisoning every kiss he ever had. Then Kane showed up and shattered the darkness like it was nothing.

"Yeah, it was him," Kane said. "He's dead, Miki."

And just like that, he was gone. They were both… gone. His cop continued talking, murmuring about fingerprints and technicians, but Miki didn't hear a word Kane said. All he could think about was that Carl and Shing were dead. Really dead. Forever taken off of the same dirt he walked on and no longer sharing the same air. He knew it was stupid. They'd never been near him over the passing years, but still he could feel the sickness and poison of their breath when he inhaled. Finally, he was free of that.

It was over.

The first breath he took after the realization of their deaths tasted so sweet in his lungs, he had to take another.

Then his eyes stung, and he let the tears gathering on his lashes fall, listening to Kane talk in his low, Irish-whiskey rumbling growl. There was some mention about a man in a beanie, but Miki couldn't focus on anything other than the warmth of the man next to him and the silence of the world around him.

He was finally… irrevocably free.

"Baby? What's wrong?" Kane reached over to smear away Miki's tears with his thumb.

The salt turned his skin slick, and Miki laughed. "Nothing. I just feel… okay, you know? I'm kind of… okay. Especially now. Here. With you."

The man turned slightly, pressing his chest down on Miki's shoulder to fit their bodies into each other. Kane's thick, heavy cock and long legs on him made Miki's skin burn with want, and when Kane's hand stroked up Miki's bare arm, he shivered with the tingling, erotic whispers his mind leaked into his consciousness.

"How much *with me* were you thinking about?" Another stroke of Kane's hand, this time on the inside of Miki's thighs, set him on fire.

"A lot," Miki murmured. "A fuck of a lot, actually."

In the middle of all the craziness, he could always find Kane, his solid and sardonic touchstone. He'd been there through the pain and confusion, pushing forward and asking questions Miki didn't want to answer. Even in the anger they first shared, Miki had *known* Kane wouldn't hurt him. Not in the ways he'd been hurt before. No, the pain Kane would give him would be like nothing he'd ever known.

"I can see you. Do you know that?" Kane whispered as he kissed the corner of Miki's mouth. "When you are about to open up to me, then something inside of you pulls in. It's like watching a flower die right in front of me, Miki love. And it kills me every time. Talk to me, Miki. Tell me what's going on inside that pretty head of yours so I don't have to watch you die in front of me."

It was about trust. He knew that with Kane, and it scared the hell out of him to fall and expect the man to catch him. He'd tumbled to the hard ground too many times, breaking everything inside of him. If he'd been smart, he'd have walked away after Kane hugged him in the police station, but as soon as the man's arms wrapped around him, Miki felt safe. *Safe* in a world where Carl still breathed, and in that moment, Miki knew he couldn't walk away from the cop. *His* cop.

"You." Miki swallowed, trying to keep the sour down in his stomach. "What happens when you don't need to be here anymore?"

"Need?" Kane's deep laugh broke free from him in full force, and his wicked, gleaming smile tugged at Miki's heart. "Oh, Miki love, I more than *need* you. You're my temptation. My sin. I've got no intentions of being anywhere but next to you. We Irish? We like bathing in our sin."

"Suppose it doesn't work?" Miki gestured between them, and suddenly the ceiling disappeared as Kane covered him, straddling his hips. Balancing his weight on his shins and forearms, Kane brought his face in close to Miki's, so close that he could taste the sweet coffee Kane had on his breath. "Suppose...."

"Sometimes, Miki, you've got to stop building sand castles just to watch the ocean take them away," Kane murmured against his cheek. "Sometimes, you just need to find someone to sit on the beach with you."

"I hate the beach," Miki whispered back. "Sand gets up my ass. I hate that."

"How about me? Getting up your...." It was a leer. That was the only word for the look on Kane's face, and Miki rolled his eyes.

"What's with you and the cheesy shit? That crap actually work out for you at some point?"

"You know, Mick m'love," Kane growled. "I think I've got better things for that smart mouth of yours to do besides talk."

It was a kiss Miki would always keep inside of him. Small things resonated with him. From the feel of the smooth duvet cover, slippery beneath their bodies, to the honeysuckle-perfumed evening air coming through the sliding glass door he'd left partially open for Dude to slip in and out of. Kane's hands were familiar now, broad and inquisitive, delving into the dips of his body as if exploring him for the first time.

Their clothes became a barrier, and Miki peeled himself free of his prison until he finally had Kane's soap-and-musk-scented skin against his body. Suddenly, there didn't seem enough time left in his life to taste the man lingering over his shoulders. The press of Kane's lips on his collarbone was followed by a teasing nip, and Miki's cock strained to fill itself.

Pushing up on his cop's chest, Miki murmured, "Get on your back. Please. I want…."

He couldn't say exactly what he wanted. Not unless he wanted Kane to think he was crazy. How was he supposed to tell the man he wanted to slide his hands under Kane's skin until there was enough space for Miki to slide under and burrow? The need to have Kane inside of him consumed him, driving all reason from his mind until the only thing Miki could think of was the heft of Kane's sex stretching him open until his soul poured out of him.

The other man's eyes were dark, the blue gone nearly black with want, and for a second, Miki wondered if Kane even heard him, but then the man shifted his hip and turned over to lie on the back.

Sitting on his haunches, Miki studied the man willing to stretch out for him. Kane's eyes unnervingly followed his every movement, but Miki ignored the man's face, not wanting to fall into the honeyed trap of Kane's lips. The light fur on Kane's legs was soft under his fingertips, and he traced through the hair, liking the springy feel of it on his palm. As his fingers trailed over the inside of Kane's powerful thighs, the man parted his legs, giving Miki free access to the heavy, wrinkled sac and hardening cock nestled in a nest of silken black strands.

Like Kane's face, Miki blatantly avoided touching Kane's sex, concentrating instead on the hard planes of muscles on the man's stomach. He discovered a tiny white scar on his lover's hip, a leftover remembrance from a childhood spent with brothers. Miki bent over and kissed it, marveling at the smoothness of it. Kane's growl gave him a happy thrill, and he spent the next minute laving the man's hipbones, using his tongue to caress the dark line of hair trailing down from Kane's belly button.

Near his cheek, Kane's sex stood hot and ready, its slit already filled with precome. Drawn by the salty pearl poised at the tip of the man's cock, Miki smeared his thumb through it. He wanted desperately to slide Kane's seed into his mouth, to savor the spread of the man's salt on his tongue, but Kane's eyes narrowed as if he was reading Miki's mind.

"Don't," he ordered, his voice Irish-bright and rough. "You don't know. Hell, I don't know. I held a man's guts in my bare hands today, babe, and I can't risk you."

Kane sat up and cupped Miki's face, stealing his breath with a savage kiss. They fought for air, stealing it back and forth from each other's mouths until there was nothing left to sustain them and they broke apart, panting hard for another taste.

"I'm not going to let you go, Miki love." Kane shuddered when Miki's hand dipped down between his legs to stroke up his thigh until the back of his hand brushed against Kane's sac.

"I don't want to let you go either," Miki whispered. "Just don't walk away from me, Kane. Please. Just… *don't*. Don't make me want this… want you… make me think this is something real I can actually have then take it away from me. That's what will kill me, Kane."

"The *last* thing in the world that I want, babe…." Kane chuckled as he eased Miki on his back into the pillows. A stretch of Kane's long arm snagged his bag from where he dropped it, and he grinned wickedly when he came up with a small bottle of lube and a string of condoms. "Is to kill you. Fuck you senseless until you wake up sore and wanting more? Now *that* is a definite possibility."

The click of the bottle being opened made Miki's ass clench, and he shivered violently at the touch of cold lube when Kane's fingers played at his entrance. Pursing his mouth, he huffed his breath out and pushed back on Kane's hands, but his fingers slid away before Miki could envelop them.

"Spread your legs, babe." Kane cupped the back of Miki's right thigh. "Can you do it this way?"

"Yeah, just… fuck me," Miki grumbled. "Why the hell do you talk so much?"

"So impatient." His lover tsked. "We're going to have to slow this down sometime so I can show you how good it is when we take our time."

"Less talking," he growled, hooking his fingers into Kane's hair and tugging the man's face down so he could suckle on Kane's mouth. "More fucking."

Kane's fingers stabbed up into him, and Miki hissed, pushing himself to take the rough skin sliding into his core. He mewled, shoving further down until he seated himself on Kane's hand, snarling when his cop tried to pull free to tease him. He knew Kane's tricks and was in no mood for them. Not now. Not when he'd make love to the first man he actually wanted deep inside of him.

Not when he could finally breathe freely without the taint of his past chasing his every waking thought.

It still went too slow for Miki's liking. Kane *liked* slow. The gentle intrusion of Miki's entrance was a torture, especially when his fingers hooked inward and slid over the sizzling core of Miki's body.

When he screamed, Kane caught it, closing his lips over Miki's gasping mouth. Another stroke brought Miki's ass up off the bed, straining his angled legs, but he threw the pain away as it crept closer in on his pleasure. Stuffed full, he squirmed, scrambling to grab hold of Kane… of anything to steady the world as it shifted and tilted on him. Fisting his hands into the duvet, Miki rode out the thundering shudders being pulled up out of him, quaking when Kane's fingers withdrew.

Shivering from the cold emptiness he was left with, Miki barely felt Kane when the man lifted him up by his hips, then carefully slid a pillow under him. Another slosh of iced oil on his entrance broke Miki from the tumbling pleasures wrapping around him. Lifting his head up from the mattress, Miki watched Kane fit a latex sheath over his thick, bulbous head and roll the condom down over his shaft until it snugged in tight on the root.

Carefully, Kane positioned himself between Miki's parted legs and hooked his large hands under the singer's thighs. The desire in Kane's eyes was for him, something Miki still had trouble accepting, but the sight of the powerful man kneeling in front of him made his cock writhe for attention.

Kane gripped his heft, circling the head with his fingers, and pressed it against Miki's slick entrance. With his head bowed, the man's black hair fell forward, brushing his lashes, but Miki could still see the sweet, liquid heat in Kane's startlingly blue eyes.

"Do you want this, Miki love?" Kane whispered, casually dragging the head of his cock over Miki's pout.

He couldn't speak. His tongue seemed glued to the roof of his mouth, and any moisture he had left inside of him seemed to pool down to his cock as it dripped in anticipation of Kane's incursion. With his hands firmly on Kane's muscled forearms, Miki gripped Kane and lifted himself up to meet his lover's thrust.

CHAPTER SEVENTEEN

Sin, you're off key. Pull it in.
You wanna try singing this shit? I'm fucking tired. I can't do it.
Dude, if I could make your life easier I would but I can't so we've just got to deal with this shit together, okay? Sin? Miki? I'm here, man. Right with you to the end, okay?
... Yeah. I know. It's just... fucked. I just need... to breathe, you know?
Yeah, I know. Take a deep breath, Sin. I'm not going anywhere.

—Recording Shattered Lies EP, 3 a.m. session.

IT CAME hot and fast. One moment Miki was cursing the loss of Kane's palm against his ass with his fingers spreading him apart and then he was stretched nearly impossibly wide by his lover's heavy cock. The odd, sweet smell of the lubricant faded, replaced by the coiled musk scent of Kane's sweat, and Miki arched up, using his tongue to lap at the hollow of his lover's throat.

"Keep that up...." Kane grunted. "Won't be able to hold it in."

They fought to find their beat, and Miki shifted his hips, raising himself up as Kane drove into him. He clenched around the man filling him, hissing when Kane dragged himself slowly out only to push down hard again. It burned, hotter than Miki thought he could bear. When the ache of being filled became too much, and Miki was nearly out of his mind from the heat building up inside of him, Kane dipped in and slid down Miki's pleasure spot, easing away the tightness at his entrance.

His world spiraled out, and Miki followed, drawn along the electric starbursts streaming from his center. It started small, a tiny tingle, then Kane found him again, and Miki was carried away by the raging tide of sensations boiling up from inside of him. He couldn't do anything, not consciously. He might have spoken words of encouragement or damnation. He wasn't sure what was pouring from his mouth other than the guttural need to have Kane drive into him deeper and harder.

Just more, his mind whispered before it surrendered to the sparkling darkness Kane drew up from inside him.

He surfaced, gasping for air and clutching at Kane's broad shoulders. The man... *his cop*... loomed over him, black hair damp with sweat and sharp white teeth made for biting Miki senseless. Their bodies slapped together, a steady beat that made Miki's heart skip. Kane's arms bulged with the effort of holding him up. His shoulders hunched forward to keep the strain off of Miki's knees. Lifted up and spread open, Miki could only moan and clench tightly down on the cock piercing him, inhaling sharply when Kane lit his nerves on fire with every other stroke.

Kane leaned back, balancing his weight on his knees. Miki groaned, complaining when his cop moved out of reach, but Kane's smile was wicked, a promise of more to come.

Tipping Miki's chin up, Kane moved his lips down the long line of Miki's throat. The touch of Kane's tongue burned nearly as much as his sex buried deep inside of Miki's body. The sensual glide of Kane's agile tongue over his heated skin was followed the brush of Kane's teeth over the thumping spot where his blood rushed to his heart. The cop teased him with faint scratches of fingernails over the backs of his thighs, and then when Miki arched his shoulders in supplication, Kane bent his head down further on Miki's body and took more.

One of Miki's stiff nipples brushed Kane's lips, and the cop took it into his mouth, suckling the tip with a fevered hunger. Unhurriedly, Kane let his cock glide back into Miki's entrance, trailing over the stretched opening in a delicious crawl while he laved at the nipple, curling his tongue around it. Groaning, Miki tightened his passage around the man's sex, his entrance suckling at Kane's tip, drawing him back in.

"Need...." Miki gasped. His hands moved up over Kane's broad chest and clung to the man's shoulders. "God, need... you."

Toying with the nipple, Kane tweaked it between his front teeth, pressing at it with his tongue and flicking the captured nub. Unable to do more than lie beneath his lover, Miki's hips churned of their own accord, caught under Kane's roaming hands and rapacious teeth.

Kane kept his thrusts shallow, slowing, then quickening the pace when Miki's writhing slowed. Moving his hips in small jerking motions, Kane set a new pace, sliding in and out of Miki's damp body. He lowered his hands to Miki's hips, stilling the singer's movements. Drawing himself as far as he could, Kane slid firmly back into Miki's tightness. Held firm by the man's strong hands, Miki moaned and twisted against his cop, straining to take in much of Kane's cock as he could.

"Damn you," Miki hissed between his clenched teeth. He needed more than what Kane was giving him, and he struck back, sinking his teeth into the cop's upper arm. Kane only laughed, a dark, sensual pleased chuckle at Miki's distressed want, and shortened his thrusts until his cock's tip barely brushed the inside of Miki's entrance. Miki gasped and let go of Kane's skin, leaving a deep, dimpled oval behind. "Fucking... son... of a... bitch."

"Such a filthy mouth. Remind me to have you wrap it around me next time." Kane stole Miki's breath with an untamed, sloppy kiss, swallowing Miki's curses.

Their world became nothing more than the bedding and the soft whisper of the evening breeze coming through the open sliding door. A delicate sweat of musk and sweet oil curled down their limbs, stomachs, and backs, curling around the deep bruises blooming dark purple poppies on Miki's taut throat and Kane's fingernail-raked arms. Long red welts dappled Kane's shoulders where Miki's fingers claimed him, and similar furrows ran up Miki's thighs and over his ass.

Miki was lost. The bursts of pleasure hit him swiftly as Kane began to plunge deep into him, losing all sense of control the cop teased him with just moments before. The heat between them boiled, and they were driving hard against each other, falling out of rhythm, but the sensual dance they played earlier became a frenetic explosion of melded mouths and joined bodies. Miki was about to reach the tip of his climax when Kane's hands cupped his lower back, and the man pushed Miki hard down onto his cock.

He could see Kane struggling to hold himself back, but Miki clenched in on him, and the tight glove of Miki's body was all it took for Kane to lose his mind. The neon and stars illuminating the San Francisco sky seemed to pour into them, and Miki felt every nerve in his body suddenly come alive under the tingle of his sac.

"So beautiful," Kane whispered, his hips snapping back into Miki's body. Struggling to keep going, he wrapped his hand around Miki's cock and stroked the slippery skin as it moved over Miki's shaft. "Let me see you come, baby."

"Almost… Kane." Unwilling to lose contact with Kane's hard length in him, Miki lifted his hips up, and Kane went deep, hitting nearly every spot Miki needed him to again. A tangle of stars buried deep inside of Miki suddenly broke free, and he gasped, feeling himself go over. "There… Kane… please."

Miki clenched and his back and legs went stiff. The tightness in his guts released, and his pleasure expanded to fill him under his skin. Gripped in Kane's palm, his cock gushed, spurting with the force of his climax. His spill ran over Kane's hand, and Miki's shaft shivered with the prickling stimulation of Kane's fingers. Another long, lingering brush of Kane's shaft along his passage and Miki's climax crested again, this time taking Kane with him.

He could see Kane's orgasm work up from his cock to spread through his body. Kane's neck tightened, and then his muscles went rigid as he rode the wave of his release. Twisting his hips, Kane nearly split Miki apart when he drove in deeper and hunched his shoulders in to pound at his lover's entrance one last time. Miki's body, already wrung nearly to exhaustion, tumbled under the force of Kane's explosive need, and his cock jerked again, spilling hot into the tangle of hair around Kane's belly button.

Kane grabbed at one of Miki's hands and held it, letting the shudders rocketing through his body carry them both. Digging his heels into the mattress, Miki found his breath taken from him, and his heart beat frantically, his hips rolling to meet the final thrusts of Kane's cock. His ass closed in on Kane, and his spasms milked Kane to his final peak. Kane groaned between his clenched teeth, pulling in sharp breaths, and gave in, the heat of his spill turning the latex glove around his cock hot with his seed.

Miki lingered in the darkness swaddling him. Then he emerged from his satiation, a brutal rebirth into a body others tore apart. His hips ached and his knee throbbed, but he didn't care about the pain, not while the remains of his orgasm lapped at the edges of his nerves. Life spun back into a sharp contrast when Kane slid himself free of his entrance, and Miki winced, feeling the tug of the condom as it caught on his furled ring.

"Sorry, Mick m'love." Kane's gentle kiss made it all better, especially when his lips skimmed over Miki's bitten-bruised neck in a swirl of butterfly touches. Easing Miki's legs down, Kane turned him over onto his side and wiped at both of their damp bodies with one of their T-shirts. Kane tossed it toward the hamper at the corner of the room and snorted when it fell short. "You okay?"

"Yeah. Sleepy," Miki murmured. He was tired. Fatigue tugged at the small of his back and dug its lazy fingers up his spine to feed off of Miki's brain, leeching out any strength he had left in him. "I should go get Dude. Shit, he could be tearing the shit out of your parents' backyard."

"I'll do that." The mattress dipped and Kane's weight shifted, then was gone. "Why don't you get some sleep? I'll be right back and lock up the room."

The bed was suddenly icy cold and lonely. Struggling to make his lifeless body respond, Miki grabbed at Kane's hand before the man could move too far away. He drew Kane's fingers into his mouth and kissed at the tips that both splayed him open and brushed away his tears. He blinked and looked up, focusing on the man standing silent at the side of the bed.

"I love you, you know." Kane crouched, tightening his grip on Miki's hand. Leaning over, he first kissed the botched tattoo on Miki's shoulder, then brushed his lips over Miki's jaw, whispering when he reached Miki's earlobe, "You're under my skin, Miki St. John. I can wait until you trust me... until you're ready to let me love you like you should be loved. Even if you let me go, I'll be waiting."

"Don't want to let you go, so no waiting," Miki murmured, feeling the fatigue in his bones dragging him under. He tugged at Kane's hand, drawing it across his chest until the man's palm was over his heart. "This... me... hurts when you're not here. I need you here. Think I love you, my stupid yelling cop. Now go get the dog so we can sleep. Tomorrow, you go catch the bad guy so I can get the hell out of your mom's house before she eats my brain."

THE smell of coffee brewing woke Kane up, and he snuffled his face into Miki's thick hair to avoid his brain clicking on and hunting down the scent. The tickle grew, and he sighed, surrendering to the bean's delectable pull. Working himself free from Miki's sprawled limbs, Kane stumbled into the three-quarters bathroom to brush his teeth and take a shower, hoping he could scrape the night's romp from his skin before the pot disappeared. Making another trip into the bedroom, Kane dug through his bag and dressed in a pair of jeans barely suitable for cop work. His button-up shirt stuck to a wet spot on his back he hadn't wiped dry with his towel, and Kane turned to hunt for a pair of clean socks, stopping when he spied Miki still asleep on the bed.

They'd lost Dude to the allure of the backyard sometime in the early morning hours when Kane woke up long enough to relieve himself. A couple of barks later, his brother Braeden called out to the dog to come to breakfast, and that was the last Kane saw of him. Taking advantage of having the bed to themselves, Kane woke Miki up enough to suckle him to spill into Kane's mouth, and they fell asleep wrapped around one another, murmuring silly things that made no sense once Kane reached full consciousness.

Leaving ibuprofen and a bottle of water on the side table next to the bed, Kane leaned over and kissed his lover on the forehead. Miki stirred, grumbling about a slight chill, and Kane drew the duvet over him, covering the singer's scar-damaged legs and belly.

"Stay here," Kane whispered to his slumbering lover. "Don't get into trouble while I'm gone either."

Surprisingly, the coffeepot was full. Even more startlingly, his father was scooping sugar out of the lamb-shaped bowl Brigid had picked up at a yard sale, measuring out two teaspoons into his coffee mug. Captain Donal Morgan glanced at his second son and reached for another mug, handing it and the spoon to Kane.

He grew up in the huge kitchen, playing under the table his mom used in the middle of the room. When he was older, Kane learned to cook there, his younger siblings playing with dolls and cars safely tucked away near his feet. The room was bright, old-fashioned double-pane windows letting sun in when the red gingham curtains were drawn back, and while the walls changed colors over the years, the knotty-pine floor remained as smooth as glass and clean enough to eat off of. Comfortable and lived in, it was the room they were usually drawn to first, either for coffee or to talk to Brigid, who'd spend hours listening to their troubles.

It was also where Kane could sometimes find his father, and in the middle of the night, right before his parents went to bed, they could be found there together, dancing to something slow playing on the radio and murmuring to one another in Gaelic.

"There's creamer in the icebox, son," Donal rumbled. "And some muffins yer mum made if yer hungry. Blueberry, I think."

Even after thirty-two years, Kane still wasn't used to being tall enough to meet his father's eyes straight on. It seemed just yesterday he needed a boost up to see the twins asleep in their cribs, Donal's broad hands circling his waist while the man instructed his wide-eyed second son that he was responsible for keeping his younger siblings safe from harm. Kiki and Riley were now fully grown, both junior inspectors in a police force their father made his... and their... lives.

Connor looked the most like their father, rough-set and seemingly hewn from granite, but Kane could still see his own face in his father's solid features. Larger than life, Donal loomed over his brood, a quiet sentinel with steely blue eyes and silver-flecked black hair who spoke in a gravelly Cork County brogue he'd never lost. He raised his children with laughter and soft words, tempering his wife's fiery hot-headedness with a steady calm. A peacemaker at heart, Donal still waded into the epic battles fought amongst his offspring, separating out the instigators from the victims and meting out punishments arduous enough to wring out the last ounce of spare energy the troublemakers had in them.

He was the man Kane wanted to be. Especially now, with Miki sleeping in the spare room, Kane longed to be able to slow dance with his lover in the middle of a kitchen before they tumbled off into bed, where Miki's melodic voice would cry Kane's name until they both drifted off to sleep.

"Yer man still out for the count?" The question would have sounded odd coming from any other Irish-born cop large enough to bench press a manatee, but Kane was used to his father's unshakeable sensibilities. "From what I hear, he's had a bit of a rough time of it."

"Yeah, it's been a shitty couple of weeks," Kane mumbled, sweetening his coffee, then taking a sip.

It tasted like every sour, bitter, cop house coffee he ever had, another legacy his father passed on to his children. For all of his good points, the man couldn't make a good pot of coffee to save his life, but Kane drank it anyway, used to the bad brew. The muffins smelled good, but his stomach wasn't ready for breakfast. Glancing up at his dad, he grinned when Donal grabbed the butter dish from the fridge, then reluctantly put it back, pulling out the heart-friendly spread his wife bought for him.

"Yer mum wants me to stay healthy." Donal grimaced and waved the tub of cholesterol-free spread at his son. "Sometimes, I think she's the one who wants me dead. Have ye tasted any of this shite? It's like sucking on motor oil. But, eh, she loves me. It's how she shows it. Ye take care of yer boy in there that way?"

"Dad, I love you," Kane said over his coffee cup's rim, "But I don't know if I'm ready to talk about Miki. Not yet. Maybe in a bit. Right now, it's too... new between us, you know?"

"Fair 'nough," Donal grunted. "Yer case, then? Ye and that caterwauling partner of yers get any further on those killings?"

"You know about that runner we lost yesterday?" Kane leaned against the stone counter and watched his father dissect his muffin into quarters. His father grunted a yes and sucked a bit of spread off of his thumb. "I'm hoping we get a hit on the prints from the knife he dropped at the second scene. Right now, it's all I've got. Bastard was fast, like he was running for his life."

"Ye figure out his connection to yer Miki?"

"No, but that's something else the print might help with." Kane frowned. "We've tried running down all of the kids Vega and his wife fostered, but so far we've come up empty there too. The ones that survived Vega's shit have gone to ground, but I'm thinking this guy's one of them. He has to be."

"Suppose he's someone yer boy pissed off?" Donal asked as he chewed a bit of his muffin. "Maybe a fan or even one of his band's family? Is there a money trail ye can follow?"

"Kel and I chased that down first. The only ones with a grudge against Miki are the Mitchells, but they've been in Montana for the past week. I've been in touch with Edie, the band's manager, and she's got nothing on her radar. No one's sent threatening letters to the record company. The other two families don't have a problem with Miki. Damien's parents... the Mitchells... are pissed off about song rights, but they've been mostly attacking him in court."

"Could they have hired someone?" Donal waved off his question as soon as he asked it. "Sorry. Ye'd have checked that first."

"Yeah, they had money before Damien hit it big with Sinner's Gin," Kane replied. "I know there's no such thing as too much money, but there hasn't been a huge payout to anyone that hasn't been there for the past couple of years. They're taking care of some aunt in a nursing home, that's the Montana place they go to visit every few weeks, and they pay the kind of bills rich people have. Hell, Dad, they pay more for their dog groomers in one month than I pay rent. They came out clean."

"And there's no note or anything to lead ye to a fan," his father mused. "It's hard to catch someone ye can't get ahold of."

"Nothing other than that one note," Kane growled, frustrated. "Guy's good at covering his tracks. And he doesn't give a shit who he hurts. Beanie boy didn't hesitate to stab that guy. He did it to slow us down."

"Smart then, at least enough to know the basics." The muffin was becoming crumbles in Donal's hands as he thought.

"And he likes knives," Kane said. "You should see the shit he's done. Last night, when we found Vega? It was like he needed to see every bit of him laid out on that floor. We're cross-checking the restaurant's employee list once we find the owner. He could have worked there. He's got the knife skills to have been in a kitchen."

"Yer mother was right, then, in dragging that boy here," Donal said. "He'll be safer here. If your killer *is* one of Vega's fosters, he might want to take out his frustrations on someone else who survived, now that those two are dead."

It was prophetic, really, especially when Kane's phone chirruped its salsa at him. He gave his father the same long-suffering look he used when one of his siblings called him, and answered the phone.

"What's up, Kel?" Kane checked his watch. "We're not on for another hour."

"Yeah, fuck you, Morgan," his partner spat. "I hope that rock star you've got in bed's a good piece of ass, because you owe me a fucking new car."

Sirens broke into Sanchez's rant, and Kane could hear random shouting in the background, with someone screaming to "get the hoses on the houses close to the front." Amid the chaotic crackle of noise, what Kel said to him finally sank into Kane's brain.

"I'm going to forgive your shit because I love you like a brother, Sanchez," Kane snarled back. "But you ever fucking talk about Miki like that again, you're going to be chewing your food in your throat, 'cause that's where your teeth's going to be. Now, what the hell is going on?"

"That bastard... he hit my mom's house, man." Kel's voice was lost in another onslaught of sirens. "I know it was that bastard. Looks like he dumped more of Vega's body parts on the front porch. That is one sick son of a bitch."

"Fucking hell. Is everyone okay?" Kane felt Donal step closer, and his hand settled on Kane's shoulder, an anchoring weight to hold him down as Kane's fears took flight. "Is your mom okay? The neighbors?"

"Yeah, we think so. Firemen got her dogs out, so that's a blessing. We're trying to keep the other houses from going up," Kel shouted above the fracas. "I parked the Porsche in her garage. She had a doctor's appointment this morning. She hates sitting that low in a car, so we drove hers."

"I'll be right there," Kane promised and began to rinse his cup out.

"Go. I'll do that," Donal ordered him. "You go on. I'll make sure someone feeds your Miki when he wakes up. Call me when you get to Marina's house. When yer mum comes back from the store, we'll start getting some things together so she's got clothes and a place to stay."

"Thanks, Dad." Kane gave his father a brief hug, slapping him on the back. "Don't worry so much about Miki. His dog'll eat you out of house and home."

"I can handle the dog, Kane." His father smirked. "I raised you, didn't I?"

CHAPTER EIGHTEEN

I am only home in the dark.
The shadows are my only friend.
When a spark of light comes on,
I know my peace is about to end.

—Cursing the Candle

THE only thing left of Sanchez's pride and joy was a twisted pile of blackened, oily scrap metal. Even the Jack in the Box antenna ball that hung from the rear view mirror was melted slag with only a smear of gray left where the Raiders helmet once sat on its round head.

The front of the garage was gone, a blown-out mess after the Boxster's gas tank heated up when the fire spread through the structure. The engine suffered the least amount of damage, although it sat partially engulfed in fire-retardant foam and what appeared to be the scorched remains of the Sanchez's Christmas decorations.

It was not a pretty sight, and Kel stood in the middle of the blocked-off street, pacing as he spoke on the phone to his insurance company. He gave Kane a tight smile. His voice was a low, threatening grumble, and Kane guessed the call wasn't going well.

"Rest of the house looks to be okay. They might be able to go in once they get a cleaning crew inside. Car's toast, though," one of the firemen said to Kane. He tried to remember if he'd met the young man before. They all seemed so young, barely out of high school and gangly despite the weight of their gear and their bulk.

"They've got to stay out of the garage area, though. The arson guy'll be here in a couple of hours. Looks like it was started close to the garage door, but I don't want to promise anything."

"Thanks. Appreciate your help," Kane replied, shaking the guy's hand as he passed by. "I'll let them know."

The air on the quiet street was thick with inky black smoke, and the tarry taste of it fouled the coffee Kane had grabbed on the way over. Marina Sanchez and Kel's younger sisters were already victims of Hurricane Brigid, having been swept off to Kel's aunt's house before the firemen stamped out the last ember. People were gathering around the house, keeping a safe distance as the firemen went through the garage's remains, pulling out what they could salvage from the fire. Boxes of family keepsakes were lined up on the sidewalk, beaten soldiers guarding their contents behind filthy, damp cardboard walls.

"Do you fucking believe this shit?" Kel walked up to Kane's side, gratefully accepting the cup of iced coffee his partner brought for him. "Bastard made my mother cry. I want a piece of his ass nailed to my desk so I can use it as a mouse pad."

"Inventive," Kane conceded with a nod. "I want him to have a prison cell next to a carnival. A cell with really thin, high windows he can't see out of, but he can hear everyone laughing and having a good time as he sits in the darkness."

"You are one weird son of a bitch, Morgan," Kel said.

"Oh, and maybe fire ants. That would rock," Kane added with a smirk. "Ones that really like the taste of his testicles."

"Like I said, weird."

"See anyone you don't recognize in the crowd?" Kane asked, skimming the people huddled against the cold.

"Nah, most of them are neighbors," Kel replied. "Mama's popular. A lot of my sisters' friends come home from school and their houses are empty so they come here. She's got cookies and listens to them bitch about homework. And before you ask me, no, I didn't see anyone I didn't know when we left this morning. Just that

Howard kid from down the street heading to school. He waved, and Mama wished him to have a good day."

"That normal?"

"Dude, I think that kid wishes he could just live with her. He's younger than the girls, but she doesn't mind him wandering over. His parents are crap."

"Crap how?" Kane leaned against his SUV. "Child Protective Services crappy or just shitty parents?"

"They've got no time, kid's a bit weird... that kind of crappy." He shrugged helplessly. "Some people are just bad parents. Hell, look at my dad. He's a piece of shit for a father, but he's a good guy. Just not someone you ask for advice about anything."

"Or stay married to."

"Yeah, that too," Kel admitted. "Mom likes him, but he was as shitty of a husband as he was a dad. When he lived with us, we were the last thing on his mind. Shit, I wasn't even sure he even knew how many kids he had. I don't think he really saw us, you know? We just weren't important to him."

"There was something Miki said to me," Kane murmured, trying to catch a stray thought buzzing around his head.

Reaching into his car, he dug through the accordion folder on the passenger seat until he located Vega's folder, then flipped it open to go through their meager findings. The file was woefully thin. On paper, Vega appeared to live an exemplary life, contributing to charities and fostering unwanted young boys. The photos they found in the dead man's house told another story.

Staring at Vega's license photo, it was hard to reconcile the image of the smiling, confident man he saw with the damage he'd done to Miki.

The man looked *normal*. Forcing aside his knowledge of the man's activities, Kane wouldn't have given him a second look. With his broad, craggy face and warm brown eyes, Carl Vega looked like the uncle who sneaked his nephew a peanut-butter sandwich when dinner that night was going to be eggplant surprise. He was the man whom a guy with kids would invite to a baseball game and not think twice about leaving them with Vega while he went to the bathroom in the seventh inning.

He was also the man who stalked Miki's nightmares, tearing him apart from inside the singer's soul.

And Kane had to find his murderer.

"Miki said to me… shit, how did he put it? 'At least he saw me,'" Kane recalled. "That's what stuck with me. That Carl *saw* him."

Kel broke off watching the firemen. "What the hell does that mean?"

"He was talking about Vega," Kane replied. "And I wouldn't tell you this if I didn't think it was important. This is Miki's privacy I'm violating here. This stays between us."

"Not a problem." Kel crossed his heart with an index finger. "Dude, if it helps us find the bastard, I'll be willing to listen to my sisters talk about shoes. Hell, I'd try them on."

"He told me the worst part about the whole… thing… about Shing and Vega was that he *missed* Vega. Not because of the shit Vega did to him but because that son of a bitch was the only person who ever really gave a shit about him. *The only person who saw him.*" Kane put his cup down and rifled through the papers. "Suppose we're going at this all wrong? Suppose the person we're looking for isn't one of Vega's fosters but some kid in the neighborhood? A kid who might have been pissed off because he was replaced. Maybe even replaced by Miki."

"Even bad attention is attention?" Kel whistled. "Morgan, that's some sick shit. Who the hell is going to miss the guy who molested them?"

"Someone who has no one *but* that guy. Miki said he knew it was wrong to feel anything toward Vega but disgust, but even knowing how much Vega fucked him up, some part of him still remembers being that little boy who would do anything to make Vega happy." Unable to find what he was looking for in the first file, he moved on to the second. "If the guy I ran down was the doer, then he's way too scrawny to take down someone as big as Vega. That guy topped out at about two hundred pounds. The guy I saw was maybe one fifty. He would need to immobilize his victims."

"Maybe he was wiry?" Kel offered. "Maybe he's Welsh?"

"Really?" Kane gave his partner a disgusted look. "We don't have tox on Shing or Vega, but there was one done on one of the fosters. The cops down in San Luis called the death undetermined. I just have to find it."

"Undetermined's a bit of a stretch, don't you think?" His partner sounded doubtful.

"Fucking A, here it is. This is Doug Zhang's suicide report. He was one of Vega's foster kids. Cop house near Vega caught the case. The apartment building's a few blocks from Vega's house." He pulled out the police report and read back the description of the young man's autopsy. "Deceased's tox screen came back with high values of barbiturates and benzodiazepine. Cause of death is undetermined due to blood loss deceased experienced following extensive injuries caused by slashes to both arms and legs. Weapon used found on scene and determined to be eight-inch paring knife. Knife found by deceased's side is a match to set found in kitchen. The injection site was found on the inside of Zhang's right arm. Doesn't say if Zhang was left-handed, but odds are good he wasn't."

"That's a pretty deadly combination. Even if it didn't kill the guy, it would have knocked him down long enough for Beanie Boy to do his work. That could have been his first kill. Or, hell, even second or third." Looking over Kane's arm, Kel skimmed the report. "If our boy still lived in the neighborhood while Vega was grooming his fosters, then he'd have seen them. Hell, he might have even kept in touch with them after they split, so he might have known Zhang, knew he was still in the neighborhood."

"Someone like that would probably have a record. Petty stuff or even animal cruelty. Some place he started off before working up to something like Zhang or Vega. There's got to be a trail. We're just not seeing it," Kane said. "Let's finish up here and see if we can't shake him out of the trees."

"Sounds good," Kel said, grinning wickedly. "You know, Morgan, the more I think about it, the more I like your fire-ant idea. Let's go rattle those trees."

MIKI woke up to pain.

It wasn't a bad pain. He actually felt pretty decent, if not slightly rumpled, but his hips ached, and there was a tenderness to his insides when he moved across the bed. A hot shower helped, especially after he scrubbed at his hair. His knee made its presence known with a subtle twinge as he walked, but for the most part, other than the complaining stretch of his thigh muscles, he was doing okay.

The same couldn't be said of his kiss-swollen mouth or the prickle-rash from Kane's stubble covering the line of love bites his cop left on his throat.

"Jesus fucking Christ, you couldn't have eaten before you crawled into bed with me?" Miki rubbed at the tiny purple blossoms on his neck. His stomach grumbled at the mention of food, and Miki sighed. "Okay, man up here, dude. You can face them. Just go raid the fridge and then go hide or something."

He'd thrown his most comfortable clothes into the duffel bag, and as he pulled out a pair of worn-through jeans, Miki wondered if he shouldn't have dug out newer pants from the boxes in his bedroom. Shrugging on a pair with the least amount of holes, he found a black Se7en shirt to put on and walked barefoot into the fires of his own personal hell.

Only to discover hell was very sparsely populated.

In fact, the only occupants appeared to the one-headed Cerberus he'd brought with him and a slab of Irish slate masquerading as a man.

He came through the mudroom as cautiously as he could, keeping an eye out for any stray Morgans lurking in the shadows. Dude barked a happy hello when he spotted Miki coming into the well-lived-in family room, and the terrier bounded over, wagging his tail hard enough to wiggle his entire back end. Bending over, Miki hissed a bit at the tightness in his ass but scruffed at the dog's neck and ears, trying to avoid Dude's nose-seeking tongue.

"Hello, ye must be Miki." A tree trunk dressed in loose denim and a T-shirt sprouted next to Miki's arm, and he looked up, craning his neck to take in the enormity of the man holding his hand out to him. "I'm Donal, Kane's da."

"Hey, how're you doing?" Unsure of what else to do, Miki accepted the handshake and swallowed when he lost his hand in the man's gentle grip. Standing, he stealthily eased Dude behind him with his foot, dislodging the terrier from his round-the-leg dance. "Um, thanks for taking us in. Sorry about the dog. He's an asshole sometimes. Shit, sorry."

"Not a problem. Our house is always yours. And don't worry about swearing around me. I've probably done worse than anything ye can say," Donal replied, nodding to the open back door. "Hope ye don't mind, Duke seems to like having the run of the yard."

"Ah, Dude. His name's Dude." Miki took a step back when Donal's frown sketched over his face. "Sometimes he even comes when you call him."

"Remind me to talk to Brae about his hearing, then. Boy told me the wrong name." The man let go an earthshaking chuckle. "Ye must be hungry. Come on to the kitchen, and I'll get some food in ye. Won't be anything gourmet, but I can turn a burger out with the best of them."

Donal Morgan had more than a head on him, and the man was about half again as wide, but he was welcoming, with a warm smile and eyes as blue as Kane's, crinkling at the corners when he laughed. A dash of silver glinted in his thick blue-black hair, and a shock of soft strands fell over his forehead and brushed at the bridge of his straight nose. Donal's work-worn hands moved as he spoke to Miki about his choices for lunch, the broad gold wedding ring on his finger burnished and nicked from years of wear. From behind, Donal looked as fit as his sons, his powerful frame moving easily under his loose jeans and T-shirt, and Miki felt more than a little weird thinking about how Kane's shoulders compared to his dad's.

"Hope Dude's been good." Miki glanced down at his begging mutt. "He's not... um... civilized. Kind of takes after me, I think."

"Ah, the dog's been fine. Other than he's collected some things from around the house and stashed them behind the couch there." Donal winked at Miki when he groaned in disgust. "It's all right, Miki boy. He's a dog, and it's all new for him. New smells and new people. We only had one small talk about dragging in the pool skimmer, but after that, he's kept to shoes and the like. Now, cheese or no cheese on yer burger?"

"Cheese would be cool." Miki caught himself before he hitched up onto the counter, remembering Kane's shocked expression. Several stools were tucked under the table set in the middle of the kitchen, and he pulled one out to sit on. Resting his elbows on the scarred wood, he watched Donal move from the fridge to the oven, gathering up cheese, meat, and onion rolls.

"Are ye a vegetable eater?" Donal asked over his shoulder.

Miki curled his lip. "Only if you make me."

"Good, then since it's just us carnivores, we shall say we had some of the greens and agree not to speak of it if anyone asks," he rumbled, shifting over to the table. After cracking an egg into a mixing bowl, Donal added the hamburger, breadcrumbs, and some seasoning, then gave Miki a look. "Ye mind me hands in there?"

"Dude, you're feeding me." Miki smirked. "I don't care what you use to mix it with."

"We're going to be getting along fine there, then. Can ye grab the ketchup from the fridge there? Add some to this while I mix it up." Donal washed his hands, then returned to massage the meat together. Miki squirted a few tablespoons into the meat and Donal nodded. "That'll do. Thank ye, Miki. Leave it out on the table in case we want some more. I'll toss some chips into the oven. We can have them with our burgers."

It was a comfortable space, and Miki glanced around, taking in the room without a battalion of Morgans surrounding him. He hadn't seen much of it the first time, relegated to a rushed introduction, then hustled off to the family room to sit on one of the soft, long couches as Brigid shoved a plate of leftovers at him. Now he took his time studying the kitchen Kane grew up in. It was bright and cheery, much like Brigid. A china cabinet held some porcelain platters and a large wooden bowl carved so thin he could see light pouring through the translucent sides.

"Did Kane do that?" Miki asked, pointing to the rough-edged bowl. It looked almost like a tiger lily, undulating up from the base, then flaring out suddenly. It was pretty, a rich golden grain run soft with darker sienna veins. "Make that bowl thingy?"

"Aye." Donal's smile was a quiet light in his face. "He's very good with his hands. I wish I had that kind of beauty inside of me but, ah, the best I can do is carve a turkey and hope there's enough left for me by the time my hellions are done snatching up theirs."

The love in Donal's face *hurt*. The softness of his pride stabbed Miki deep into his broken, screwed-up mind, and he had to look away, pinching his lips together to swallow the uneasiness welling up from his chest. Donal continued, but Miki couldn't make sense of what the man was saying. Just hearing the affection in his voice stung, and Miki shook his head, scolding himself to pull it together.

"What's bothering you there, Miki?" Donal's voice rolled over him. "I'm gathering it's not the cheddar cheese."

"Nah, the cheese is fine." Under the table, Dude gnawed at the end of a bone he'd been given, and Miki tsked at him to be quiet when he started making slurping noises. "Just thinking."

"About being in this crazy house while waiting for Kane to figure all of this shite out?" The man lobbed Miki's unspoken anxiety into the middle of the kitchen, smiling as it went off. "I know that look on yer face. I had it myself when I met Brigid's family. There's eleven of them there, all underfoot and talking up a storm. It was like wading into an Irish tidal wave wearing nothing to protect me but a pair of stolen knickers."

"Those are panties, right?" Miki gave him a sidelong glance.

"Aye, big blue ones, with flowers on them, even. My gran had a pair like that. She hung them out on the line to dry, and I used to worry they'd catch the wind and the house would sail away like it was on a kite." Donal winked and tossed the heel of the bread loaf to a waiting Dude. "Don't ye be telling my bride I've been feeding the dog in here, or she'll have my nuts."

"Only one who'll say shit about it would be Dude." Miki shrugged. "And he knows keeping his mouth shut means more food for him."

"So if ye can imagine me, at the ripe age of twenty, sitting at a long table at the Finnegans' and waiting for my girl to sit down next to me, when her da ambles up and whispers into my ear, 'Boy, yer in me seat.'" Sliding the cheese over to Miki, he continued. "Unwrap a few of those for us, Miki. Four should do."

"What'd you do when he said that? Your father-in-law, I mean." The package proved to be difficult, and when Donal turned his back to grab a frying pan for the stove, he tore at the corner with his teeth.

"Well, I'm pretty sure I went white with fear," Donal laughed. "Ye see, Brigid's da is a short man, shorter than me, anyway, but he's built like a fireplug. He worked the docks for years, and I'd seen him take down men three times his size when they spoke ill of his wife down at the pub. I knew he could lay my scrawny arse out like I was a gnat buzzing about his ear. So I did what any Irish man would do. I stood up, apologized, and made for the door. Without any supper, mind ye."

"And she married you anyway?"

"She had to," Donal said. "I loved her. With all of my heart. But see, my family… the Morgans… they're not one for joking and laughing as much as the Finnegans. No, we're a more sober family, so while her da was joking with me, I didn't have it in me to understand that. The Finnegans, they're a clan that spends most of their time having fun, so it took me a while before I was comfortable around it. By the time my first boy, Connor, came along, I knew that's the kind of house I wanted him to be raised in. Someplace he'd feel warm inside, able to laugh. Do ye understand me?"

"Yeah, I think so," Miki replied, frowning.

"What I'm saying to ye, Miki boy, is that I know how ye feel about being caught in the storm of this family, and if ever it gets too much for ye, you come over to me, and I'll stand in front of ye until the winds die down a bit." Donal put his hand over Miki's wrist and gave it a loose squeeze.

"They'll take some getting used to, and they'll have to get used to you too. Push back if ye need to. Some of mine are a bit dense, and they need a bit of a slap across the brain sometimes to get them going," Donal continued. "Ye got a good one there with Kane. He's got a good heart. My temper, though, so I apologize to ye for that, but he'll never do more than raise his voice at ye. And then probably feel bad about that afterwards. If I've taught them one thing, it's that they're strong, stronger than most. They've got to take care with that. Ye'll never have to worry about him taking a hand to ye."

"I'd kill him if he did," Miki snorted. "He's got to sleep sometime."

"Good for ye." Donal beamed. "Just remember that snarl when my bride comes at ye with her succotash. Love her to death, but that shite's nasty. Don't let her feed it to ye. Once it passes yer lips, she'll be shoving it down ye for the rest of yer life."

"Got it. I didn't even know it was real," Miki conceded, passing over the unwrapped cheese slices. The sizzle of meat hitting the hot frying pan was followed by the heavenly aroma of burgers cooking, and Miki's mouth watered. "Can I ask you something?"

"About Kane?" Donal glanced at him, and Miki nodded. "About him being gay or a cop like his da?"

"Gay," Miki murmured. "I can't see him being anything *but* a cop."

"True," the man replied as he added rings of onions to the pans to grill. "Even as much as he loves making things, he'd rather wear a badge if he had to make a choice. Go ahead. Nothing ye can ask that someone else hasn't already."

"How'd he know he was gay? I mean, for sure?"

"Okay, I was wrong, that *is* something I haven't been asked before." Donal grinned. "How'd he know he was gay? Simple, Miki boy. He likes men. Easy as that. A man's body makes him sit up and look. Kane's the easy one. He knows himself and what he likes... what he wants. He brought ye here, or at least didn't butt heads with his mum about it. He'd have taken ye out before my bride could take a breath if he didn't. Kane wants ye here, in the place he learned to live and love. That's how I know that yer someone special to him. Quinn, now… that one's got a bit of trouble in his heart, but he'll find his way soon enough."

"And you're okay with that? With them liking guys?" Donal was an aberration. Even as free-spirited and open as the city was, Miki never really knew any parents okay with their sons loving men. Damien's parents treated his sexuality like it was a mole on his nose, something to be ignored and not mentioned in public.

"Miki, I can tell ye one thing for sure," Donal said, waving the spatula in the air to make his point. "I taught my sons to be men. I don't care who they love. I care about how they act. The moment they stop having manners or treat someone poorly, then we'll have words. Other than that, I only want them to be happy, and if you make Kane happy, then all I have to say to ye is welcome to the family. Now pass the salt, boy. I've got to season the meat, or it'll be like eating a stale cracker."

CHAPTER NINETEEN

Her tears are long gone, stained with ice and despair,
And no one knows why. 'Cause they sure don't care.
A rose on her stone gave me grace from above.
The dirt on my hands is as cold as her love.

—Dirt and Stone

THE trip out to Zhang's apartment building was a bust. Doug Zhang's life was a bleak trail of blood and sorrow through the San Francisco foster system. Removed and returned to his parents more than a dozen times, he was in and out of temporary homes, a typical statistic made more depressing by the abuses he suffered under Carl Vega's hands. According to his file, Doug was a simple but quiet child, unperturbed at living with strangers and obedient to a fault. The perfect gift for a man like Carl Vega.

Before his death, Zhang lived in a run-down cinder block former motel. Scraggly clumps of weeds filled most of the thin scrap of landscaping in front of the structure, and the building's white walls were grayed from dust and peeling at the foundation. It was a depressing, lackluster place to live.

And surrounded by an elementary school and two day cares.

After nearly two hours of pounding the sidewalks, they found no one who'd cared enough about Zhang to pay attention to who visited him. Kane thought it was a sad commentary about the man's life. Sanchez grunted in sympathy, then complained his stomach was empty.

Inching the unmarked sedan into a parking space in front of a taco shop, they both sighed with relief that the car made it back to the City. They'd secured the black Crown Vic from Motor Pool with a stern admonishment from the administrator to return the car in pristine shape. Kel grumbled they'd have to get someone to do body work on the Ford before they came back, and Kane resigned himself to a lifetime of motor pool rejects following the sour look they got.

The sedan wasn't going to win any prizes. The backseat's vinyl was cracked and smelled, strangely enough, of lavender and burnt chicken feathers, but the radio worked, and up until Sanchez took a bump in the road too fast, the onboard computer linking them to the SFPD database responded smoothly. After their reenactment of an old *Starsky and Hutch* car jump shot, the Crown Vic rattled back onto its tires and the computer screen turned blue, leaving a few lines of squiggling white code behind. It also hesitated a second when Sanchez hit the gas, as if it needed to contemplate going another foot forward.

"Odd place for someone like Zhang to live." Kel slid a tray of chips and salsa onto a bright orange picnic table. Passing a carnitas burrito over to his partner, he opened up his Styrofoam container and inhaled the aroma coming from his carne asada fries. "Single guy. Place is crawling with kids. It was creepy."

There'd been piles of toys in front of many of the apartments' doors, and Zhang's old place on the first floor faced the street. Anyone sitting in the living room would have a clear view of the schools' playgrounds and the children who frolicked there.

"Just because he was molested doesn't mean he passed it on down the line." They both knew the stats and the high likelihood of Zhang reaching out to normalize his shattered world in the only way he knew how, but Kane wasn't ready to hang Vega's crimes on one of his victims. "Maybe he liked listening to kids laugh. Doesn't sound like he had much of it when he was young. Neighbors said he was nice. Didn't bug anyone."

"Makes me want to shoot every single asshole who's ever touched a kid, you know?" Sanchez's voice was soft but hot with emotion. "Someone pull that kind of shit with my sisters, I'd kill him. I know it's the job, man, and if this asshole wasn't fucking with St. John, it'd be hard to hate this guy."

"That asshole gutted a man just for smoking outside. Get some food in you so we can find Beanie Boy." Kane bit into his burrito, sucking at the juices filling the wrapped tortilla before the liquid dripped down his hand. "Maybe we'll be lucky and get someone who recognizes him from Vega's neighborhood. We just need a damned name. Shit, anything. I just want Miki safe."

"Have you thought about what you and him are going to do when this is all over?" Kel sprinkled spicy red sauce on his fries, not meeting his partner's quizzical glance. "You know, when you go back to being a cop and he goes back to being a rock star."

"We never stopped being those things," Kane replied. "I figure we'll eat together, have sex, and argue about him getting some physical therapy for that leg of his."

"So you really think this…." The man waved his hand around in the air. "This thing between the two of you is going to last after this?"

"Yeah, Kel. I do." Kane put down his food and leaned his elbows on the table. "See, I get it now. For a long time, I couldn't figure out how my dad and mom stayed together. They're too different. They like different things. Hell, they can't even agree on what kind of Christmas tree to get, so it never made sense that they were… inseparable."

"And now you do? Because of St. John?"

"Yeah, I do," he replied softly. "People like my mom and Miki are like kites. They need the sky. They *need* the wind. Me and my dad? We're the people holding the string. We're their anchors to the earth. Miki and I can feel each other through the connection."

"Huh, how does that work out? You're… wait, you're not the string. You're holding the string."

"Yeah, dude. I'm holding the string." Kane laughed at Kel's confused look. "I can feel the power of the wind catching Miki, lifting him up and dropping him down. He can feel the world beneath me, and he knows… he trusts me not to let go… not to let him drift off into the sky. And when he gets too tired of flying, he knows I'll reel him in and take care of him. Just like my dad does with my mom."

"And what do you get out of that? Huh?" Kel asked pointedly. "What the fuck happens to you when he flies off?"

"I have to trust him not to." Kane smiled at his skeptical partner. "Trust has to go both ways. I love him, Kel. I love his singing to himself as he scribbles in the damned notebooks he leaves everywhere. I love kissing the ink stains on his fingers and the flush he gets when he's had half a beer. I *know* him, Kel."

"He's fucked up, Kane." Sanchez shook his head, worry creasing his forehead. "You've gotta see that. Hell, I was in that room with him for what? An hour? Hour and a half? And I could tell he's messed in the head."

"It's what I was dealt, dude." He shrugged. "It's what he was dealt. We've got to deal with it. Vega and Shing? They're the least of it. He's missing part of his soul, Kel. When Damien died, Miki's music died too. He writes lyrics and leaves the other side of the page blank because that's where Damien used to score their music. Miki *knows* how to love and, damn, he knows how it feels when he's lost it."

"He and Damien Mitchell were together, then?" Kel made a face. "Shit, man. You're screwed."

"They weren't lovers, Sanchez. You aren't listening, man. They were… brothers. Hell, closer than brothers," Kane said. "They got one another. I can respect that. Hell, I wish I could take that kind of pain away from him, but that's going to haunt Miki for the rest of his life. But I've got his heart and soul, even the shredded pieces where his best friend used to be."

"You, my friend," his partner pronounced. "You are stupid in love."

"Yeah." Kane knew the grin on his face was silly, and it hurt to stretch his cheeks out that much, but he liked how he felt, even as Kel shook his head in mock disgust. "Kel, I'm lucky he lets me love him, and I'm going to take care of what he's given me. I have to, Kel. Or I'll be as dead inside as Miki used to be."

"Sounds like you're getting the raw end of the deal there, man," Kel sighed, picking at his fries with a fork.

"Not if you never thought you could fly," Kane murmured. "With Miki, I can feel the wind. He lets me have a taste of the sky every time I kiss him. That's not something I even thought of before, and now I can't imagine my life without it."

"YOU'RE doing what?" Edie's voice screeched out of Miki's phone, and he pulled it away from his ear, shooting the taxi driver an apologetic glance. "Are you insane? Turn the cab around!"

"No." Keeping the phone angled away from his face, he spoke quietly into the headset. "I kind of have to do this, Edie. It just feels right to do."

"Right to do? You thought it would be okay to have chickens on the tour bus because you wanted scrambled eggs! You think *this* is the right thing to do, and I can't get you to see a therapist to talk about your messed up head?" She ranted for a moment, and Miki spent the time tracing the snippets of a song in his mind. After he circled round to the chorus for the third time, he took advantage of Edie's need to breathe.

He loved Edie. In a very real way, she'd been the only family he had left after the accident, but as she inhaled quickly and continued to disparage his decision to see the Vega house one last time, Miki remembered why it'd been so important to come back home to San Francisco instead of living in Los Angeles where she could watch him.

"Hanging up on her would be bad, right?" Miki leaned forward to whisper into the driver's ear. "I mean, really bad, right?"

"Is she your wife?" the older Russian man asked. "Because if she is your wife, yes. If she is your girlfriend, maybe a little bad, but you can make that better. If a wife, then no. You listen and shut up."

"No, she's my manager," Miki said, wincing as another round of berating began. "Kind of like an aunt."

"Oh, then, *no*." The gray-haired man adjusted his cap. "If your mother or aunt, worse than your wife. For them, you say yes and do what you need to do as a man behind their back. Then hope they do not find out."

Sitting back, Miki slid his remark in between Edie's admonishments. "Okay, I'm heading back to the Morgans. I'll have the cab guy turn around."

The Russian met Miki's eyes in the rearview mirror, lifting his eyebrows in question. Shaking his head no, Miki made a face when the cabbie grinned widely at him, showing the large gap between his two front teeth. Edie wound down her tirade with a dark promise to descend upon San Francisco as soon as she finished filing lawsuits on his behalf. Ending the call, Miki turned off the phone and sank into the vinyl seat, tired out from the battle.

"Good! Well done!" The cab driver grunted. "You have no father, yes? Or he would have taught you these things."

"Nope, but I know one now I can ask." Miki's mouth lifted at the corners as he thought of what Donal Morgan would have to say about Edie. "I think he'd have told me the same thing. Well, I hope so. He's kind of the reason I'm heading up here. Just need to say… good-bye. To everything."

"Good man, then." He flipped off the meter. "You, I give you the ride for free. Then you call me when you're done there. I'll come get you."

"Deal," Miki said, taking the man's card when the driver handed it to him.

After directing the Russian to drop him off at the corner, Miki gave the driver a hefty tip and another promise to call him back. Giving the man a friendly wave, he gripped the walking stick he borrowed from Donal, easing the weight off of his injured knee.

They'd tussled a bit about Miki heading to Vega's house but in the end, Miki's desire to put his ghosts to bed outweighed Donal's apprehension. As a concession to Donal's suspicious nature, he took the ancient walking stick Donal pulled from an umbrella stand.

The shillelagh was a gnarled piece of blackthorn Donal's grandfather used while tramping through the wilds of Ireland, and Miki'd been reluctant to take it with him, but the older man scoffed at his reservations.

"That shillelagh there's been through greater battles than you'll find here in San Francisco, boy." Donal's lilting scold was light, a cheerful reassurance for Miki to take what seemed to be a Morgan heirloom with him as he climbed the hills of Vega's neighborhood. "It'll be good to have a piece of the family with you as you chase your boojums. If you want to do this alone, then at least have us with you in spirit. Now take the damned thing and go. Before the driver starts charging you for sitting there at the curb."

"I feel like a goddamn leprechaun," he groused. His knee gave him a little trouble, sending off a twinge or two as he walked up the hill toward Vega's house, and the blackened, stout piece of wood made it easier to walk. "Or one of those hipster douches at the coffee shop. I could start a new trend. McPimp Mac Daddy fashions."

It was too damned easy to reach the middle of the street. Miki suddenly found himself staring at his own personal hell. His fingers ached until he realized he was gripping the cane's knob too tightly. He forced his hand to relax and the tension flowed out into his arms and shoulders, locking his legs with a rigid purpose.

Coming up to the house seemed like a good idea when he'd been cradled in the relatively insane warmth of the Morgan home. Surrounded by echoes of laughing children and steady adults, Miki found a longing inside of him, something whispering a promise that he could find a place at the table during the holidays or even a comforting word from a battered veteran of the fathering wars when he got too lost to find his way out of his head.

Donal asked him if he was ready to say good-bye to the past and step toward a better future. Miki couldn't answer the man. There'd been too many shadows lurking behind him, and in that moment, Miki knew he had to make a clean break with his demons. He owed that much to Kane.

A tiny, frail voice in the back of his head whispered he owed that much to himself.

The house looked... smaller than he remembered, more worn down and tired around its edges. A bright orange paper was taped over the doorframe, warning people off the property. Fragments of yellow tape flapped their ragged edges from the hedge near the front stoop, more remnant of a tragedy than a warning against entry.

Time slipped away from Miki when he finally took a step forward and his foot hit the concrete walk. Within a blink of an eye, he was a child again, edging past the house in a slink. The boards fencing off the backyard were still loose, and he used the shillelagh's heft to hold them to the side so he could slip past the splintery wood. Familiar scents assaulted him: a drift of pine from the trees bristling between the houses, a whiff of mildew from the partially open basement windows, and the odd pungency of the cheap paint Vega used to coat the house in its weary colors.

The ground beneath his sneakers was damp, and he nearly slipped when his foot hit a patch of lichen spreading outward in a black ripple. Miki slammed his hand against the house's outer wall and hissed at the pain of his palm being scraped open on the rough paint. Shaking off the weeping sting, he picked his way through the weeds and recycle bins filled with empty aluminum cans to reach the ramshackle shed sitting at the back of the property.

At one point in the shed's past, it served as a place to park a car. Adjacent to the alley running behind the houses, its single open wall had been boarded up, rendering it useless as a garage. Past owners made the space their own, either as a workroom or a space to tinker on mysterious projects, but the Vegas used the space for storage.

Miki had used it as a place to hide and dream.

He'd spent several afternoons moving boxes around until he carved out a good amount of space along the far wall. Now confronted by a wall of cardboard, Miki wondered if his hidey-hole was gone, but the flap of a washing-machine box remained in place. Slender windows cut along the eaves of the old garage let in enough light to see, and dust motes clotted the air, spiraling away in great waves as Miki moved about.

"Shit, I was a skinny kid," he grumbled when he whacked his elbow against the wall trying to squeeze through the space. The shillelagh tucked under his arm rattled against the wood frame with each crab-walk step he took. A few seconds of dimness, and he was free of the tunnel and standing in what he'd always thought of as his lair.

It was as if time stopped and he was a kid again, trembling in fear at hearing Vega's car rumble down the alleyway to park behind the house.

The painful-to-the-eye orange beanbag he'd rescued from a trash pile was still there, covered with a thin layer of dust. Strips of duct tape stitched together its torn sides, keeping its guts from spilling out. The edges of the tape were lifted up from age, and while he wouldn't trust it to sit on, Miki grinned at the idea of it lying in wait like a vampiric tangerine blob. Shelves above the beanbag held what he came looking for, treasures he'd hidden away from grasping adult hands and judgmental eyes.

Pulling out a large box marked "roofing nails," Miki eyed the beanbag suspiciously, deciding the decrepit vinyl probably wouldn't hold its guts in if he sat on it. Squatting was another option, but an upside-down milk crate served readily enough as a stool. Miki opened the box flaps and stared down into his remains of his childhood.

A curled-up Playgirl held a prominent spot against a cardboard wall, and Miki laughed when he pulled it out and leafed through the pages. He couldn't remember spending a lot of time on the images of the heavily endowed men between the covers, recalling only reading the sexual encounter stories, but the stickiness between the middle pages told him otherwise.

"Huh," Miki murmured, turning the book so he could stare at the sculpted, muscular form of the blue-eyed centerfold model. "Guess this means I'm really gay. Kane'll be happy."

Emptying out the box took very little time. A few CDs he ripped off from the music store at the top level of the Japantown mall rattled when he drew them out. He set the L'arc disc aside, promising himself to go back and pay for them now he had money.

A few papers boasting test scores low enough to qualify as Death Valley residents reminded Miki he'd hated school and an insect got to the string of gold stars he pasted together during a nearly funerary art class he had to take in the seventh grade. The art teacher showed up drunker than one of the unwashed men loitering down at the pier, and he'd taken great care to rub his leg against Miki's thighs when he went around the class to look at their art projects.

"Maybe I can get Kane to shoot him too," Miki sniffed. He reached down to stroke at a furry ear that wasn't there and then sighed, suddenly missing his dog terribly. "Come on, it's got to be here."

It was under the papers. He'd not been careful with it, not as careful as it probably deserved because, like the beanbag, it showed the wear of time and the grimy effects of belonging to a little boy. Still, Miki drew it out with a special reverence, a tiny flicker of warmth flushing his cheeks as he uncovered his first friend.

Like the house, the plushie was smaller than he remembered, a little bit longer than his hand but squishable. With a black body constructed more like a flattened X than any similarity to an animal, its white head was topped with floppy round ears. Two black button eyes were set above its squished, dirty pink embroidered nose.

He'd been eight and at a street carnival, scrounging about between the booths for dropped money or game tickets. Fifteen tickets meant a small popcorn. Thirty gained him a hot dog with the works. Miki couldn't remember how many he had when a woman shoved a handful of tickets at him but all of it been enough for cotton candy, two hot dogs, and the oddly shaped black and white plush dog-panda he spotted at the prize booth.

It wasn't pretty, but it hung alongside the other toys as if proud of its cobbled-together appearance. The guy at the booth thought he was crazy for wanting it. Miki couldn't imagine taking anything else home.

"Hey, Dude," Miki whispered into the stuffed animal's ear. "How about if I take you home now? There's a guy I want you to meet. Oh, and I've got a dog, but I don't think that'll be a problem. He's mostly into tennis balls."

After stuffing the toy into the inside pocket of his jacket, Miki made his way out again, banging his elbow on the garage's framing. He stumbled out of the shed and into the full daylight, blinking away the tears stinging his eyes at the bright sun. Patting his chest, Miki gripped the head of the shillelagh and dug its tip into the backyard's scrabbling weeds. He took one step forward then the back of his head exploded in pain. The world spun around him, a battalion of stars swimming through the blackness edging around his vision.

He hit the ground face first, his stomach aching where the shillelagh dug into his side. The pain across the back of his head was nothing compared to the agony of his twisted knee, and Miki nearly threw up when he flipped over to face his attacker.

And saw nothing but the black muzzle of a gun as it was shoved into his open mouth.

CHAPTER TWENTY

When you said you loved me, I believed you.
Then when you needed to be free, I deceived you.

—Junie's Lies

"YOU like sucking on my things, bitch?" The gun jammed further down Miki's throat and he gagged on it, its crust and oil filling his mouth. "Here. Suck on this. Just like you sucked on *him*!"

He didn't recognize the guy shoving a gun into his mouth, but Miki knew what he was intimating. The gesture was obscene, a vulgar rape of his mouth with a piece of dirty steel. The knit beanie pulled down low on the man's face was meant to intimidate, but it only emphasized his greasy shank of hair and flushed, pocked skin. The man spat as he screamed at Miki, his words a string of nonsensical profanities. From the way the young man held the weapon, he believed he had the upper hand.

If Miki had learned one thing in his life, it was to even the odds. And when the odds were evened, cheat.

He grabbed a handful of dirt and flung it up into the man's face, spraying rocks and fertilizer into the gunman's wide, crazed eyes. The gun slipped out of Miki's mouth, its muzzle slick with Miki's spit. His knee buckled when he turned over, but Miki kept going, reaching for the cane Donal had pushed into his hands before he left the Morgans' home. Staggering to his feet, he spit out the taste of the gun and got a good grip on the shillelagh's shaft.

Right then, he couldn't care less if the man was a saint and it was all a horrible mistake or if he was some crazy person who knew him and came in from San Francisco's streets. Miki would ask questions later. Better to apologize for kicking someone's ass than to end up dead because some asshat got something wrong in his head.

Feeling the weight of the wooden cane in his hands, Miki smiled when the familiar tingle of adrenaline hit his nerves. Donal's shillelagh would go a long way in evening the stacked odds.

The first swing connected with the man's jaw, and the crack of the wood knob against bone seemed to echo in the small yard. Staggering back, the man tried to bring the gun up, his finger squeezing down on the trigger, as Miki rounded back and struck again, slamming the end of the shillelagh across his knuckles.

A loud boom burst from the gun, and its bullet whirred past Miki's arm. He felt the bite of something on his shoulder, and then a creeping burn spread down his arm. A numbing shockwave hit his hand, and his fingers convulsed around the shaft. Shaking, Miki shifted his grip and held on harder, flinging the cane up again, knocking the gun out of the man's hand.

He didn't know where it landed, but from the crazy, wild-eyed stare on the man's face, Miki guessed his assailant knew. The man leaped toward the thick weeds by the garage's open door, and Miki jumped after him. His knee screamed in agony as he tackled the guy to the ground, and his shoulder set up its own refrain, throbbing and oozing a wet trail inside the arm of his jacket.

"He was fucking mine!" The man's breath was foul and he spat as he spoke. "You shouldn't have come back. I could have had him back! *I* wanted him. You didn't, and he *still* fucking chose you."

"Fucking hell." Miki's breath caught as a terrifying realization spread through him. "You're one of *Carl's*."

It was like staring up into the face of his own personal nightmarish mirror. The man twisting around underneath him was a brother of sorts, bound to him in the sticky, emotional strands of Vega's sickness. They'd had their blood spilled and their bodies torn apart by the same man. It should have bound them closer. Instead, it was driving the other man to kill.

Miki wasn't going to argue with a crazy man. Especially not one with a gun in arms' reach. Doubling over, he twisted his legs around the man's torso and pinned him to the ground. He brought the cane up and slammed its knob into the man's head, splitting open the skin by his eye.

An enraged insanity seemed to fill Miki's attacker. A gleam burned feverishly in his unfocused gaze, a nearly evangelical fervor strengthening him as he threw Miki off.

Miki landed hard, losing his hold on the shillelagh. It bounced out of reach, and he lay on the ground for a brief second, forcing the air back into his lungs. Out of the corner of his eye, he saw the man scrambling on his hands and knees toward a clump of weeds.

He came up with the gun as Miki got to his feet with Donal's shillelagh held out in front of him.

"I don't know you, dude." Miki shuffled to the side, testing his knee. He didn't need to. As he moved, his jeans' leg tightened around the swollen joint. There was very little give to the fabric, and fire was shooting up his thighs and roasting his balls in pain. His arm hurt like hell, with blood dripping down his hand and onto the wooden shaft. "You can walk away from this. We both can."

"I don't want to walk away from this… from you. Uncle Carl was mine." The gun shook in the man's hand, the muzzle drifting back and forth off of Miki's chest. "Until you came along."

"Um, did you kill him and Shing? That was you, right?" Miki reminded him, then blanched when the gun steadied to point at his head. Not for the first time, he cursed his own mouth. "Just saying."

"He didn't want me anymore." He began shaking again, tears tracking through the dirt marbling his face. "I was too old, too ugly. He didn't want to see me anymore."

"Carl wasn't…." Miki took another step closer, gritting his teeth against the pain. "Dude, he wasn't worth this. What he did was wrong. You know that, right?"

"It *wasn't* wrong!" Spit flew in long strands from the man's mouth, splattering Miki's face. "*You* were the wrong one. *You* should have stayed away."

"Trust me, man, this was the *last* place I wanted to be." The grass crackled under his feet, and Miki inched closer.

"How can you say that? He wanted you so much! What's wrong with you? He would have given you everything!"

"Look, being here wasn't what I wanted. Shit, you shouldn't have wanted it either," Miki said. "It fucks with your head, you know? The shit that he did gets into your brain and chops up all of your mind."

Miki left off that by killing Vega, the man pretty much doomed himself to never gaining Vega's attention.

"He used to tell me I was his special boy. *Special!*" The gun wavered again, its muzzle drifting toward the ground. "You know what he told me when he woke up from the drugs? When I had him in the room?"

"Can't even fucking guess," Miki said, shrugging, then wondered if he shouldn't have, but the other man seemed not to care.

"He didn't recognize me!" The spit began flying again, joined by a run of snot as he began to sob. Clutching the gun tightly in his hand, he lifted it up and waved it at the clouds, his outrage filling him. "When I told him I loved him, you know what he told me? He said I was stupid, and he couldn't have ever wanted someone as ugly as me. Even tied up and on the ground, all he could think about was you. So, fine, he fucking wants you. He can fucking have you."

"Pretty sure I wasn't what thing he was thinking about there, dude." Miki shuffled again. He needed to get the guy distracted. Anything to give himself enough time. "Did you tell him your name or just say, hey, I was one of the little kids you fucked up?"

The man spun quickly and stepped closer, bringing himself nearly to Miki's nose. "I told him my name. I leaned over and whispered it into his ear when I started cutting him. He started crying. Then the begging started. 'Andrew Coons, I remember you now.' *Now?* That's all he could say before I took his lips off. I didn't want to be *remembered*. I wanted him to *need* me."

"Seriously?" Miki took a breath and hefted the shillelagh into a tight grip. "You are more fucked up than he was."

It wasn't a fair fight, not with the years Miki spent on the street and singing at backwater bars where his pretty face drew more animosity than compliments. The shillelagh's weighted end was something he'd never have used in a bar fight, but Miki wasn't going to split hairs. He was more interested in splitting open Andrew's head.

He swung, a fierce upswing that would have done any homerun hitter proud. Connecting with Andrew square in the teeth, Miki grunted when he stepped forward to follow through. He tried keeping his eyes on the gun, but it slid around too much for Miki to watch, and then, when he cocked his stance for another hit, Andrew wavered and squeezed the trigger.

The shot went wide, but Miki's swing connected hard, and Andrew went flying backward, landing in the dried grass, speckled with his blood and spit.

"Drop the fucking gun!" Miki screamed at him.

Andrew's answer was to bring it up and fire again.

Miki felt the bullet hit his jacket shoulder, but other than the burn of leather in his nose, he was pretty certain Andrew missed. The second shot didn't. It pinged off the shillelagh and shattered the bulbous knob at the end of the shaft. The lead weight drilled down into the wood and scattered splinters into Miki's hands and cheek.

It was enough for Miki, and holding on to the wooden shaft with one hand, he flung the shillelagh at Andrew's head, bashing him across the nose with the truncated shaft, then balled up his other fist to deliver another blow. His fingers took the shock of striking bone with a jolt, and Miki's stomach turned at the crunching sounds Andrew's face made when hit. He tangled his legs into Andrew's and they both went down, fists flailing wildly. The shillelagh was lost somewhere in the grass near Miki's feet, but he didn't care. Not when the other man still held the gun in his hand.

Andrew's knee came up and caught Miki's balls. The sharp impact squeezed his sac into his thigh, his jeans forming an unforgiving brace of pain when Andrew jabbed at him again. Roiling nausea struck Miki's stomach, then the curling sensation of his dick being peeled apart hit and Miki gacked, choking on the back of his tongue.

He rolled, trying to separate himself from Andrew, but the man held on tight, jabbing his knee up again. This time, the hard stab caught Miki on his injured knee and he screamed, his world turning a bright pinkish red. Miki hadn't felt as heavy a pain since he'd been in Carl's hands. It wasn't a pleasant memory, and the angry uselessness he felt back then resurrected itself, sinking its venomous teeth into his will.

"Yeah, fucker," Miki panted. Spitting out the pain-thickened saliva pooling in his mouth, he shoved himself past the wall of ache to grab Andrew by the throat. "I'm not taking any of your shit."

The roughness of the grass under his other hand reminded Miki he wasn't gripping pilled cotton sheets to keep from shoving at Carl's heavy body. It was worse when he fought back then. Now it was retribution. He'd come too far, endured too much to let Andrew Coons take his freedom away from him.

Especially when, somewhere out in the city, Kane was waiting for him.

His fists were enough. They were going to have to be. Shoving Andrew back with all of his might, Miki straddled the man's knees, pinning him to the ground, and began to whale away.

Miki's knuckles bit into Andrew's face, pummeling the meat beneath his skin until it glowed red from the sharp impacts. He didn't care if he could hold onto the man long enough to make him see reason. Reason was a lost cause. The only thing Miki wanted from the other man was blood.

And even then, he might want more.

It was too much to take in. The pain in his legs mingling with the burning fire coming up from his hands and ripping through his shoulders. Andrew's hands shoved at his chest, trying to get Miki off of him, but the singer hooked his ankles under the man's knees, anchoring himself in place. Retaliating, Andrew balled up his hands and struck Miki where he could reach, slamming his fists into Miki's shoulders and knees.

Andrew got a few good licks in. Miki's head snapped back when his chin took a hit, and there was a taste of blood on Miki's lip from another errant blow, but it wasn't enough to make Miki stop. He couldn't risk it. He finally had too much to lose.

Miki's vision remained red, this time the color of Andrew's blood mottling his hands and running over the man's face. Andrew flailed, catching Miki's throat with his fingers. He felt the trapped man rake at him, then the bite of air when his skin peeled up under Andrew's dirty fingernails. The wound wept, trails of watery pink running down Miki's neck

The exchanged blows were furious. Then Miki hit something in Andrew's face that gave way. A nasty crunch reverberated through Miki's skin, and his knuckles bloomed their own spikes of pain. Miki's eyes watered, and the middle finger on his right hand quickly swelled, curling his fist into a rigid claw.

Then he noticed Andrew's unnatural stillness.

Miki rolled off the other man's legs to rest on his hip and hand, leaning to the side. His right knee refused to uncurl, and he cradled his hand to his chest, panting from the exertion of nearly beating a man to death.

Andrew's face was a mess, barely recognizable under the blood and swelling. Turned slightly to the side, his chest stuttered as his lungs struggled to breathe. A chattering sound rattled from somewhere below his collarbone, and bubbles of snot and blood clogged his left nostril. Miki's fists had pounded at the bridge of bone until only one passage worked. Andrew's mouth didn't look much better, and somewhere under the tangled clot of hair, spit and more blood were Andrew's eyes, his lashes barely visible beneath the crimson swirls.

Miki's knuckles were raw, and the dried weeds were pricking into the scraped skin. Blowing on the spots only made matters worse, and Miki shook his hands to rid himself of the sting. His own breath was as jagged as the skin on his palms, and Miki forced himself to stay upright. Despite the scratchy burrs around him, he wanted to fall over and close his eyes. Every inch of his body ached where it wasn't on fire from pain, and he doubted he had the strength to do more than just breathe.

The shakes hit him fast and hard, and his fingers barely had enough strength in them to pull his jacket forward so he could check its inside pocket. The worn plush was secure in its nest, its bobble-black eyes staring up at Miki from its stained white round head. Twisting one of the bear-dog's ears between his trembling fingers, Miki let go of a shuddering breath and let the shock take him. Overwhelmed, he retched up a watery cocktail of stale coffee and mostly digested burger. Staring down at the weeds, Miki couldn't help but think his contribution could only help the disastrous lawn.

"I have thrown up more in the last couple of weeks then I have all the time I was on tour." Miki spat his mouth clean. "This is fucking insane."

When sirens began to close in on the Vega house, Miki's insides clenched. Then he heard a very familiar Irish-tinted voice announcing he was a member of the San Francisco Police Department and that whoever was around should come out with their hands up.

"Oh, fuck me," Miki sighed, rubbing at his sweaty temple with the back of his hand. "Fuck me to hell."

"Hands in the air! Let me see them!" Kane came around the side of the house and leveled his gun at Miki. Miki obliged his lover, raising his battered hands so Kane could see his palms. Swearing, Kane jerked his weapon up when he recognized his lover, then dropped it again to cover the man lying facedown in the dirt a few feet away. "Miki?"

"Hey, how you doing?" Miki gave Kane a negligent wave. "If you want to point that thing at someone, keep it on that guy. He tried to kill me. I think. Don't try to finish off what he started."

"Sanchez! Back here!" Kane shouted toward the street and squatted next to Miki. Dropping his voice to a whisper, he studied his lover's tear-streaked face. "Dear God, what did you do to yourself, Mick boy?"

Glancing at the prone man a few feet away, Kane holstered his weapon and ran his hands over Miki's body. Kane plucked at the bullet holes in his jacket, and then he cupped Miki's face. His fingers made a mess of the blood and spit on Miki's face, smearing trails over his skin.

"It's not my blood. It's Andrew's. Dude, you're going to get that all over you," he protested weakly at being touched. "I'm okay."

Miki found himself being kissed soundly. He gave in to Kane's assault, his lips parting to let the other man's tongue in. It was short but intense, enough to steal the rest of the air from Miki's lungs.

Even through the pain, Miki was left panting and wanting more.

"I am seriously fucked in the head," He muttered under his breath. "Kane, stop trying to rearrange my face. It hurts."

"Are you sure you're okay, Mick?" The Irish was strong, bleeding into his words. His thumbs brushed over Miki's lips, and he stiffened slightly when the wind rustled the weeds around them.

Reaching for his gun, Kane visibly relaxed with relief when he saw his partner emerging from the brittle, dry brush at the other end of the house. Kel's face was bright red from exertion, with a sweaty sheen covering his cheeks. Panting, he bent over to grip his knees as he caught his breath.

Sanchez glanced at Andrew's still form, then motioned at the man with his gun. "That Beanie Boy?"

"Looks like it," Kane assented. Then his eyes narrowed, and his hand dropped to the swell of Miki's knee. "What happened? Are you okay?"

"He kicked me." Miki shrugged. The touch of Kane's fingers on the joint nearly made him crawl out of his skin. "Kind of pissed me off. Beanie Boy?"

"It's what we've been calling him. He's the guy I chased down the alley." Kane stood and pressed a hand on Miki's shoulder, preventing him from getting up. "You stay right there, Slugger. I'm calling for a couple of ambulances. One for each of you. Talk to me, love. How'd you get here? Did he bring you here?"

"Russian guy brought me." Miki waved Kane off when the cop frowned with worry. "Cab driver. I asked him to bring me here. Guess Andrew either followed me here or I walked into his spiderweb."

"You know him?" Sanchez carefully rolled Miki's assailant over onto his side to cuff his hands. Kane walked through the weeds, hunting for Andrew's gun.

"His name's Andrew Coons." Miki shifted the weight off of his hip and tried to get his leg underneath him. "He used to be one of Carl's… boys." Kane turned, fixing a steely blue eye onto his lover. Miki gave him a light shrug. "He's a bit off in the head, Kane. He *liked* what Carl… did. Or at least the attention. I don't know. I don't speak that kind of crazy."

"Why'd he kill them, then?" Sanchez frowned, pointing Kane over to a clump of weeds. "Over there, man."

It happened too quickly for Miki to see. One moment Kane was reaching for the discarded gun then Andrew Coons was up on his feet, wrestling with Sanchez for control of his weapon. The handcuffs jangled from one of Andrew's wrists, and Kel began shouting at Kane to draw his gun.

Despite the pain eating through him, Miki got to his feet when Kane pulled his Glock free from his holster and drew down on Andrew and Kel. Taking a step toward the cops and Andrew was a big mistake, probably one Miki would regret for the rest of his life.

He took that single step. Then an ear-splitting boom fractured the neighborhood's eerie silence, and Miki's world went black.

CHAPTER
TWENTY-ONE

I like that riff, D.
Yeah? Wrote it yesterday when you were in the shower.
Was that when you flushed the toilet?
Yeah. Sorry about that. I was just thinking about the chord
progression.
Next time, think about the singer in the shower, dude.
Song came out kick ass though. Isn't that worth a little burnt skin?

—Studio 5, Take 17

Three months later

THE dog was underfoot. Again.

No matter where Kane was—even in Miki's warehouse—the damned dog seemed to always be underfoot.

Kane nudged Dude aside and reached for his drill, checking its screwdriver bit. One last screw and the two doors he'd dragged over from his workshop to Miki's place would be hung from the newly installed hinges. At the very least, they'd be able to close off Miki's bedroom from his mother's prying eyes when she came over to visit.

Fixing the final piece into place, he stepped back to admire the job and test the swing of one of the doors. Inspired by the warehouse's elaborate metal-and-wood front door, he'd replicated the design for the bedroom doors, using thick frosted glass for the interior panes so more light could pass through the room.

"Not like he closes the doors," Kane told the dog panting near his feet. "But with my mother sniffing around, doors aren't a bad thing."

The warehouse gleamed, smelling of spices and lemon oil. In the days following Coon's suicide-by-cop, Kane and Kel put their administrative leave to good use, moving the furniture down from the second floor to fill up the emptiness. Miki grudgingly agreed to have his mattress put on the iron four-poster bed the designer originally purchased for him, and he grunted at Kane when Kane pointed out the mission-style furniture looked nice against the former dining room's pale walls. The sectional wasn't negotiable, and they'd come to a compromise to have it re-covered. Miki chose a soft brown bomber-jacket-style fabric and sulked for the few days it took the upholsterer to do the work.

He spent the time filling the cherrywood barrister cabinets with the seemingly millions of CDs Kane discovered in stacks of boxes in one of the upstairs bedrooms. With the furniture finally in place and the sectional returned to a glory it'd never known, the warehouse was an eclectic blend of old and new pieces.

Neither of them spoke about the storage boxes with Damien's name scribbled on with black markers. Instead, Kane designated the smallest upstairs bedroom as a storage area and stacked the unopened boxes carefully against the wall. Dusty guitar cases, laden with memories and loose-stringed instruments, joined the boxes. Kane was about to close the room up when Miki stopped and walked to the middle of the room, breathing in the dusty memories of his dearest friend. After grabbing one of the guitar cases from its place against the wall, Miki headed downstairs without a word, leaving Kane to shut the door behind him.

The acoustic guitar was as battered as the sectional had been. It showed its age by its wood and the stickers from various diners and dives across the country covering its back. Resurrected from its tomb, the guitar now spent half of its time in Miki's ink-stained hands, a soft, murmuring refrain of music coming from its strings while Kane cooked in the kitchen or lounged on the couch next to Miki's feet.

Most of the time, Miki played songs Kane knew from the Sinner's Gin CDs he'd scavenged from the piles of extras in the studio next to the garage, but sometimes there were others, unfamiliar and faltering. Miki alternated stroking the chords from the acoustic and scribbling in one of his notebooks, the cheap ballpoint pens he favored smearing globs while he wrote. There were a few tentative ventures of love songs, but mostly Miki wrote of a bit of pain he couldn't shake. Kane grinned when Miki sang to him of wickedly sinful nights, and kissed him soundly during the times he mourned his best friend.

Dude was often Miki's audience, especially when Kane groaned at Miki's mocking rhymes.

With the door checked out, Kane had just reached for a hand towel when Dude's ears perked up at the sound of a car's tires pulling up in front of the warehouse. The terrier was pawing at the jamb before Kane could put down the drill. Barking in a high pitched yip, Dude shuffled back quickly as the front door swung open.

Seeing Miki never failed to take Kane's breath away.

"God, I fucking hate learning how to drive," Miki growled at his dog, bending over slightly to pet the undulating terrier. "At least this guy hasn't quit on me yet."

And as usual, right after his breath was taken away by the singer's pretty face and lithe body, Miki's off-kilter brain and loose mouth brought a laugh to Kane's lips.

"How was it?" Kane brushed a few curls of wood from his jeans and crooked his finger at his lover.

"I didn't run into anything this time," Miki grumbled under his breath. "And I can't be blamed if someone walks into the car, right? It's kind of like he hit me."

"Were you moving at the time?" Kane shook his head. Miki was on his third driving instructor, and not for the first time since the singer took it into his head to get his license, he was glad they decided Kane wouldn't teach him how to drive.

"I was starting to," Miki confessed. "He *walked* into the side of the car. By the passenger door. *Totally* not on me."

Chuckling as Miki approached him, Kane caught the man by the waist and pulled him in to cup Miki's ass in his palms. He loved the feel of his lover's ass. The round, muscular curves fit perfectly in his hands, and Kane kneaded Miki's jeans as he took Miki's mouth. Their kiss began as a tender exploration, their tongues teasing one another until Kane felt Miki's hands slide under his T-shirt. The man's fingers should be declared lethal weapons, because the delicate brush of his fingertips on Kane's ribcage was enough to drive him wild. When Miki sucked on the tip of Kane's invading tongue, Kane decided it was time to take even more.

Kane turned him around, introduced Miki's back to the newly installed doors, and hoisted the slender man up as an invitation for Miki to wrap his legs around Kane's hips. When Miki's legs were secure around him, he pressed in and took as much of Miki's kiss as he could, slanting his mouth to savor his lover's taste.

There was nothing more sensual for Kane than the slide of Miki's velvety tongue along the roof of his mouth. The nip of the man's teeth along his lower lip was a close second. With a satisfied smirk, he leaned in, supporting Miki's weight with one hand on the man's pert ass while he wrapped his other hand into the silken chestnut hair at the base of Miki's neck.

As mouths went, Miki's was a sublime experience, full and kissable with a hint of a wicked smile ghosting its corners. Kane took his time exploring every millimeter of it until Miki was left gasping. Clinging to Kane's shoulders, he panted heavily, straining to get some air into his lungs. Taking advantage of his lover's distraction, Kane slid his hand down from Miki's hair to tuck his fingers into the loose waistband of his jeans.

The skin there was soft under Kane's fingertips, and he raked at the delicate span of flesh with his fingernails, making Miki hot enough to grind his hips against Kane's waist.

"Shouldn't be doing this," Miki gasped when Kane's fingers slid down further and teased at the top of the cleft parting his ass cheeks. "Edie…."

A crisp, feminine voice finished Miki's sentence for him. "Edie is standing at the front door wondering if she shouldn't get a hotel room. Hello, boys. Good to see you… fully recovered from your traumas."

The tall woman was a sharp arrangement of angles and planes. Dressed in a dark red power suit, she removed a matching pillbox hat from atop her short black bob and perched it on the handle of her rolling suitcase. Slender nearly to the point of being too thin, she looked down her long nose at Kane and arched one eyebrow at the couple.

"It's good to see you are back on your feet, Miki." The eyebrow remained in place, and Kane felt a flush start to creep up his neck. "Well, feet being a relative term."

"Shit." Kane carefully lowered Miki to the floor, waiting for the man to have his legs in place under him before letting go. "Um…."

"Why don't you wash your hands first before I shake hello?" Edie crossed the room, her heels clicking on the polished floor. "You appear to have… an oily substance of some kind on them."

"Grease from the hinges," Kane admitted. "Very innocent. I promise."

"Hey, Edie." The hug Miki gave the brittle-faced woman thawed her to putty, and her smile was enough to brighten the room. "I'm glad you could come up to visit."

"I'm glad you finally let me. Now, let me look at you," she said, leaning back only far enough to study his face. "Are you sure you're okay? No more bullet wounds?"

"I didn't have any to begin with," Miki snorted. "My *knee* gave out. The guy kicked me right in the broken spot."

"He fainted," Kane interjected. "Well, passed out from the pain, really. Not a single extra hole in him to be found."

"Okay, so long as you're fine." She sniffed and let Miki tighten his grip on her before lightly pushing him away. "Squeeze me too hard, and I'll make a mess on your lovely floor." After kissing his cheek, Edie looked around the warehouse. "This certainly looks much better than the webcam chats I've had with you. Is the bathroom in the same place? I need to freshen up. The flight wasn't long, but the person sitting next to me... well, he was a nervous flyer. Very nervous."

"Uh, yeah," Miki mumbled, scratching the back of his head. "Through that door over there. It's the room with the funny seat."

Kane waited for the woman to disappear into the depths of the warehouse's hallway before wrapping his arms around Miki's waist from behind. Resting his chin on the man's shoulder, he nibbled on Miki's earlobe and whispered. "You webcammed with her in the bathroom?"

"I had to go pee, and I took the tablet with me." Miki went hot over his cheeks. "I didn't even think about it. Shit, she's seen everything already. She toured with us."

"I don't think I'm too happy knowing a woman's seen all your goods there, babe," Kane teased in his deep, whiskey-laden lilt. "I might have to inspect you for damage."

Miki eyed Kane suspiciously. "Put your hands on me and we're going to forget about Edie again. I don't think I need her to see that much of me."

"Hmmm, probably not the impression I want to give," Kane agreed.

"I think she's already got that impression," Miki scoffed. Fending Kane off with one hand, he dug into his pocket. "Hold up. I got something for you."

"You made the driving instructor do a pit stop?"

"No, I asked the taxi driver to." Miki drew out a pair of keys strung on an iCat pull-apart. "Here, I want you to take these."

"Mick love, I've already got a key to your place," Kane reminded his lover gently. "Shit, I practically live here."

"These aren't for the house," Miki said. "They're for the GTO. I want you to drive it. You know, because I... can't."

"Babe, Damien—"

"D wanted me to have the car to drive," Miki cut Kane off. "The way I'm going, it'll be years before they let me have a license, and... I want my life to go on. I *need* my life to go on. And I want it to go on with you in it. So for me, will you drive it around? Maybe with me in it once in a while?"

"Yeah, I will," Kane murmured, closing his hand over Miki's fingers and the keys. "Love you, Mick. You know that, right?"

"Love you too, K," he replied, ducking his head down. "With everything I've got."

Miki moved first, sliding his tongue across Kane's lips. Kane barely heard the roar of his blood in his ears, lost in the flavor of Miki in his mouth. Every man tasted different; he'd kissed enough men to know the truth of it, but Miki was different. In each of his lover's kisses there was a vastness Kane couldn't imagine until his mouth brushed the other's. The keys jangled when they hit the floor, and Kane's mind went blank when Miki pushed him back against the doors to the bedroom.

Reaching up under Miki's shirt, Kane stroked at the line of Miki's lower back, teasing the silky skin there. Responding, Miki's kiss grew rough, his passion hardening beneath Kane's stroking touch. The delicateness of Miki's frame was deceiving, the power in the singer's lean body evident as his legs trapped Kane against one of the doors. A steely strength lay under the loose clothing swaddling the singer's torso, hard muscles under his smooth golden skin.

"Those things open, right?" Miki gasped when Kane's fingers dipped below the waistband of his jeans.

"Yes. That's what makes them doors," Kane said, leaving a trail of kisses along Miki's throat until he found the spot he was looking for. The cop nipped and tugged at the skin under Miki's jaw, plucking up dark pink welts with his teeth. Kane's fingers were everywhere, pulling at the pebbled nubs of Miki's chest while his other hand trailed up and down the cleft of the singer's ass. "All you need to do is turn the knob, baby, and let me in."

The click of the latch did little to prepare Kane for the door giving way behind him, and he laughed when he stumbled back. Snagging Miki's jeans by a belt loop, he pulled his lover in, dragging Miki in with him. Neither of them saw the woman coming down the hall nor heard the quiet snick of the door closing behind them as they fell into bed, more intent on getting one another undressed than anything else.

"Well, puppy, it looks like they were the ones to get a room," Edie said, looking down at Miki's blond terrier mix. Grinning up at her, Dude shook the red pillbox he clenched in his teeth, as if daring her to say something about its theft. "Let's see if they've got some beer in the fridge, and then we're going to talk about you giving me back my hat."

The prophets and the wicked both wear black.
How do I tell one from the other?
When both want to kiss me,
And ask for my soul.

—The Consuming of Me

AS PRISONS went, Stephen had to admit, Skywood was a beautiful prison. The majestic, sweeping landscapes were filled with burbling rivers, tall evergreens, and a cobalt-gray range of mountains that turned icy blue when the winter months came around. He clearly remembered seeing the leaves turn brittle, and a few weeks later, what greenery remained was buried under the frosty kiss of icicles and swirling snow. Spring now had a firm hold on the grounds, and bright colors dominated the greenscape, giving the residents of Skywood Chateaux a vibrant expanse to walk or be wheeled around in.

Stephen hated every minute of it. Especially when the staff began to talk to him in a perfected singsong tone that left him with no doubt they thought he was crazy.

"How are we this morning, Mr. Thompson?" The beefy, bald-headed orderly carried in Stephen's meal on a wooden tray. After placing it on the table near the window Stephen sat at, he removed the silver dish coverings and placed them on the trolley. "Are you thinking of taking a walk outside today or maybe heading over to the entertainment room? Doctor Hanline thinks it would be a good idea for you to try the game systems again. Maybe something interesting, like Katamari."

"No Rock Band, huh?" Stephen sniffed at the hollandaise sauce on his eggs.

"Probably not, sir." He caught the sour look on the orderly's face before the man could mask it. "That did not... go well for you last time."

"Yeah, you could say that." The eggs were good, and the bacon had a sugary crispness he liked. The English muffin accompanying the meal was toasted to perfection, and the orange marmalade tasted handmade, a likely possibility considering the exclusive facility's attention to detail.

It still was his prison. Despite its beauty and the suite of rooms he occupied, everything was either screwed into the wall or monitored to within an inch of his life. Even the reading material was carefully gone over so nothing would set him off into a rage. The homogenized atmosphere was driving him more crazy than the smug politeness of the staff or the overwhelming blank bits in his mind.

He'd also kill for a cup of coffee, Stephen thought as he stared down at the glass of apple juice. When had he ever *liked* apple juice?

"Here are your supplements, sir." The orderly handed Stephen a small cup of pills, watching carefully beneath hooded lids to see if Stephen swallowed all of them.

They both knew the pills weren't vitamins. What Stephen didn't know was if the orderly was aware he knew it. The meds brought a numbness to his mind, and he hated the lethargic response of his thoughts. He tossed the pills into his mouth, gulped down the entire glass of juice, and wiped his mouth with a napkin. He set the balled-up paper down on the tray and waited until the orderly took the tray to the trolley.

Taking advantage of the man's turned back, Stephen slipped the pills into the space between the chair's back and seat, letting them rattle with the others he'd stashed there.

"Your parents will be visiting you today, sir," the orderly mentioned, stacking the tray with the dish covers. "They'll be joining you in Entertainment Room C."

"Lovely," Stephen drawled.

They were waiting for him, a well-dressed, elegant couple whose every movement spoke of money and privilege. Stephen didn't have to look hard to see himself in the older man. They shared the same inky black hair, light blue eyes, and strong features. Nearly the same height, they both towered over the delicate-boned blonde woman picking at the edges of her nails in boredom. She smiled when Stephen approached and murmured an air kiss near his ear before drawing quickly away. The man patted Stephen's arm awkwardly and sat down next to his wife on a tapestry settee. The orderly closed the door as he left, leaving them alone.

The room was on the small side for the facility, offering a private venue for family gatherings, and Stephen wished they'd been able to meet in one of the larger areas so he could have some room to pace off his frustration. He was halfway to the window when the man who called himself his father broke the silence.

"Why don't you come sit down with us, Stephen?" Hell, they even sounded alike, but for the life of him, Stephen couldn't remember a damned thing about the man he resembled. "We want to hear how you're doing. Do you need anything? Maybe more books?"

"What I need is to get the fuck out of here," Stephen said, staring down at the parents he didn't know. "Look, you seem nice and all, but I don't *remember* you. I don't want to be here... I.... This isn't my life."

"Stephen, we've gone over this," his mother said in the same damned lilting singsong the staff used to speak to him. "You're our son. You were in a car accident... a very serious car accident. It's okay that you don't remember anything—"

"See, that's where you're wrong. I sure as hell don't remember *you,* but I remember a lot of things," he interrupted. "I remember that my name's not Stephen Thompson. It's Damien Stephen Mitchell. I know I was in a car accident, and I know Johnny and Dave are gone. What I don't understand is why you're not letting me see Sinjun or even letting me talk to him. So if you want to do something for me, let me out of here. Because what I need... who I want is *Sinjun,* because I need him to take me home."

RHYS FORD was born and raised in Hawai'i, then wandered off to see the world. After chewing through a pile of books, a lot of odd food, and a stray boyfriend or two, Rhys eventually landed in San Diego, which is a very nice place but seriously needs more rain.

Rhys admits to sharing the house with three cats, a black Pomeranian puffball, a bonsai wolfhound, and a ginger cairn terrorist. Rhys is also enslaved to the upkeep a 1979 Pontiac Firebird, a Qosmio laptop, and a red Hamilton Beach coffeemaker.

Visit Rhys's blog at http://rhysford.wordpress.com/ or e-mail Rhys at rhys_ford@vitaenoir.com.

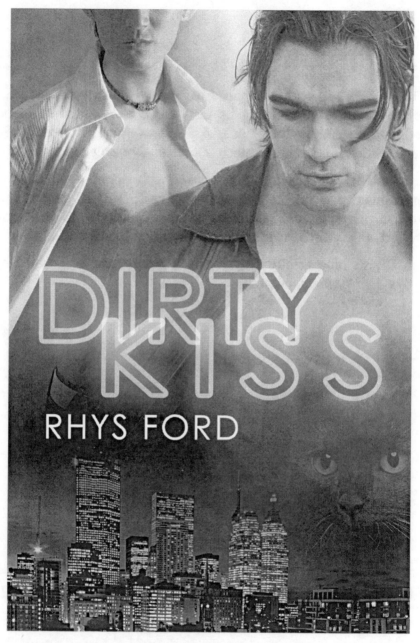

Also from RHYS FORD

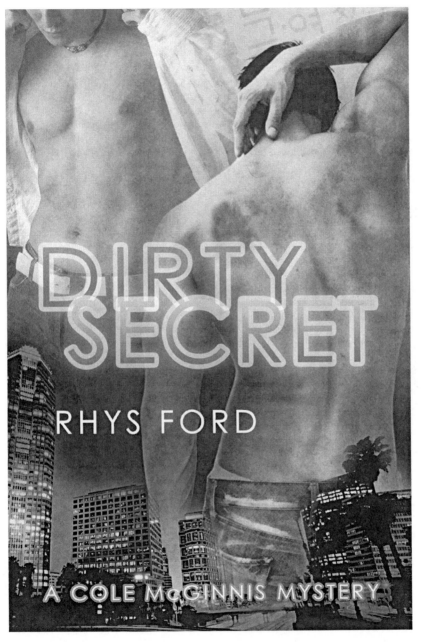

DIRTY SECRET

RHYS FORD

A COLE McGINNIS MYSTERY

http://www.dreamspinnerpress.com

Billionaire's Row

Sullivan Wheeler

http://www.dreamspinnerpress.com

CPSIA information can be obtained at www.ICGtesting.com
Printed in the USA
LVOW070247261212

313181LV00016B/580/P